HEART'S JOURNEY IN WINTER

JAMES BUCHAN was for ten years a foreign correspondent of the *Financial Times*, reporting from the Middle East, Germany and Central Europe, and the United States. His first novel, *A Parish of Rich Women*, won four major literary prizes in Britain, including the Whitbread First Novel Award. He now lives in London and writes for the *Independent on Sunday*, the *Telegraph* and *Esquire*.

JAMES BUCHAN

❋

Heart's Journey
in Winter

THE HARVILL PRESS
LONDON

First published in 1995 by The Harvill Press

3 5 7 9 8 6 4 2

© James Buchan 1995

The author asserts the moral right to be identified
as the author of this work.

A CIP record for this title is
available from the British Library.

ISBN 1 86046 000 3 hardback
ISBN 1 86046 001 1 paperback

Photoset in Linotron Garamond No. 3 by
Rowland Phototypesetting Ltd, Bury St Edmunds, Suffolk

Printed and bound in Great Britain by
Selwood Printing Ltd, Burgess Hill, West Sussex

Heart's Journey
in Winter

1

The absolute truth is that without a revolution in Germany, we shall perish.

LENIN

Gretchen Lightner opened the apartment door. She looked older than in West Germany. I smelled piss and brown coal. Behind her, a chair scraped on board or lino. She said:

"Have you come to kill me, young man?"

She laughed and slammed the door on my hip and face. My jacket, as I kicked the door open, tore on the lock-plate. As I stood in the room, opening my arms wide to show I had no weapon, stunned by coal-heat and rage, taking in a formica table, a big old man askew on a chair, two plates of sausage and potato salad, a scummy beer glass, I felt I'd left my cheek and hip out in the gritty stairwell. I felt I'd been dropping pieces of me the length of the Leninstrasse from the Fairgrounds or beside the rails coming east, in smears of orange streetlight and *Jugendstil* streets that ran away like bad children and filled me with homesickness, and station-names that glided out of the screeching darkness; and there was nothing left of me but breath.

I said: "I don't give a tinker's fuck if every State Security agent in Leipzig hears what I have to say. But you might, Mrs Lightner. And your brother."

I put down in front of her a photograph of a man and a child skating.

I

"Turn that thing on, Manfred."

On a dresser was a Grundig television set. Some kind of Hollywood Dickens came on, in blizzardy black and white, dubbed into deafening German. A door detonated. Carriage wheel on cobbles burst like grenades into the hot room.

"What's your name, young man?"

"Fisher."

"Manfred, this is Mr Fisher. A BRITISH ASSASSIN."

"Shit," he said and turned back to his plate.

I said: "Who killed your husband, Mrs Lightner?"

"But you did, young man! You brave Britons! You fair Britons!"

"Who killed Pastor Lightner?"

She leaned on her fists on the table. She said: "Go away, Mr Fisher. They don't care about Maggie Thatcher in Bautzen! They don't care about Lady Di!"

"I don't have a lot of time, Mrs Lightner."

"You won't even get to the Fairgrounds!"

Perhaps I won't. Perhaps I'll get to Bautzen concentration camp. Perhaps not even there. But whether or not I get out of here, you certainly won't, so you might as well tell me: not who killed your husband – which I don't want to know, no ma'am, that's just for show – but about the little girl in the picture, skating on a frozen canal.

"I need to know who killed your husband."

"GET OUT!" She sat down with a bump at the table. It came up to her chest. Her brother turned to her, eyes like saucers. She said: "You'll be the death of me, young man."

When Gretchen Lightner gassed herself in the spring of 1989, the year the Berlin Wall came down, Klaus Hofmeyer wrote an obituary in the feuilleton of the *Frankfurter Allgemeine Zeitung*, headed "Gretchen Piotrowska: A German Life"; in which he said that Mrs Lightner, having survived National Socialist barbarism, Ravensbrück, persecution in the Federal Republic, her husband's assassination and, finally, flight to the GDR, had retained an existential sovereignty over the disposal of her life which she had now

2

unflinchingly exercised. People used to write things like that when Germany was divided.

He didn't know, because I didn't tell him, that Mrs Lightner exercised that existential sovereignty (if that's what it was) back in 1983, on May 1, when she picked up in two hands the picture of Sebastian Ritter and his daughter skating; or, to be quite precise, the previous Saturday at her husband's funeral at the Old Cemetery in Bonn, the other side of the wall. A chair had been brought for her and she sat, a little sideways, in a headscarf and dark glasses, a stick propped against her leg which pointed, rigid with arthritis or some like illness, into the grave. The spruces dripped. The cheeks beneath her dark glasses were wet from tear gas. Above her, Sebastian Ritter was saying, in fabricated anger: "The Constitution of the Federal Republic has judicial precedence over the Public Resting-Places Act!" I must have known that her hold on life was slipping, that she was falling out of the world.

I suppose that's why I made this journey east, which is the direction you take in Germany if you have business with death: to extract, out of this dying statelet, its last secret: in all these miles of beetfield, pine, sand, cities, steelworks and overgrown railway yards, the only thing worth knowing. Though my head and guts rebelled and my ignorance, nursed in the broad lap of Yalta and the British oligarchy, pleaded for a moment longer.

"WHO KILLED PROFESSOR LIGHTNER?"

Her hands trembled as she picked up the photograph. Manfred Piotrowsky stood up.

In 1983, I knew these would be the capital events of my life. I couldn't know that the missiles deployed in West Germany that November would be the final shots of the last action of the Cold War. I didn't know the Soviet Union would abandon forty years of military competition with the United States, central economic planning and bureaucratic socialism; leave its friends to go to hell, and then itself explode, scattering weapons and nations to the four winds; while the peoples of Western Europe, the siege lifted and the Americans sailed home, would fall to fighting among themselves. Who did know that in 1983? Even Polina didn't, damn her.

When the Berlin Wall fell down six years later, it buried not just the division of Germany but a way of looking at the world. The Cold War petrified the map of Europe at the state of mid-century, and also the societies on both sides of the divide, notions of history and right, the way men and women arrange matters between them, habits of ruling and doing business. In the crackup, a new language came into use which could no longer describe the old order. Between that day in Leipzig and today, there runs a river of forgetfulness, and I guess it's all best forgotten, though I can't forget it.

Let me explain that for nearly fifty years, the world was ordered according to understandings reached by the powers of the anti-German coalition in 1945 at the little Crimean resort of Yalta. The purpose of these agreements, though this was never actually said, was to prevent the war in Europe going on for decades between different adversaries, like the wars of the 18th century. The continent was divided into spheres of influence. The United States took the west, the Soviet Union the east. The front between them ran down the middle of Germany.

Yalta was both a success and a failure. It gave peace in Europe, in as much as there was no Continental war for fifty years; but it could not give peace of mind, least of all to the Soviet Union which felt acutely its backwardness, and devoted almost all its wealth to building armaments. The rivalry between the two Great Powers was transferred from the real continent of cities and fields on to battlefields of the imagination: ideology, though this had become degenerate by 1983; subversion; and the accumulation of nuclear weapons whose power to terrify and persuade depended not on their detonation – for that was too terrible even for the game at issue – but on their value as entries, as my father wrote in the 1960s, in some imaginary ledger of terror and might.

The chief theatre of this mental war was Germany, and that for obvious reasons. It was where the fighting had stopped in 1945, leaving battle lines that expressed the situation at that moment rather than the convenience of the population. It was the country where, if there was to be any real fighting, that fighting would most likely start; and the Germans, who had rebuilt cities turned to rubble by British and American bombers in the Second World War, knew they had most to lose from any deterioration in the balance of terror between the two Great Powers. Both Germanies were military camps, overflowing with armed men of all nationalities, bristling with nuclear weapons, churned up by tank manoeuvres, deafened by low-flying fighter aircraft.

The Federal Republic, as the western state was called, was divided both territorially and between the generations; for when, in the late 1960s, West Germans born during or since the Third Reich came to understand the nature of the Nazi regime, they conceived for their parents an implacable hatred. Among the parricidal youth of 1968, whose heroes were not the founders of their prosperous republic but the peevish Marxists of the Frankfurt School such as Frank Lightner or the revolutionaries of remote and picturesque ex-colonies, the Soviets found a field ripe for subversion and recruitment. In the eastern state, known as the German Democratic Republic or GDR, men and women felt absolved of war guilt by the unremitting hopelessness of their lives.

That the Soviet plan failed so miserably does not mean it was doomed from the beginning. What the Soviets wanted was not so much to administer Western Europe as that the Americans should go home; and they devised a weapon to prise open a gulf between the United States and its European allies. This weapon was the SS-20, a missile capable of destroying cities and military bases all over the continent but not of crossing the Atlantic and, therefore, in the Soviet view, of no interest to the US. As these missiles appeared on satellite images in the second half of the 1970s, the Americans were indeed indifferent, but were brought to order by the incessant hectoring of the West German Chancellor, Helmut Schmidt, who saw quite clearly what the Soviets were up to. In speeches and apoplectic lectures to American officials, he warned that unless the SS-20s were dismantled, warhead by warhead, the balance of terror in Europe would be tipped, the Soviets would blackmail and bully the western states and a continent would be lost. Since nobody imagined the Soviets would remove these useful and expensive weapons voluntarily, a stick was needed: President Carter reluctantly agreed to send to Europe a mixture of ballistic and cruise missiles of countervailing destructive power, should the Soviets refuse to withdraw the SS-20 from the European theatre by the end of 1983. Both sides, for reasons of political show, agreed to discuss the issue in the neutral opulence of Geneva and two elderly diplomats of great experience and hawkish disposition, Yuli Kvertsovsky and John Chauncey Polk, were despatched to waste their time in interminable plenaries and their livers at fancy restaurants.

Back in West Germany, Schmidt's career foundered. His party, the Social Democratic Party, rediscovered its pacifist roots and accepted the Soviet claim that the SS-20 was merely a long overdue modernization of the antique rocketry captured from the Nazis in 1945. Schmidt's coalition collapsed, the Christian Democrats under Helmut Kohl took power in a Bundestag vote of confidence and new elections were called for July of 1983. The election had the trappings of a world-historical event. The Reagan Administration feared that victory for the Social Democrats, in their pacifist guise, would cause the Western Alliance to collapse and bring Soviet hegemony over Europe. Outright victory seemed unlikely but a new party, the Greens, had been knit by Frank Lightner out of the disgruntled sixty-eighters and various other radical oddments – vegetarians, ramblers, feminists, Christians – who were united only in the certainty that no Pershing ballistic missiles would be brought into Germany. There were the makings of a coalition. When on April 16, 1983, Lightner was found in the little pergola of his Berlin garden, dead of a bullet wound, it appeared to all that the war had erupted from its imaginary realm and invaded the world of every day.

This is the official course of events, which has been told and will be told again. But beside it, and obscured by it, is a secret history, which has never been told and only I can tell, for it left its protagonists dead or stunned into silence. It is the history of the Golden Plough.

In 1983, the two opposing systems were in such perfect equilibrium that the fall of a feather would tip the scale; and great events, for the only time in my life, came within the agency of individuals. Polina and Lightner and Sebastian Ritter step out from the tedious shadow of the official history. Day-to-day affections – jealousy, ambition, love – shake empires till they totter. Love, in particular, is the circus hoop through which history is forced to jump, over and over again.

I first met Polina Mertz in Bonn, West Germany, at a house on the Lennestrasse by the Hofgarten on April 17, 1983. The house, a big Bismarckian thing with stucco wheatsheaves on its pale yellow facade, was rented by the British Embassy for Nik Tully, who was head of station for SIS, the British external intelligence service. Tully, who'd been in his time a soldier and a lecturer in German at Lancaster University, liked to give parties. He invited people from the Soviet and East European services and mixed them up with journalists, Social Democrat Bundestag deputies, university people, actresses from the Bonn and Cologne operas, even on one occasion two Australian nannies he'd met in the Münsterplatz. I suppose he thought this mixture would combust and throw off a shower of usable intelligence. I didn't like Tully or his guests, but I always went, just in case.

I watched the nine o'clock news at home. It was raining outside and there was a shoe-high puddle across the Poppelsdorfer Allee where it went under the railway tracks. The house in the Lennestrasse crackled with central heating. The lights had been turned down and people lounged stiffly on cushions covered in a bad Iranian bazaar print: if diplomats and journalists bring back junk from their

7

foreign postings, how much more so spies! Suspicious or inquisitive looks flickered over me. Beneath the party noise, there was boredom so concentrated and acrid that, for a moment, my stomach churned. I couldn't see Tully or a clean glass. I picked up a dirty one and an open bottle of Alsatian Riesling and went into the kitchen.

Two women stood with their backs to the kitchen sink. One was Caroline Barchard, the wife of the British Head of Chancery. The other woman had a strikingly slim waist. She had her eyes down and her hand out.

"Hi," she said. "I'm Polina."

"How do you do? Richard Fisher." I shook her cold hand. "Hello, Caroline."

"Polina knows all about nuclear weapons. Isn't that interesting? And Richard's father . . ."

"You're the guy who knew Lightner?"

"I saw him a couple of times," I said. "First in Berlin, when I was a student . . ."

"You're with MI6, right?"

"Richard! With MI6! You must be joking."

"I'm doing a book on the Red Army Fraction, you know, the Baader-Meinhof group. For an American publisher."

I was bored with my phoney book, being British, Germany, diplomatic conversation, Caroline Barchard, acute sexual desire, espionage, answering direct questions and the Cold War. I could have asked Polina to move away from the sink, washed the glass, poured everyone some wine, said something friendly or interesting, gone next door to register myself with Tully and then left the party. I'd decided to do this, except Polina pinched my right sleeve. She reached up to my wrist, unclasped my fingers, took the bottle of wine, put it to her mouth and drank from it. She handed the bottle back to me and said: "So what are you doing here?"

I said that for thirty-five years, Britain, France and the United States had been fighting the Soviets and one another for control of West German public opinion. Suddenly, it was as if a shell had burst overhead and exposed this dreary struggle to a blinding light.

I went on a bit about Pershings and SS-20s, missile throw-weights and explosive yield and the de Honschian electoral system in the breezy and precise way I'd borrowed from Brian Barchard, eyes on the ceiling, as if I'd said it many times before. Actually, I didn't want to look at Caroline's clever face. I said we were now in the midst of a pitched engagement, the first since Cuba in 1962; the Soviets would again be beaten; but I just wished . . .

"I meant here: Lennestrasse 43."

"Shsst!" Caroline put a finger to her lips and said (in German): "Dear Mr Makhaev!"

Sergei Makhaev was head of the *Tass* bureau in Bonn and a more or less overt KGB agent. He kissed Polina's hand like an operetta count, bowed to Caroline and slid his arm briefly through mine. We talked about the inconvenience of early closing. Makhaev opened a book on the election result. He asked Polina about something he'd read in *Der Spiegel*, about a test flight of the Pershing II off the coast of Florida which had, apparently, not gone so well. As his sentence clunked towards its verb and auxiliary, Polina crossed and uncrossed her stockinged legs. She looked up at him and waited, as if to make sure he had nothing more to say. In the hail of her technical German, Makhaev seemed to wilt. Then she said: "You should not handle secondary material of questionable authenticity. The Army range reports have been partially declassified. I'll have our press folks bike them round."

Makhaev turned briskly to me and asked about a farmer he'd met near Bielefeld, during the spring manoeuvres, who'd lost his entire potato crop under the tracks of VIIIth Armoured Corps, and what was the procedure for compensation in such a case? Caroline put her fingertip against his chest and said she was leaving before he caused any more trouble.

"Let us all leave this dull party," Makhaev said.

In the big room, Tully and a woman I didn't know were sitting on the floor. John Lennon's "Imagine" was playing from expensive speakers. Caroline had gone off, I suppose to find her husband. Tully got up clumsily, though I'm sure he wasn't drunk. He put his arm round Polina on the way to the door and said something in Russian over his shoulder to Makhaev, who laughed. I thought: If you touch her, Nik, I may break your neck.

Tully propelled her gently by the small of the back, let his hand drop to her bottom and then swept it up to run through his thick hair. I followed Makhaev into the wet evening.

We parted, the three of us, in the Hofgarten. Polina had a car the size of a boat. Makhaev proposed we go to the Altstadt, to a place he knew called the Goldener Pflug, make an evening of it, but Polina shook her head and we watched her pull away. Makhaev bustled off to the taxi rank and I made my way across the Hofgarten and splashed through the tunnel under the railway lines. I thought: Here is the famous Poppelsdorfer Allee, laid out by the Prince-Elector, and stretching all the way to that pavilion you can just see in the floodlight, now the Botanical Faculty of Bonn University. This is the Mozartstrasse, built, like all the streets round here, after Sedan, when French reparations reduced the cost of money to nothing and speculative neighbourhoods erupted all over Germany in the pretty style known as *Jugendstil*. And this, the most beautiful of all these houses, is mine; or rather contains my apartment, two rooms to bourgeois scale, one thousand marks a month and a thousand marks security deposit. Come in, why not? Have some Kirsch and a piece of this *Linzertorte*. Tell me about yourself. Or about old Sergei. And by the way, what or who is the Goldener Pflug? You see, it's not in the phone book.

I don't imagine this is news to anybody, but I'll say it all the same. You don't know you're irretrievably in love until you're running for the U-Bahn, or washing up your breakfast things or sitting at your sunny desk over *Die Zeit*, and you realize someone has come in and sat down in your thoughts: not necessarily a whole person, but a fragment of speech (in this case, the expression *fragwürdiger Zuverlässigkeit*, which I translated as "questionable authenticity"), or of sensation, the touch of her finger on my wrist, the swinging belt on her raincoat, her car moving away from the wet pavement.

I'd wanted to let three days go by before I called her. I got as far as five o'clock on the Thursday afternoon. She wasn't at the US Embassy and her secretary didn't give out home numbers as a matter of State Department policy. I walked back from the Tulpenfeld along the railway lines, which I often did when I couldn't face the Mozartstrasse. I could feel the Inter-City behind me, burrowing through the town, till it burst past and, for an instant, slammed the solitude right out of me; but it was back, to the left and just behind me, with the windows still tinkling in the tall houses on each side.

I stopped at the Käfer, a bar by the level crossing that the *Realo* faction of the Greens — that is, those favouring a coalition with the Social Democrats after the election — used for their caucus, but I knew nobody there. I stayed all the same. It was eleven when I got home.

I was opening another beer in the kitchen when the phone rang. "Is that Richard?" an American woman asked.

"Patty! Sweetheart!"

"Patty? It's not Patty. I'm Polina. We met at Nik's. On Tuesday. In the kitchen. With Mrs Barchard . . ."

"Lady Caroline."

"Who?"

I gave up. "I've been trying to call you."

She didn't reply. I tried to think of something more to say, but it wasn't easy without a picture of her at the other end of the telephone; not her house or apartment, but her face or eyes, whether she were dressed or in a nightgown. Do me a favour, woman: say something.

I said: "Do you need to meet now?"

"No. What for?"

Silence filled the receiver. Polina coughed: a woman's cough, prissy, American-genteel, abbreviated by a hand or fist. Then she said: "I need to talk to you about Lightner."

"You what?"

"You're working on Professor Lightner, right?"

"Come to the funeral. Saturday. Everybody'll be there. It'll be fun."

That sounded foolish to me, too, but it was too late to find a new manner. I said: "We could go to lunch after. Maybe go to the Osteria. You can explain the difference between a Pershing II and a Pershing I."

Down the telephone, Polina took a breath. She said: "Enhanced accuracy. Lower yield. Rather dramatically improved survivability. There's not a whole lot I can tell you that's been published. Maybe I can point you at the specialized press. Look, I'll call about Saturday, OK?"

Jim Dole was crossing the lawn to the Tulpenfeld, carrying his mail. Everything about him was neat, brushed, clean, folded and put away, except his belly; and that was partly concealed by trousers he wore so high they exposed his socks and ankles. He came from Jamestown, New York, but had for fifteen years been Bonn correspondent for Radio Free Europe, a station in Munich financed jointly by the CIA and the State Department to broadcast to Eastern Europe. In his manners and interests, Dole had about him an authentic whiff of the American Occupation. As if aware of this, he affected an interest in House of Commons debates and the rules of cricket.

"You can play the tape, Richard. My notes may not be perfect."

"You are kind, Jim."

Dole's cassettes were arranged – like his notebooks, Chancellery press bulletins, copies of the metropolitan German newspapers, *Neues Deutschland* and *Izvestiya*, radio transcripts from the BBC in Caversham and *Deutsche Welle* in Cologne – chronologically on home-made wooden shelves. He was wired into the Bundestag plenum hall and, while he set up the tape, I listened to a caustic and echoey debate on student loans.

I said: "It's the very long question. Hofmeyer's, I think."

"I remember: the joke."

Over Gromyko's Russian drawl came the German interpreter, pained and self-assured: "That, sir, is a question . . . is a question with three independently targetable warheads."

Laughter burst from the cassette player. Dole, seated behind his clear desk, smiled in professional recollection. Then he leaned forward and frowned.

"Do you want it again?" he said.

He replayed it anyway. This time, he looked at me. He was smart, Jim Dole, as well as industrious.

I said: "'The rumours of progress, purporting to emanate from delegation circles in Geneva, do not in the smallest degree correspond to the truth. There is no golden . . . there is no golden instrument . . . no golden solution, not even silver!' I thought it sounded odd, that's all."

"Sure."

What I came here for, Jim Dole, is the Russian word Gromyko used that so bothered his interpreter. I came here because you know Russian and I, through poor education, do not. But I cannot ask you because you're already suspicious as hell.

"I guess you could say 'tool' or 'implement', like in a factory or on a farm."

OK, let's leave it at that for now. I'll see you right, Jim. If I can. Only not now.

"OK?" he said.

Who is that girl?

The Osteria Ischiana is an Italian restaurant in the Remigiusstrasse in Bonn. Its wonder years were the late 1940s, when Christian Democrat politicians, de-Nazified and with certificates in their waistcoat-pockets to prove it, spun webs of intrigue between the padded booths; when the Bundestag still convened among the stuffed animals at the Museum König a hundred yards away; and the political city had not yet marched south into the villa gardens, fields and allotments between the railway lines and the river; before the journalist-hutches and diplomat-silos had sprouted at the Tulpenfeld.

By 1983, the restaurant had fattened in the yeasty Rhineland air. Women in hats and fur collars worked their way through extended midday meals. Flour and cream glutted the sauces. The pasta burst with egg yolk. But you could still sense, under the Rhenish phlegm, the warmth and genius of Italy.

There used to be – maybe still is – a baize curtain over the street door to keep out draughts. On this Saturday, April 21, 1983, the day of Frank Lightner's funeral at the Old Cemetery in Bonn, I paused for a moment before pushing through it. I wanted to assemble Polina from the pieces in my mind – small waist, a side-parting like a Thirties actress, alarming clothes – and then project this image on to the teeming restaurant gloom. A waiter unwound himself from the racing pages, picking up a menu. There was nobody else there except a young woman in yellow, sitting under a big fresco of the Bay of Naples, not reading the newspapers or correcting a telex, not looking at anything at all. I waved, Britishly. I thought, as I strode across the room on British leather heels: I didn't know, Polina Mertz. I guessed, but I didn't know.

"Polina Mertz! You came! Hey! You haven't got a drink! Let's have some grappa! It's home-made and makes you Rip-Van-Winkle drunk, which is what I need!"

We shook hands feebly. She said: "Rolf Hartig said it came within a hair's breadth of the use of firearms at the cemetery gate. I heard him in the car. *Eine Haaresbreite*: was that your assessment?"

"Commissioner Hartig wants to get ahead."

I thought: That is not the right tone, Richard; worse, in its way, than the display of old-fashioned national characteristics at the door. Also, Richard, you should attempt to stop eating radishes. You have just eaten a dish of radishes, which anyway taste of CS-gas, as does the Osteria's celebrated grappa; and as for you, Polina Mertz, don't look me in the eye, I'm not that kind of bloke: I'm shifty, British-ironical, affectionate, asphyxiated.

She said: "Frank was a bad guy. You know that, don't you?"

"Cock!"

The word startled her.

"I mean, forgive me, but are you telling me that Professor Lightner was a Soviet agent? Or an agent of the GDR?" I chose a spot on her long neck to look at, and spoke quickly: "I'm sure you know . . . *And in Spite of That, Walk Upright!*, Frank Lightner's Russia book. In it, you'll remember, there's a very full account of the POW camp near Tulagai in Yakutsk where he was moved in the winter of 1945 and which he presents as the most laboured metaphor for Soviet society at large. In *The Faith Principle*, 1972, that swansong of Western Marxism which I can say, with a conviction bordering on certainty, that I am the only person in Germany (excluding, of course, Sebastian Ritter) to have read in its entirety, he speaks of Soviet communism as the 'capital problem', *das Hauptproblem*, of philosophy. You will recall" – and I would be grateful if you would stop looking at me in that compassionate way as if I were half-witted – "that he was never a member of the official German Communist Party, either as KPD or DKP; and Gretchen Lightner quit over Krushchev's secret speech to the XXth Party Congress and the invasion of Hungary. Lightner vigorously resisted Soviet front politics, tried to keep the Party and its agents out of the Easter Marches and the Tübingen Appeal, spoke against Soviet external policy not only in 1956 but after the crushing of the Prague Spring, during the African adventures of the 1970s, Afghanistan, you name it. His obituary in *Neues Deutschland* . . ."

"I saw the obituary . . ."

". . . was two lines long and said he 'represented ultra-Left, small-bourgeois/utopian and anti-communist social theories', which is hardly a ringing endorsement from East Berlin – or what do you think?"

"You can talk for as long as you like. You may even want to use facts."

"What facts? Who have you been talking to?"

She stiffened. "Our sources."

I thought: If you go on patronizing me, woman, I'm going to clock you one. No, no: I take it back. I said: "Polina . . . Can I call you that?"

She nodded.

"Polina. Sebastian Ritter was at the funeral. He thinks . . ."

"What does Sebastian think?"

"Let's order, why not? Then I'll tell you what he thinks. The black risotto is outstanding, if you like good things."

Ritter was listening, with intense concentration, to a punk girl with a bad nosebleed. A helicopter roared in my ears. I bent down to greet Mrs Lightner and his concentration broke.

"Is there something I can do for you, Mr Fisher?" He leaned protectively over the widow. "Please excuse me, Mrs Lightner," he said; and to the girl: "I assure you that I shall be bringing a general action against Commissioner Hartig and the Minister of Interior." His voice soared: "The Constitution of the Federal Republic has judicial precedence over the Public Resting-Places Act!"

A cry went up. The crowd surged, thickened and clogged. At the head of the grave, Petra Kelly seemed to be lifted from the ground by the crush of reporters and microphones. Her eyes were bruised and wet, her blonde hair like the flare on a gas-well. I said: "I wonder if you would do me a favour, Dr Ritter?"

"What would I not do for our NATO- and EC-partner, Great Britain?"

The girl gave a bitter little laugh. I took a step back from the grave. Ritter followed.

"I understand you are Pastor Lightner's executor."

"Indeed." He made an ironic bow.

"I would be somewhat grateful, Dr Ritter, if you would permit me to examine the Lightner archive. As you will remember, I did eight semesters at the Free University Berlin at the turn of the 1970s and came powerfully under the pedagogic influence of Professor Lightner as well as the political currents circulating in the student body. It has occurred to me that, through a scrupulous examination of the origins of the 1968 unrest, I might succeed . . ."

Ritter looked hard at me, and then over my shoulder. He said: "That would not be proper." He raised his harsh voice, so that people began to drift towards us. "I find it intolerable that certain of Pastor Lightner's papers, including documents of the most compelling *prima facie* interest to my proposed Bundestag Commission of Inquiry into his death, are sealed under the orders of the Berlin Public Prosecutor, who is as yet unwilling to state whether or not she intends to open her own investigation."

"Shameless!" said a woman behind me.

I moved off, but Ritter came with me. His black hair, with its exhausted streaks of grey, curled in damp bangs on his forehead: it was as if one of the stone monuments had come alive and stepped out from under the wet trees, a Schlegel or an Argelander, who named a thousand stars, or the man who saw the structure of the benzene molecule in a dream of a snake swallowing its tail.

He said: "Pastor Lightner spoke in 1968 of a 'Long March through the Institutions'. Here, belatedly and at the limit of our strength, we are in sight of the end of that Long March. Do you not find it a little curious, Mr Fisher, that on the eve of this fateful Bundestag election, the chief candidate of the Greens, an evangelical priest, a man who had fought for justice and peace since before Hitler seized power, and the only personality on the German Left with the authority to dispel sectarianism and hold together a Red/Green coalition – don't you find it surprising that this righteous and right-handed man should be found dead at his desk, from a bullet agreed even by the Berlin Public Prosecutor's ballistic expert to have entered his right armpit?"

"Highly curious, Dr Ritter."

The crowd surged again. A TV crew scampered between us, articulated like a dragon at Chinese New Year.

Ritter said: "Please call my assistant, Mrs Müller." He turned and walked back to the grave. I nodded respectfully to Gretchen

Lightner. Her hand trembled on her tweed skirt: I couldn't see through the dark glasses whether she was looking at me.

Outside the cemetery gate, a police van was on its side, burning. Crash-barriers lay twisted and helpless as crushed beetles. In the wet, littered street were paving blocks, a cracked red gas shell, a white scarf, a gymshoe with the sole torn, and a splintered police shield. Commissioner Hartig, the commander of the State Police Department, lounged half-in and half-out of an unmarked white Mercedes, speaking into a radio telephone. In his left hand, he held a police helmet with a neat gash through the crown. He crooked his finger through the hole, smiled and shook his head.

"Thirteen of my men hospitalized, Mr Fisher," he said. His suntanned face was striped with dirt and tears. Weeping officers stood back to let me through.

For the eulogy, Ritter took as his text the first sentence of Marx's eleventh thesis on Feuerbach: "The philosophers have merely interpreted the world in various ways. The point is to change it!"

Polina was eating fettucine. She cut up the pasta, then transferred her fork to her right hand and crossed her left arm under her bosom.

I said: "However hard you find this to believe, you're wrong, Polina. Ritter is a German patriot, though he wouldn't use such a phrase, which has been ruined for him and his generation by National Socialism. It ain't easy to be German, you know. You can't look for yourself in the past, which is what, for example, makes most British people feel British, because you bump into a dwarf with a dead-mouse moustache, blocking every avenue into history. In the United States, I know, the past is also somehow distant . . ."

"I was born in Europe . . ."

". . . I just meant that American life is in such flux that even quite recent events seem to belong to another place and era. For you, I mean to Americans, the assassination of John Kennedy is more remote than the Congress of Vienna is to us."

Why am I being so eloquent, when I don't believe I like you?

"Imagine you're German, Polina. You inhabit an irremediably fallen world, like Parsifal. You can't get at the past; the present is all messed up, the country split by a fence and churned up by foreign armies; and your culture – your high culture, by which you set great store, your poets and philosophers and musicians – all messed up by the Nazis and by ideological division; and if these new missiles are deployed in the south . . ."

"As they will be . . ."

Fascist. ". . . or even if Jackie Polk . . ."

"Ambassador Polk has no . . ."

". . . even if Mr Polk . . ."

"SHUT UP!" Her hands were in fists on the table. "Richard, you don't listen. You just go on talking all the time. And it makes no sense what you're saying." She let her shoulders drop and looked down at the tablecloth. She turned the stem of her glass, which was sticky with grappa. She said: "This is off the record. In fact, this entire meeting is off the record. I never came here. Right?"

In some ways, Ms Mertz, I wish you hadn't.

"OK, Richard?"

"Sure."

"Whatever happens in Geneva, we're bringing the Pershings to Germany. It's not just the military and the Pentagon civilians, guys like Dick Perle that you've read about in the press. Heck, even the State Department wants deployment and it's reportedly so soft on the Soviets. Only one person in the Administration wants a treaty and that is Ambassador John Polk. Well, OK, two, but I don't count, being a girl. Are you sick or something, Richard?"

"I got gassed. Everybody did. It's fine."

"Who's Patty?"

Don't flirt with me, lady.

"My stepmother."

"Your stepmother! Nobody speaks to a stepmother like that."

I suspect, Polina Mertz, that I positively dislike you. "I thought you were her. She's American."

"You've got some dual-nationality thing?"

"No."

"But you have a green card."

"No."

She said: "I need to go. We need the check."

"I'm doing this."

"Don't be a jerk."

Outside the Osteria, the sun had come out. The glare off the wet streets made me weep again. The colonnade of the university ran down through shade, sunshine and fly-posters into the empty Saturday afternoon. In a butcher's shop across the street, a blue venetian blind covered the window. Beneath it, a big car, green with a black roof and diplomatic plates, was parked half in the street and half on the pavement, with two parking tickets under the windscreen wiper.

Polina said: "Do you need to see Ambassador Polk? For your book?"

Glass and Detroit metal blinded me. Bursts of hot plastic rolled out of the opening window. I thought: If I put my hands round your waist, my fingers and thumbs would meet.

What I need, rather urgently, is to sleep with you, Ms M. Otherwise, I shall certainly die.

"What do you think, ma'am?"

"Come at five thirty. Earlier, if you care to." She smiled, with what seemed like relief. She had straight, white, American teeth. The need to kiss her was like a weight on my shoulders. She said: "He's in town to brief the Chancellor before the new Geneva round. There'll be something to eat, I guess. I don't cook."

"Today? Dinner today? At half-past five?"

Polina pouted. "We're Americans. Plittersdorfer Strasse 36, in Godesberg."

"At *five-thirty*?"

"OK, six, you British snob." She put a hand through the window for me to shake.

I kissed it, KGB-fashion.

Little city of dentists! I think I forgot to say I loved you. Little city of tax accountants, politicians, innkeepers, newspaper columnists, policemen! You're going to make me famous, you and Polina Mertz and Sebastian Ritter, even if right now my head aches, my chest is mucky with chemicals and my balls feel like number six shot. Little city, how sweet are your shut department stores, your cake shops and drapers with their Fifties signwriting, your switched-off fountains, your empty railway station and Saturday silence, your men stacking mangled crash-barriers, your tear gas drifting up from the cemetery! Little city of drinkers and dossers, faces red as farmers in August, adrift in the underpass on patches of twitchy sleep! Little city of driving instructors, simultaneous translators, secretaries, Nazis, spies!

Little city of my solitude, you were my companion! How we have walked and talked, along the middle of the Poppelsdorfer Allee, feeling through our shoes the faint, brittle geometry of German absolutism; past the Botanical Garden and over the booming motorway, past the swimming pool where the first summer housewives knit, bare-bosomed, on the grass. Here, at an indestructible bunker from the Reich, a road forks to the right, falters, recovers, then climbs up through blackberry brambles and calvaries. From a squad of boys in breeches, one breaks out, and in a single liquid movement, skims two fingers of water from a stoup and joins his moving friends higher up (rather as, at the funeral, a paving stone would come arching down to rattle off the police shields). At the top is the Kreuzkirche, where a marble staircase soars and vanishes into a vault of painted angels, which I would climb on my knees, but for some Dutch tourists, as once the Prince-Elector did in a bout of remorse. I turn and pick out the low British Embassy in the haze, the Bundestag and the old waterworks, and the Rhine slithering into the Siebengebirge. The Inter-City appears against the green of the Poppelsdorfer Allee.

Little city of pensioners and postmen! I take my other way down: beside an apple orchard, shedding its last rain-stained blossom, and into the allotment gardens, past rusty swing-seats and plywood summer houses, to the College of the Sacred Heart, where, between 3 November 1943 and 8 November 1943, 341 fellow citizens of Jewish extraction from Bonn, Beuel, Poppelsdorf and Endenich, men, women and children, were detained in unspeakable conditions before entraining for the East, may God have mercy on their souls! And on ours! *Wimmelnde Weltstadt der Dichter und Denker und Frisörlehrlinge, hasda not net geschnall, dass die Einsamkeit, ständige Begleitung meines bisherigen Lebens . . .**

Little city of joggers and bargemen! Have I not walked the Rhine to Godesberg, breathing in the taste of stale water, keeping step with your moving islands of sulphur and coal, your saloon car perched on the wheelhouse, the smell of Dutch tobacco riding over the water to me? Have I not gaped at the villas of dead chocolate millionaires, the palaces stolen from affectionate Jews?

"You're British! You're Dick! Right!"

"Right!"

"Hi. I'm Bill. Poll's husband."

"Don't tell me! You're British! You're Dick! Right?"

"Right."

"I'm Bill Spratling. Poll's husband."

"OK. Fair enough."

I shook hands with a short man with a neat, black beard and a thinning scalp. He had on a butcher's apron. From the open front door, I could see through the house into a garden where people

---

* Teeming world capital of poets and thinkers and barbers' apprentices, ain't you seen that solitude, my lifelong companion . . .

were standing about in pastel yellow, blue and pink. I was in the suit and black tie I'd put on for Frank Lightner's funeral. My feet ached from the walk down the Rhine towpath in leather shoes. To my right was the curved street I must have come up, with bungalows and American trees and unfenced lawns running down to the pavement, and a brick church which might have been picked off some New England common and air-freighted to Germany. A child in padded football strip did tight circles on a bicycle.

"I'm Bill Spratling."

"It's kind of you to invite me."

"Come on in. I'll tell Poll."

The house passed in a blur of tears. In the paved garden, I repeated names: Jim and Nadine Dole, another Bill, Bart and Nancy, Binky Sharma, Mr Hofmeyer of the *Frankfurter Allgemeine*. They held drinks and napkins in their right hands.

I turned and Polina was at my shoulder. She had on a lime-green dress with ruffles at the shoulder, black stockings and high-heeled pumps. I thought: A matronly costume, madam!

"Mrs Spratling?"

"Why not call me Polina?"

"How do you do?"

Spratling came between us. "Drink, Dick? We do a single Islay malt. Beer: German and American. A raft of sodas."

"Scotch whisky, please. With water."

"No ice, right?"

Why the hell not?

"I know Brits."

"I'll get it," said Polina. Her high heels clicked on the paving. At the small of her back was a lime-green bow.

Spratling was forking chicken quarters on to a grill. The charcoal still glowed red. I thought: They'll scorch, you prat. Beyond him, walking slowly towards us, head on one side to catch some twaddle from the Indian Ambassador beside him, was Jack Polk. He was very tall. His hair was whiter even than in newspaper photographs. His suit had a faint chalk stripe. He seemed quite out of place in

23

this outpost of Middle America, insulated in his celebrity and the history – Yalta! SALT! – he embodied. (In one of the Yalta group portraits, he stands behind Roosevelt's wheelchair, looking as if he'd just come off the tennis court at Piping Rock; beside him is a sleek and black-haired Gromyko.) Two US Secret Service agents followed at a distance.

"Guys," shouted Spratling, waving his barbecue tongs. "Isn't anybody going to ask Mr Polk one little question? He's come a ways."

Hofmeyer had his pipe out of his mouth. I got in first:

"Are the Soviets serious about a treaty?"

"No, sir."

Somebody laughed. Hofmeyer had begun a speech. I felt a tap on my shoulder. It was Polina with my whisky and a paper napkin.

"Dick here is *the* expert on the German Left," said Spratling. "He's read all those crazy clowns. You know, the guy who lived down at La Jolla and thought all the surfers and beachbums were Nazis. That old parson who did himself in in Berlin. He's got this humongous advance from . . ."

"May I ask you a question, young fellow?" said Polk. "Was it suicide?"

"No, it wasn't."

Hofmeyer took his pipe out. "On the contrary. My sources . . ."

Nobody asked your opinion. Piss off.

"Jack, it's a classic piece of GDR disinformation."

There was a whoosh of flame from the barbecue. Spratling shrieked. I went into the house.

A grey carpet dipped and righted itself. The room was cluttered with furniture in some Asian wood: a sofa, armchairs, a dining-room table laid with place-mats and a pyramid of pine cones in the middle, six matching chairs. On the walls were an Andrew Wyeth print, a bombastic photograph of the Rockies, another of Bill with Gerald Ford, a facetious diploma, and a pair of sculls with signatures on the blades. In the lavatory, where I tried to piss away the ache in my groin, purple towels were arranged in order of size: biggest, big, smaller, smallest. I was paralysed with indecision. I thought: Polina, I'm a conceited little prick, a snob, a piss artist and a flirt, but I'm all heart. I don't care that you're married or what you're up to with that sleaze Sergei. I'll teach you everything I know. We'll see Schloss Brühl, the Lochners in Cologne, the Elisabethkirche in Marburg, the Veit Stoss altar in Cracow. I'll show you how to grill chicken the American way. I'll cook you anything you want, even venison in rosehips. I'll put ten inches on your waist and a baby on each breast, if you'll just . . .

I opened the door on Jack Polk. He inclined his fine head and said softly: "I admired your father terrifically. We lived on L Street when you fellows were on Olive. Patty and Mildred just did everything together. We had fun."

"I barely knew him."

Polk looked at me sharply. I suppose he was rummaging in the 1960s, found some hot Georgetown evening, martinis on the back porch, Ed Fisher in a lounger, Patty Fisher in shorts, no kid. Then he lost interest and said: "You're on the team, boy. Got that?"

I nodded.

He straightened and said: "I wish you'd persuade these good people to move house. I never did care for waterfront property." As the lavatory door closed on him, I saw into the garden and into Spratling's eyes. They were cold and alert.

Promptly at nine, the Hofmeyers got up and said their goodbyes. The Indian Ambassador looked into his glass of Chivas, sighed and rose. Polk left with his security detail in two cars. On the lawn, he spoke quickly to Polina. At the front door, Spratling put his hand on my stomach. I jumped.

"Quite a gut you have, Dick. You should run. Do sports."

I take neurotic walks and run after your wife. I get enough exercise.

He said: "I have a racketball court at the club, the American Club, at ten tomorrow. I need a work-out myself. I have a long, long day ahead with Jack and the Chancellor."

"I'll be there."

"Where's your car?"

"I haven't got one. I'm taking the U-Bahn."

"You don't drive! How do you live, man?"

"I'll take him," Polina said. She ducked under my arm and out of the door. My heart turned over. "You're impaired, Bill," she said.

"Me? Drunk? You're full of shit, girl."

I said: "You shouldn't bother, Polina. I can walk to the station. It's no distance."

"Shut up, both of you," she said, reaching back in to a raincoat pocket for car-keys.

The car had imitation velvet seats. We turned on to the Ollenauerallee, the main road into Bonn. The engine crept up through its automatic gearbox. We kept pace with a lighted U-Bahn. Polina drove past one station and then another.

She said: "You don't have to play, you know."

I thought it best not to hear this. "An excellent barbecue. Thank you."

"I said: You don't have to lick my husband's ass just because he's my fucking husband."

The U-Bahn caught up, swayed and rattled past. In the light, her face was rigid with anger: it occurred to me she might have been hard used at one time. I said: "I was most interested to meet him. I don't believe you'd mentioned you had a husband."

"Just tell me where to go."

In the Mozartstrasse, Polina double parked. I kissed her on her left cheek, and on her right. Then I kissed her mouth, which opened vertiginously: for an instant, I saw hills and villages of happiness. I could feel her struggling to get her shoes off.

"Will you come in and sleep with me, Polina Mertz?"

"No," she said. She lifted her dress and slid on to my lap.

"Why not? If I may ask?"

"I'm through sleeping with guys."

She moved off my lap and sat, curled up, her cheek against the velveteen seat-back, looking at me. I opened my door and tried to stand up. She leaned right over my seat, her face turned up at me in the streetlight, her dress on her hips. "You have to help me, Richard. I mean it."

I shook my head wearily, like a man of the world; or as if somebody were watching me from the headquarters of the fascist *Deutschlandpartei* across the street, or the Borussia student corporation under its snapping tricolour, or the doctors' practice specializing in the urinary tract.

She said: "Jack needs to see Sebastian."

"Why?"

"Because, come July 5, Ritter'll be running German arms control policy, that's why."

"So?"

"So you can do it?"

"Sure. Who couldn't? Do it yourself. You're the superpower."

"You're his friend."

"For the fourteen-millionth time, I haven't got any friends. And who told you that?"

"Shut up! You talk so loud always, Richard."

I knelt down in the road, at her level.

She said: "Jack has a Nuclear Planning Group meeting in Brussels on the 29th, which is next Sunday. It's felt maybe he could drive up from Geneva, take in a monastery or something, whatever you guys do, eat lunch or dinner in a restaurant . . . Look, I haven't thought it through, OK?"

"Will you sleep with me, if I fix it?"

"NO."

I said: "I need time. We could go to Brühl after my game. I'd like to show it to you and it's on the way to the Ruhr, where I have to make a speech."

"I don't have the car."

"What's wrong with the train?"

Polina said: "Brühl. Not Brool. Your u-umlaut needs urgent remedial attention. I'll call, OK?"

I stood up. The wind sighed in the neo-Nazis' monkey puzzle.

27

The leaves fluttered in the weedy pavement birches. I said: "In 'On the Proposed Divorce Law', which was published in the *Rheinische Zeitung* at the end of 1842, Karl Marx wrote: 'All ethical relationships are by their very concept indissoluble, as one can easily find by assuming their truth.' A true state, a true marriage, a true friendship is indissoluble; but there is no state, no marriage, Polina, no friendship that completely corresponds to its concept. Actual friendship even within the family is dissoluble; the actual state in world history is dissoluble; and so, Polina Mertz, is actual marriage in the state."

The long car pulled away.

"You should try doubles one time, Dick. It's fun."

Spratling led the way down glassed-in courts. The place boomed and roared. A man sat on a bench with his wet head in his hands. Spratling said: "You need a bunch of guys who like to run around, use the ceiling. It's kind of quick."

My shorts squeezed my balls. I stank like an apple cellar.

"You've got to work on the back-hand court, Dick." We were in the changing room. A naked man was blow-drying his hair. "You've got to go for the high ones, really go for them. Once they're in the hole, you'll never dig them out."

I sat down. Spratling had his shirt off. His chest was pale. In the middle was a whorl of white-black hair.

He said: "I've got Polina really working on her game."

There were no partitions in the shower. Bending down to pick up the soap, I peered wetly at his bony feet, athlete's thighs, circumcised cock, soapy chest. I knotted a towel about my waist, but it kept slipping.

He shouted: "Did I hear your dad did something?"

"He taught at Georgetown in the Sixties." He also invented the rational study of nuclear weapons, as you bloody well know.

Spratling sat on the bench, legs apart, pulling a white sock on to his right foot. The German was now combing shiny hair.

"So you grew up in the States?"

No. My parents divorced when I was young, as it happens, and I grew up with my mother in the United Kingdom. "Thanks for last night."

"We're Americans. Americans barbecue. It's our contribution to world culture." He looked round and said quickly: "Jesus Christ, Dick! That guy Polk would give away the store! You wouldn't believe it!"

The German was still there, prick-naked, doing something to his ears.

Spratling leaned forward and hissed: "That guy's so hungry for a treaty, he'll give them our planes, your rinky-dink submarines, those land-based French systems that don't fly. He's an incorrigible problem-solver. Jesus! I've got a President who thinks he's still in Hollywood in some kind of labour contract negotiation with Louis B. Mayer. I've got civilians in the Pentagon who think we should destroy Kiev or someplace, protectively. I've got a Secretary of State who doesn't know his ass from an open-cast mine. And I've got Mr Present-at-the-Creation Jackie-Striped-Pants-Polk who's got it into his head that Russia's going to blow up if we modernize a few theatre rockets."

"My father . . ."

"You know something I don't know? You got live sources in the Central Committee of the CPSU? Grow up, Dick! We just have to do it, that's all. Deploy the mothers. And your Maggie Thatcher is right in there."

I picked up the plastic bag which confined my unspeakable sports clothes. I said: "I'd better be on my way, Bill." I'm not bothered by this homosexual threat and blandishment. I am going with your beautiful wife to the Alte Hirsch in Cologne – arguably the pinnacle of small-bourgeois cookery in the Rhineland – where, at a minimum, I shall take a drink. After that we are going to Schloss Brühl, that pearl of 18th-century German absolutism, where I intend to secure the peace of Europe for a generation; or, as an interim measure, and exemplarily, as it were, my own happiness.

Spratling said: "Watch out, pal."

"What does that mean?"

"I said: Take it easy."

We spent too long at lunch, and the house and park at Schloss Brühl were closed. I waited an hour for my train. Polina walked up and down the windy platform, hugging herself. I suppose she was dying to pee. In those days, her hair went right down her back. At the front, it was parted low on the left (right as you looked at her). I said: "What or who is the Golden Plough?"

Polina closed her eyes and shivered. She raised her fist to my chest, extended her forefinger, squeezed an imaginary trigger. The train came in behind her. She started walking down the platform, stepping carefully. The conductor, who wore a red sash across his chest, as if he belonged in a children's picture book, swung himself down. Polina stooped and slid off her shoes and, where it said RIGOROUSLY FORBIDDEN TO CROSS! MORTAL DANGER!, stepped over the railway lines and out of sight.

I gave my routine speech in Herder in the Ruhr, at a sports centre smelling of *Bockwurst* and beer. Adelheid Müller had left a message, thanking me for finding time, in an undoubtedly busy schedule, to address Dr Ritter's constituency party within the framework of the Bundestag election campaign. Dr Ritter had himself proposed that we travel back together on the Inter-City, if that were convenient.

I spoke for an hour, with many interruptions. I gave a little history of the arms race; of the effort by the Soviets to catch up; of the triumph with Sputnik in '57 and the disastrous short-cut in Cuba in '62. I talked about the SS-20: 250 of the brutes, each with three independently targetable nuclear warheads, and all pointed at West Germany; and not at military bases and missile silos but at the heart of the Social Democratic Party; and all with the purpose of terrifying the West Germans out of the Western Alliance, so the thing fell to bits and the Americans lost patience, and sailed off home with their men and missiles and junk food, and Russia ruled a continent. At this point, Ritter called for order: he reminded his party-friends that tolerance of uncomfortable opinions was a tradition of German Social Democracy. Beside me, Sergei Makhaev took furious notes.

Ritter was sitting in the restaurant car when I got on. He was sipping lentil soup, with his briefcase open on the seat beside him. A waiter lounged in the coupling, eyeing the celebrity. I sat down, ordered a can of coffee and the fruit brandy known as *Obstler*, and spoke to Ritter's bowed head. He said nothing and then nodded.

At Bonn station, he said: "Don't forget your work."

A fat brown file peeped out of a plastic Kaufhof bag. As a record of seventy years of struggle and subversion, it don't look much, but then maybe Frank wasn't the sort of man to keep a diary and collect his letters. Still, I am very, very grateful, Dr Ritter.

"Thank you."

We stepped down on to the cold platform.

He strode off, but then stopped. A little girl in yellow trousers, blue shoes and a blue mac, had detached herself from somebody and was running, crying, down the platform, her arms above her head. She looked four or five years old. Ritter dropped into a crouch, set his briefcase upright beside him, and the child cannoned into him. As I went by, the girl was standing perfectly still between his knees, her face in his raincoat, her hair across his cheek. An Asian woman was standing two steps back, smiling and out of breath.

It is Saturday afternoon, and I have not spoken to Polina for six days. I have still not washed my sports clothes. The surface of my desk is cold to the touch. The light through my net curtains (which my landlord tells me are required by law) reminds me of snowy mornings in England. I feel a sensation akin to vertigo: that if I think about Polina, I'll fall and, falling, lose the terror of thinking of her, but at some unmeasurable penalty.

My eyes ache in the snowy light. I look through the curtains and down the crazy paving, past the Japanese cherry which bursts into blossom, past crocuses springing through the gravel, to the iron gate and through it, where – in my imagination – the bonnet of a green Dodge Aspen keeps bumping to a halt; a door opens and bangs; the gate whines; and Polina is walking up the path, stepping carefully in high heels, her raincoat open on her beautiful waist, furious and – *mein Herz!* – she's cut her hair off!

"It's good, Polina. Better than Jean Seberg."

She pushes past me, clacking down the passageway to my apartment. Upstairs, my landlord's baby, Ka-ha (for Karlheinz), begins to cry.

Polina has her back to me, looking at the photographs I've put up along one of the long walls. I try to take her awful coat, but she shakes my hand off her shoulder.

"You don't have chairs," she says.

"I don't have friends."

Polina stamps her foot. She says: "You're wasting your time."

I say: "I most certainly am not. I have a good memory and I'm thorough, which is why I find out things nobody else finds out. If Frank really was a Soviet agent, I have to establish what he was up to and why. What I have to do, if I'm to get anywhere, is to reconstruct the Lightner circle at each period. Let's do this one first. The conference called 'The Rule of Law in Peril!', March 16–18, 1972, Evangelical Academy, Tutzing, Bavaria. In the chair: Professor Doctor Lightner. Source: *Süddeutsche Zeitung*. The bloke seated in front, gesturing with the pencil, is, you are right, a long-haired Sebastian Ritter. The girl in the flares – got her? – is none other than Beate Beck. Butter wouldn't melt in her mouth, would it? Here she is again, here, all done up like a dog's dinner in her lawyer's cap and gown, at Peter Klein's trial, Stuttgart-Stammheim, October 22, 1977. The photograph doesn't show it, but she is

32

concealing an automatic pistol, presumably in her sleeve. Source: the *Spiegel* archive.

"This is the best of the monitor pictures. The camera was above the bench, quite high. The figure on the left is Ritter. He has his hands to his stomach. As if he thought he'd been hit. The other one is Warrant Officer Kurras, who is dead, or about to be. It's reproduced in the report of the Disciplinary Commission of the North Rhine-Westphalia Bar Society, November 1978.

"Now. This is Norderney, on the North Sea coast, no date, but probably 1979 or 1980. Source: private collection. The man with his back to that boat or breakwater thing, with sunglasses and the pipe, is Lightner. The other man, with his eyes covered by the floppy hat and the child's arm, talking, is Ritter. The little girl with the fair hair, clambering up his back, looking at the camera, remember her. OK?"

I touch her on the upper arm, but she stiffens.

"Have you got her? Because this is also her, at the beginning of January this year, also from a private source, the girl on ice skates. The man standing on the ice is Ritter. I believe this little girl is about five and is called Rosa, no doubt after Rosa Luxemburg . . ."

She turns away. "You're nowhere."

Ah Polina, let's call it off. I mean: one last time. "I'm sorry for whatever it was I did."

Polina stamps her foot again, walks past me to the door. I hear the clatter of her heels and the front door open and close. I pick up my jacket and run out. She is standing by her car door, in the dead street.

She says: "Don't you ever pull that stunt or I'll never talk to you again."

We're getting there! There is a set of possibilities where you will speak to me again, whereas the excluded set consists only of my pulling that stunt again, whatever that stunt was.

"Which stunt?"

"You know fucking well what you said. On Brühl train station."

"What? About making a baby?"

"NO!"

"Polina, I'm slow, but I always get there in the end. You'd be better off telling me."

Her left hand is tight on the door-handle; but the stiffness is going out of her and something else is coming in: something authentically feminine: a sense maybe that she's come all this way to the *Bahnhofsviertel* on a Saturday and it can't have been to bawl me out, because she's done that already: it must have been for some other purpose.

"We should go to Gut Zons," I say. Best not to give her any time. "It's quite nice." I touch her on the hand holding the car door and, this time, feel her tremble. "Show Germany your new hair."

Polina sidles into the Meckenheimer Allee and joins the stream of sunny traffic on the motorway. The act of swinging on to the highway, the way she turns all the way round to see over her left shoulder, how the back of the big car pulls and then straightens – like a fish released into a current – these things are factual delight.

"Would you follow the Königswinter signs, please?"

I feel weary and formal, as if we have just reached an understanding in business. Let the lawyers and investment bankers earn their fees for once, the principals are going out to celebrate! On the bridge sky floods the car. The Rhine runs through me and I gasp with the sweetness of it. Lord, how did this happen?

"Yes. Left. All the way up the hill."

We are going to a wine garden which is, by the near universal consent of experts, the best in the world. At some moment this evening, though my heart may liquefy, Polina will drive back with me to the Mozartstrasse. This is such an escalation of risk that I can't think about it: I lack her capacity for abstraction. What I can say is that God, or whoever it is that handles these questions, in His unfathomable mercy, has answered prayers I never prayed.

Weingut Zons consists of an unmown field scattered with red plastic tables and chairs and big oak trees. Vineyards rise steeply on three sides. On the open side is a tarmac car park and a wooden barn, where the wine is sold from behind a counter and a small kitchen does goulash soup and sauerkraut: the sort of food you're looking for in a dream. There are no customers, which ditto.

"I'll get us some wine."

"No," she says, picking up her purse and putting it under her arm. "It's my turn." Her heels sink into the grass. Polina Mertz. Mrs. Frau. Ms. Everywhere about us are things that don't bear thinking about: that'll take off a foot or a hand, put out an eye, mess up your face; but this field has been cleared, this evening, this night, this dream. You walk back in perfect safety, in a shiver and ring of glasses, lopsided where your heels have gone into the field, my now-and-tonight-and-tomorrow-morning Polina.

Of that evening at Gut Zons, I do not have continuous memory. This is not because of the drink. Gut Zons is the northernmost vineyard in Europe and its wine has an alcoholic content of 5.7 per cent. It was not so much drink as happiness, which seemed somehow independent of me and was expressed in the world of phenomena, so that when the coloured lights in the branches came on, that was a definition of happiness; or when the big oaks seemed to march towards me in the twilight, that was also happiness; or when I took Polina's hand off the sticky plastic table and touched for the first time the tight wedding ring on her finger; or when the twenty-fifth anniversary outing of the Koch Driving School got rowdy; or when Polina shivered and borrowed my jacket; or when the light came on in the barn, and a beam came shooting across the grass and pierced me with happiness; or when Polina came back with some cake and I saw she'd taken off her shoes; or when she gathered, in one unforgettable motion, her feet up into her chair and settled on her heels, her cropped head under the racing moon.

I did most of the talking. Polina did not grit her teeth, when she saw, before I did, my sentence plunging towards the obvious or nonsensical. She did not finish my thoughts for me, then dispose of them, American-hygienic. She didn't interrupt. She watched, across the table, as ideas that had been stacked like aircraft over the Cologne-Bonn district for three years came hurriedly and safely in: things I'd said only to darkness and to brandy and my granite Ikea bed; about the melancholy of small German towns that Dostoyevsky talks about in *The Gambler*; and Nabokov in Berlin, refusing to learn a word of German lest it dislodge a piece of Russia, and all the while the windows of Jewish drapers' shops staring about him; and the passage about the Realm of Freedom and the Realm of Necessity in Marx; and Goethe's journey through the Harz mountains in the winter of 1776. In retrospect, maybe I should have kept Goethe out of it, but space and history seemed to be converging on us, on our implicated wills, our polarities of sex and temperament, on the glitter of her eyes.

I said: "I never did meet Lightner, but I saw him. In 1968, just before Easter, because Sebastian Ritter was still in one piece, in the Auditorium Maximum of the Free University, where I did my degree. I knew Ritter and most of the others on the podium by sight: Rudi Dutschke, Krahl who died in a car crash, Thyra Pohl, Gabriele Koch who was killed at Mogadishu, Bernd Rabehl. There was an older man there I didn't know. He was bald, had pebble spectacles, was wearing a suit; Ritter kept turning to him from the lectern, as if it were one old professor he had to win over to his analysis of existing conditions and not the Berlin student body, that vanguard of the proletariat in the unfolding revolutionary situation.

"I was in the back row, as I used to be in those days. On my right, in front of the swing doors, a student was smoking a reefer the size of a truncheon. I suppose the smell of it made me turn and notice him. He had on a white coat like a laboratory assistant's and he was carrying one of those two-handed saws loggers use. The doors swung in and another guy entered backwards, labouring under the weight of a bright red stepladder. There may have been a third person, I can't remember. They passed me, the ladder bumping on the rubber steps of the aisle. At the dais, they bowed elaborately to Ritter and the old man, then set up the ladder – with a lot of tripping up and falling over and bashing each other on the head – under the wooden emblem of the Free University which hung from the high ceiling of the Audimax. I can't remember the coat of arms but the motto was 'Truth Freedom Justice'.

"My neighbour wore a weary Leftist smile. 'The lads from Commune One,' he said.

" 'Commune One?'

" 'Hedonist-Spontaneist,' and then in English: 'Hippies.'

"They were sawing. Ritter looked up and round. I remember the shiny elbows of his suit looked laughably small-bourgeois. 'Comrades,' he said, 'your understandable and, in my opinion, highly rational vexation . . .' or something like that. Somebody laughed. Somebody else clapped and it caught on. My neighbour shouted 'Shame!' through a cupped hand. One of the wooden chains was cut through and the shield swung from the other. At the table on the stage, the old man was on his feet, packing paper methodically into a briefcase of the kind doctors carry in Britain, you know? He came up the aisle on my right. There was a crash on the stage, laughter, wolf-whistles, dust, Ritter saying something hurried into the microphone. The old man pushed at the door. At the back of his head, behind and below the ear, was a scar. I saw stitch-marks. There was something brutal and old-fashioned about the work, though I can't say that I was then (or am now) expert in Red Army surgery of the Lower Volga region, circa January 1943. As the door opened, the man said, so quietly that maybe only I heard him: 'Infantile actionism!'

"Infantile actionism! The phrase fizzed in my head as they made a bonfire of the coat of arms on the lawn in front of the Rector's lodgings; and there were joints doing the rounds; and a girl with hennaed hair and a purple-and-white scarf which hung down to her shoes said across the fire to me: 'Why are you afraid, boy?' Infantile actionism! I tagged alongside the demonstration, because I was worried about my scholarship: along Kurfürstendamm, trying to catch my reflection in the glass from the splintered shop-cases on the pavement, while her face and name – which was Beate: Beate Beck – swam in and out of view. And again, the evening Sebastian Ritter was shot on the Ku'damm and I heard what had happened

37

at the Springer Building down by the Wall: infantile actionism! Except the phrase and Beate were slipping away from me and I saw, my stomach churning with disgust and fear, that Germany wasn't England with a fence down the middle and a verb at the end but a place of torment and horror and unfinished business, a theoretical Bedlam.

"There is something in here, that possibly I alone know but do not understand. At some point, I will need to go and call on Ms Beck, wherever she is, and pray to God Almighty she doesn't shoot me. I don't want to think about that now. Goodbye, Polina. It is four in the morning in the world's hardest bed, in the world's loneliest apartment, in the world's most melancholy city. I am naked, drunk, masculine, impotent. I'm not going to think about Beate Beck or Sebastian Ritter. I'm going to sleep, and failing that, to dream of Weingut Zons."

I say: "Actually, you're quite wrong. If I could understand what Goethe meant, it would help me, I know it would. As the hunting party canters off, a part of him goes with it, busy, ambitious, sociable, censorious. The main party leaves the path:

> Who's that turning off the ride? His track vanishes in the thicket.
> The bushes whip back behind him. The grass springs up again.
> The waste engulfs him.

That's easy enough. But the next verse is already hard. What does he mean by 'found only hatred in the midst of love'? And what is 'junkie egoism'?"

I stop because someone is singing.

I could translate the next verse, give the voice-part in musical notation,

even recommend a recording. Nik Tully, my British interrogator, had a record biked down from Saturn in Cologne. It was made for

Decca in 1944 by Kathleen Ferrier, the British alto known in German musical circles as *die schöne Telefonistin* because she'd worked for a time as a switchboard operator in Bolton, Lancashire. Nik listened with an air of rapture.

Better to say what I saw and heard and felt: how Polina looks up, gains in confidence; how conversation at the tables falters and drops; the driving instructors freeze in their carnival hats; the waiter sways on the balls of his feet; a woman spins on her chair; the cook stands, back-lit, smoking, in the barn doorway; and then Polina stops and says, loudly: "Excuse me."

Somebody claps, then others, then the garden. A big man comes up, mouth agape, and rolls his hips in a dance. Another man stands at his table and bows. A woman says: *Doch! Schubert!* Someone says Eichendorff. Someone says Brahms. *Iss da Goedda!* And Goethe and Brahms it is, running from table to table, crackling through the warm evening like a crownfire in woods. Polina has her eyes down and her shoulders in the Polina slouch. She says:

"I'm sorry. Let's go."

In the black car park, I say: "I didn't know you sang."

"Oh baby, I can do everything. I'm in your dream."

"Can you say you love me?"

"That, too."

A couple giggles towards us. Polina puts her hand on my shoulder and lifts off a shoe to shake out an imaginary stone. Then she tumbles against me. I search all over for her mouth. She undoes my belt-buckle.

"Are we done, Polina? Can we go to bed?"

She pulls the belt tight and threads it neatly home. She says: "You're not going to believe this. It's going to put you right off."

"It doesn't."

"CUT THAT, JACKASS!"

She pats my belt and stands back. She says: "Richard, Mrs Lightner's in East Berlin. It's on ADN. Statement. Greeting by Honecker. *Grosser Bahnhof.* The works."

"Leave me be, Polina."

"You can get the GDR news at seven. Time to wake up, babe."

The red VW beetle was parked at Euskirchen station. With a dent in the rear passenger-side wing. Key under driver's seat, stick shift, can you work a stick-shift? It took me ten minutes to find reverse.

In Ohrfeld, at a traffic light, a man opened the door, slid in and gestured me to go to the right. I thought: We're going to the Schule Elmersdorf, the better of the two, really, she's right, the cow! The agent had a plug in his ear that crackled nonsensically but he said nothing. At a pub at the beginning of the Elmer Valley, he signalled me to stop and got out. There seemed to be cars ahead and behind, as I wound up the valley. Trees were coming into leaf on the steep slate hillsides. At Elmerswede, the sun broke into the valley and filled me with warmth: I felt secure and public, a part of some authorized and well-rehearsed ceremony. I parked at the usual place, by an old camper van with Pforzheim plates.

Ambassador Jack Polk was sitting at the base of a rowan tree, a fly-box open on his knees. An old cane fishing rod, strung with what looked like silk line, leaned against the bole. His fishing vest had lost its colour; also his cap, which read *King Ropes, Sheridan, Wyo.* over fine white hair, his wading boots, his blue jeans, a leather creel in the grass. Everything about Jack Polk was faded, cracked, oiled, supple, expensive, fraudulent: as if he'd just fitted himself out on Madison Avenue.

"Looks like it's going to be bright, young man."

"That's all right. Should bring on a hatch."

"What? Mayfly? So early?"

"And sedges."

The flies in his book were vast things of moose-hair, turkey-feather, raccoon-tail: useless for this little Old World river.

"Yippee!" he said, and then: "They've been down the stream."

"Excuse me. The agents have been down the stream? In the stream?"

"I'm afraid so, young fellow." He smiled, as if to say: You must forgive us uncouth Americans, but those chumps from the Secret Service have just walked through every pool of the best trout stream in divided Germany. There was something of pride in there, too, as when my American stepmother used to talk about her clothes closet.

"I think we need to wait a bit. To let the water settle. At least fifteen minutes."

"I've got some coffee in the truck, Richard."

"Yes, sir."

When I came to Germany, in the spring of 1981, I asked Brian Barchard of the British Embassy if he knew of any place I could go fishing. I wanted everyone to know I had a hobby: outdoor, solitary, time-consuming, old-fashioned. He said I should speak to Pierre – everybody said I should speak to Pierre – who was the French charge d'affaires and so popular, evidently, that he went without a surname.

Caroline introduced us. He was a big man, fat even, and he spoke English so beautifully it was a pleasure merely to listen to him. We drove through the suburbs of Cologne and then Greven-broich, where, running between a pebble-dashed house and a tractor dealership, a path led us into a strippy wood with, some distance in, a square pond.

We sat on stools for about twenty minutes, apparently fishing for tench. Pierre LaFrance kept changing his rod. He disappeared and came back a little later with some morels; then he busied himself with lunch, rabbit stew with dumplings, which we ate off embossed French Embassy china, and a bottle of 1978 Chateau Beychevelle; then I fished a bit more and he read *Die Zeit*; then he drove us home, introduced me to his wife and to his son (who was thinking of the LSE), and made an incandescent martini. Pascale LaFrance laid another place beside her and went to the kitchen, halfway through dinner, herself to cook the morels. I never went to the pond again (and I'm sure Pierre LaFrance didn't either); or to their house; or ate morels; but the excursion left a memory of unbearable delight and security, which I felt throughout 1981 and 1982 was mine to recapture, if I but bided my time.

41

Instead, I bought a copy of *Fisch und Fang*, which advertised a fishing club called the Amici Petri Colonienses eV. I telephoned the club secretary, a tax accountant named Manfred Köhler, who said, why not, they were doing the stocking that weekend and he'd come by the Mozartstrasse. A black Mercedes drew up, bristling with telecommunications equipment. Hooked on Manfred's fishing vest was a mouse used, I think, only for wild rainbow trout beyond the Arctic watershed. He fished in a Walkman.

We went every weekend. We exchanged gruff little comments on party politics or the business outlook. I asked about Manfred's girlfriend, who never came; and we talked about his fishing trips: the mahseer in the Jhelum, bonefish in Guadeloupe, bluefish off Nantucket, Nile perch in Lake Victoria.

Beside those fabulous waters, the Elmer was a trickle. The beat ran for two miles through meadows where the farmer kept cattle. Miraculously, he used no chemicals, except their shit. Alders and rowans grew on each bank. To fish the river, you had to use a rod no longer than four feet, crouch or kneel on the bank, and cast upstream under the trees, retrieving line as the fly swam down. After a day's fishing, when my nerves were still and my cast was without splash or effort, I felt I'd passed into a submerged world and could see, in the crazy refraction of the fish's vision, in a riot of prism colour, a swimming fly; and could rise with a flick of the tail and an open mouth, and, turning down again, feel a stab in the cartilage of my jaw.

Manfred usually had a big bag, but I found it hard even to kill the one I gave to Angelika Simrock at the Jagdhütte, to cook in clarified butter, three minutes a side.

But this Sunday, April 29, 1983, Manfred was on the Helmsdale; Heinz-Jochen was with his in-laws in Kassel; and the others never came, or if they did, well, *der gute Fisher ist doch immer da,** and he has a guest with him – it's permitted, *ja klar*, in the bye-laws, two days a season – an American gentleman, it seems. I know nothing

* Old Fisher's always there.

42

about intelligence cover, but I presume that doing the same thing on a Sunday that you always do on a Sunday is good cover.

"So where's the hot spot?"

After five minutes, Polk was restless. The coffee was good enough to have been made in Geneva. He poured it from a silver flask, cased in scored leather, Tiffany, circa 1938.

"Do you know what I mean by the Yalta Conference?"

I nodded. Sod off, Jack Polk.

"I was kind of the baby of the delegation. The President and Mr Hopkins thought maybe we should get to know some of the Soviets socially. I asked Mr Gromyko back to my cabin, he was my age. He drank out of that cup."

I licked my lips.

Polk was smiling at me, as if to say: It never fails, that one, even at the hundredth telling. And then, the point:

"Gromyko said: 'We'll bury you, Lt Polk. Just watch.'"

I said: "We'll start at Manfred's Pool. It's the best, and I don't know how much time we've got."

We strode off down the meadow, two weekend anglers.

"Nice rod," I said, still shaken by the touch of Gromyko's lips.

"Gee, it's old. John Leonard, Sr made it for me," he said and then: "Some damn fool would probably give me $50,000 for it." It occurred to me that Polk, too, was bewildered that his past had been overrun by the Madison Avenue notion of it: that he was now just a name and a set of accoutrements. For the first time in my life, I thought: All this is going to end soon, in war or peace.

Manfred's pool was where Manfred always started. At the head of it, the channel narrowed to two feet or so between crumbly clay banks and clumps of flag irises; opened out into a pool some fifteen feet across, at the tail of which was a patch of muddy shingle where the cows came to drink; and then went out in a fast run. The pool always held one big fish and sometimes one or two smaller, which lay downstream and took the insects and nymphs the big guy thought beneath his consideration. Even if you were heavy like Manfred, you could stand on the shingle and cast without sending a wave upstream. I put Polk on the shingle. I laid my rod down and put on the polarized sunglasses Manfred had given me for Christmas.

"You're not fishing, Richard?"

"I'll get you started," I said. "Here take my book." I slid my fly-box into the back pocket of his vest.

Polk seemed relieved. He looked greedy for fish, like Manfred.

"It's by way of being small," he said sadly. "What we'd call a spring creek. I cut my teeth on the Beaverkill, of course. You know the Beaverkill? We used to get together, a whole lot of fellows. In those days, Wall Street went to sleep on Fridays. We'd ride up to Roscoe and stay in the Silver Fox there. You know it up there, Richard? Junction Pool? You needed a long line up there, believe me."

"I've heard of it."

When the Hendrickson mayfly hatches on the Beaverkill in late April, you can stand on line for four hours at Junction Pool. I knew this because I'd just read it in Manfred's *American Flyfisher*. Also, in the 1960s, US Route 10 was extended into the Beaverkill Valley, and carried back and forth across the creek on concrete stilts. The Silver Fox burned down in 1971: eventually, the loss adjusters paid up. I didn't say it, because many things are better not said and because I'd seen something splashing and skittering on the surface of the water, a hatching mayfly trying to dry its wings, spinning round and round, rising an inch in the air and then falling back, to vanish in a boiling rise.

"Two o'clock! Five rod-lengths up! What you've got on is OK! Nice fish!"

Polk bent slightly at the waist. On his face, as he drew line off his reel, passed a series of looks: concentration, anxiety, reminiscence, a smile. He false-cast twice. His line shot out and fell about two feet short. He started to retrieve it, but I put my hand up and he let the fly swim down to his feet. I could see he wanted to speak.

He cast again: right length this time, but about a foot and a half to the right. He took a step forward in exasperation. A tidal wave moved up the pool and broke on the flags. He turned to me with a look of comical horror and contrition.

I said: "Let's hold on. He may hang around."

Polk said: "How much did Mrs S. tell you?"

"Nothing."

"Not that I've wandered off the reservation? Or that there's a posse with two chuck wagons after me? That the White House ain't picky, dead or alive?"

"No, sir."

"Good girl," he said and then: "I like a fellow to put in some time on Wall Street. Bit in the bank does no harm? No exaggerated idea of human worth, eh? Your father never cared for money. Ed was such a damn prig when it came to money."

Look: Why is everyone round here talking about Polina Mertz? Are you in love with Ms Mertz, too?

I said: "He's still there."

It was a nice, slow, fat rise, probably to a nymph: six feet or so upstream from his last, but still in the pool. I heard the farmer's bird-scarer. Polk's line bellied out behind him. I thought: He'll catch it in that willow, and that's the end of this pool; but he didn't. The line came forward sweetly. The fly landed among the flags, caught, then slid down and dropped into the stream, where it spun histrionically and began to swim down. I thought: You've got him, you old ham. There was a flash of white, not at all where I expected it, and a strange and beautiful colour, between pomegranate and clean copper, but a colour of water not air, which was the fish's belly as it rolled down with the fly. I shot my arm out just in time to take Polk's rod painfully in the wrist: his strike would have broken his hook or leader.

The line tightened, raced up the pool. I thought: He still doesn't know it's in him, poor guy. Then the water boiled and something came surging up – a brown trout, three or even more pounds – and plunged on to the line. Polk dropped and then raised his rod. I sensed that muscles hardly used for forty years were being extended,

45

and also a strange and sweet melancholy: as if Polk knew this would be the last wild fish he'd catch in his life.

"Do you want him?"

"Are you crackers?"

I unclipped the net at my back. The fish came out again, rolled again on the line then ran for the head of the pool. The line veed into the gap as he tried to entangle it in the flags; but Polk held the rod upright. It bent double and then straightened. What had happened just then (that burst heart, those ruptured guts), I didn't want to think about. I dropped the net under the fish and, before he could see me, put my hand under his jaw and broke his neck. I walked back down to Polk on the shingle, with the fish on two hands. The strength of the fish's neck still ran through my arm.

Polk said: "Mr. Fisher, I never expected in my life to catch a German trout. And on quarter-pound gut, dammit!" His eyes sparkled.

It's going to cost you, mate.

"Did you hear a shot?"

"It's the farmer's bird-scarer."

"I believe not," he said.

Oh yes, very good, often hear single shots in the country, bird-scarer, ho ho!

He strode up the shingle, impatient to get out of my world and back into his own, shaking his head. I looked up and, asquat on each bank among ox-eyed daisies, were Secret Service agents.

Polk said: "I believe we should leave your car, go in the truck. A German fish! Well, well." He pulled back the camper door to reveal two more agents, eating sandwiches out of clingfilm.

Of the two venues I'd offered, I thought the Schule Elmersdorf the better. It was in the firs back from the road, with trees cleared fifty yards on all sides and only one door in. It was surely not beyond the agents' ingenuity to break the padlock on the gate, clamber in through a window (as once Manfred and I, in a thunder-storm in late season), get in some food and furniture. She had rejected it, no doubt for banal reasons: that it was cold – how she

46

hated to be cold! – or that Polk was too grand to sit in a classroom, before the remains of a blackboard and still the faint smell of chalk and the ghosts of Sixties schoolchildren.

We stopped twice on the way. The red beetle overtook us and Polk simply pulled in and we waited and listened, the agents leaning on the bonnet or murmuring into their handsets. A helicopter rattled over. We made a big detour into Belgium, then swung back through Kirchenroden. At one point, Polk said:

"Don't you love this covert stuff?"

"No, sir."

In front of the Jagdhütte, we got out and the cars were taken away. As he climbed the rustic wooden steps, Polk said: "The fishing party." Or: "The Fishing Party."

I was still holding the fish, wrapped in dock leaves. One of the agents took it from me, went through my pockets, printed two of my fingers on a pad, and patted the insides of my legs. Polk passed on ahead of me, unmolested. The cuckoo clock sang. I thought: Mrs Simrock and her daughter will have done something amazing, like that eel thing Manfred loves. Blast! I can't think about that now. The agent pointed to the *Stammzimmer*. My heart shivered.

In the room, a wood fire was blazing. The false panelling, with its satyrs and bunches of grapes, its Gothic scrolls and drinking mottoes – all Horst and Waltraut Simrock's suburban yearning and nostalgia – had been stripped and stacked against the walls. The tables had been cleared, except the big one in the middle, which had four chairs, four notepads, four pencils, four glasses and four bottles of Apollinaris. Polk had his back to me, still in his fishing vest, standing in the bay window. On his right was Sebastian Ritter, in his shiny dark suit. Also, in a brand new, matching turquoise coat and skirt, was Polina, shut as tight as a clam.

"Good day, Dr Ritter! Mrs Spratling, hi!"

Polina said in German: "I believe we should start immediately. Time is not limited, but not abundant either." She walked backwards, her arm outstretched towards the table, and just missed an oak chair. Calm down, baby, it's only the fate of the continent.

We sat down. At that moment, and perhaps simultaneously with Ritter, I realized we were on the same side of the table and what that meant: that whereas Polk had with him a translator and adviser, from the same US Administration, Ritter was sitting beside a part-time British spy of doubtful allegiances. I tried to shift my chair to the left and banged my knee agonizingly against the oak table leg. Polina bit her lip. Ritter smiled. Polk rubbed his hands together and said in slow English: "Well, here we all are."

Polina swallowed the first part of her speech. I got it from here: ". . . issues relating to the Geneva initiative in an informal and secure setting, from a Federal German perspective. All participants are aware that the fact of this meeting, its agenda and content are deniable."

Ritter nodded his head a flicker, which quite put her off.

". . . for listening devices and no record, written or electronic, will be kept. You are free to take notes, Mr Ritter, but these will be destroyed at the meeting's end, when your own papers will be returned to you. Mr Fisher will translate into English and I shall translate into German."

Little Miss Efficiency! I toyed with the notion that if I couldn't catch her eye, I could at least try to touch her leg under the table, but then thought better of it: in Polina's present state, that would be dangerous. Also, I felt I should try and grow up: We are here to dispose of the fate of Europe, and all I can think of is Polina's legs! Polk, who was presumably quite ignorant of the turbid current running between his translators, leaned back and twiddled a pencil in his fingers.

He said: "You will be aware, Mr Ritter, that since I first sat down in Geneva in November 1980 to discuss with Soviet representatives a treaty regulating nuclear weapons in the European theatre, I have made no progress whatsoever. For reasons of delegation morale, I had my staff analyse several force configurations and totals; but since our first meeting, the plenary sessions have been a stage for Soviet speeches, grandstanding and abuse."

Polk made no pauses for his interpreter. She was leaning forward, frowning in concentration, staring straight at Ritter or rather through him and his ironic smile and into her vast German vocabulary: How many words in there? Twenty thousand? Thirty thousand?

"All the time, you will understand, my hands have been tied by the President's endorsement of the so-called Zero Option, a proposal for which my thanks are due to the arms-control theorists of the German Social Democratic Party, led by your good self, Mr Ritter."

Ritter bowed.

"As you formulated the proposal, and the President and the Congress endorsed it, the Soviets were given until November 1983 to withdraw and dismantle the SS-20 force in the European Soviet Union. If they refused, NATO would match this force with a deployment in Western Europe of modern cruise and ballistic missiles with nuclear armament. No SS-20, no Pershing. Zero.

"It was clear from the outset that, for the Soviets, Zero has only ever applied to the proposed Western counter-deployments; and that, in the Soviet scheme, their armed forces should be permitted to deploy any number of land-based intermediate-range ballistic systems with targets in Western Europe and Asia. However, it was also clear to me that, at the margins of the plenaries, the Soviets were prepared to deal somewhat more creatively. I did not consider it my duty to talk bunkum ['*Quatsch*' translated Polina] for three years. On the contrary, I did consider it my duty to explore every possibility for a settlement, as long as this did not compromise the security of the countries of NATO or our allies in Asia. I, therefore, in accordance with the spirit of my instructions from the President, on October 12, 1982, extended a personal invitation to Mr Quertsovsky . . . Mr Kurtsovsky . . ."

"Shall we agree to call him Mr K.?"

Ritter was evidently unaffected by Polina's aggressive or tactless seating plan.

"Thank you, sir," Polk said. "Never could pronounce the fellow's name. I therefore invited Mr K. to Sunday lunch at a restaurant called the *Charrue d'Or* – the Golden . . ."

". . . dem goldenen Pflug . . ."

". . . Plough in English – in St Julien, a mile over the French border from Geneva. You will also be aware – and Mrs Spratling can brief you further on this, if you require – that the deployment figures and schedules on the NATO side express military and political concepts that are by no means immutable. The Defense Chiefs selected a figure of 572 missiles for despatch to Europe, because they believed anything much less would be a political nuisance without any material security yield; much more and we'd be running out of worthwhile targets."

"Even in Moscow Military District?"

"Specifically excluding the MMD, Mr Ritter. Beyond that, if you'll permit me, Defense resolved on 108 Pershing II ballistic missiles, because there existed in the Federal Republic, at Mutlangen Air Force Base in Swabia and elsewhere, that number of launchers for its predecessor-system, the Pershing I. Since cruise missiles are typically deployed in flights of 16, an appropriate figure for these weapons was 464.

"After lunch, Mr K. and I took a walk to work off some of the effects of Madame LeClerc's kitchen. I had with me a draft treaty in my coat pocket, which I gave to Mr K. to read. He made some alterations in ballpoint. I recollect we sat down on a log. I will not speculate about Mr K.'s instructions or his career ambitions; but he did volunteer that he could present the draft treaty to his masters as a back-channel American proposal. I said I would take it to Washington and present it as a high Soviet official thinking out loud. You must understand, Mr Ritter, that the initiative is wholly deniable on both sides."

Ritter nodded.

"The chief feature of the draft treaty, and by far the most audacious, is its abandonment of a zero solution in either its NATO or Warsaw Pact formulations – that is, no SS-20s, cruise missiles or Pershing IIs on the one hand, and no NATO deployments on the other – in favour of some deployment on both sides. We envisaged a European total – we can come to Asia later, if you're interested –

of some 300 nuclear warheads: that is, 100 SS-20 missiles, each with three independently targetable warheads, and 19 batteries of cruise missiles."

"And the Pershing II?"

"The Pershing II would not be deployed, sir."

I gaped at Polina. But she was staring intently, rudely, at Ritter, who was saying something careful and precise. "Please remind me, Ambassador," I said, translating, "of the deployment schedule envisaged by the deploying countries in the NATO Nuclear Planning Group?"

"Ah, that, Mr Ritter, is one of the genial features of the Golden Plough initiative. The Federal Republic would not be asked to take its allocation of cruise missiles until the fall of 1985, at the same time as the Netherlands and Belgium. The initial deployments are intended for the United Kingdom and Italy where, for different reasons, nuclear force modernization is relatively uncontroversial. The six batteries of cruise missiles allocated to the US Armed Forces in Germany would arrive, two years later, unannounced and as an agreed element in a ratified treaty between the US and the Soviet Union."

Polina relaxed. Ritter put the tip of his pencil to paper, held it there a moment, then set it down.

Polk continued: "I reported back in person to my government after the April 15 plenary. I will not expose you to the horrors of Washington political competition, but I would be misleading you if I said that the so-called Soviet back-channel initiative had been warmly received. From Moscow, the silence has been as of the grave."

"How, may I ask, will Mr K. approach or contact . . . ?"

"Out of court, Mr Ritter."

Ritter nodded in feigned apology.

Polk said: "I asked Mrs Spratling and Mr Fisher to arrange this meeting for two reasons. First, because I was interested to hear your views on this issue as it affects the security of the Federal Republic; and, second, because I hoped you could assist me. Let me be quite open about this, Mr Ritter. If a German Chancellor were to support this initiative, neither Washington nor, with respect, London, nor Paris could easily or elegantly reject it. I am most reluctant to speculate about Mr Andropov or, particularly, Mr Gromyko, the Politburo member with responsibility for the Geneva process; but I am confident that the Soviets, having failed to foment civil war in Germany, would settle for a treaty which leaves them with a substantial force of modern, land-based, intermediate-range missile systems and keeps the Western counter-deployment within very manageable limits."

Polk paused. He had spoken for thirty-five minutes by my watch, without notes. He said: "I guess that's all I have to say at this stage. Do you need a break, Mr Ritter? I'm sure we could get some tea here, for our guest. Mrs Spratling, perhaps . . . ?"

Polina blinked, then, hesitating, made to get up.

"No, thank you," I said, translating. "I shall naturally consider the proposal — the Golden Plough: Medium-range missiles into ploughshares! — scrupulously and in confidence. In the meanwhile, may I be permitted to sketch in a preliminary response?"

Ritter turned his pencil over and tapped with the eraser on his clean pad. He said: "First, and as a jurist, I have the most profound legal objections to the deployment of first-strike nuclear weapons on Federal German territory. Article 26 of the Constitution, drawn up with the approval and co-operation of the United States and the United Kingdom, states unequivocally . . ."

"No speeches, please, Mr Ritter," Polina said.

Ritter raised his hand. Polk's forehead creased in a small frown. Ritter said: "Please be patient, Mrs Spratling. Article 26 of the Basic Law of the Federal Republic asserts that preparations for aggressive war are by definition unconstitutional. In this context, Mr Polk, may I say that, notwithstanding any other objections to the NATO deployment, a renunciation of the Pershing II has the law to recommend it. We could discourse for hours, like medieval theologians, as to whether the Pershing II can or cannot annihilate the city of Moscow. I'm sure we can agree that a modern ballistic missile, with a short flight time and acute vulnerability to attack, will be employed early in any imaginable conflict − I believe the Anglo-Saxon phrase is 'Use 'em or lose 'em!' − and in that respect is a glaring provocation to the Soviets."

"We cannot and do not agree, Mr Ritter!" She seemed beside herself with frustration.

Polk looked at her in surprise. Her shoulders dropped.

"My second point concerns the political situation within the Federal Republic. Public attitudes may be defined under three headings. There is the NATO-right-or-wrong group, embodied in the person of Helmut Kohl. The second is its diametrical opposite: that element of the Federal German peace movement which is under the actual or intellectual influence of the CPSU and the SED* . . ."

"Gretchen Lightner, for example . . ."

Ritter stiffened beside me. He said: "Let me say, briefly and for your information, Mrs Spratling, that Mrs Lightner would only have moved her residence to the GDR under the most pressing threats to her objective security. A woman who ran messages for the Resistance in National Socialist Thuringia, who survived Gestapo interrogation and Ravensbrück would surely be unlikely to have moved address capriciously.

"The third and by some distance the largest of the groups comprises those Germans who are exhausted by living on the frontier between two ideological systems; who believe they can contribute more constructively to the prosperity of nations than as galley-slaves or cannon fodder of the Great Powers; who suspect that six thousand is an abundantly sufficient number of nuclear weapons to deploy in a country no more extensive, I am told, than the state of Oregon; and who fear that the post-war security system, devised at Yalta and Potsdam, with its intention of keeping the Soviets out and the Germans down, is in a condition of perilous senility. This position is represented by the Social Democratic Party, which I serve.

* *Sozialistische Einheitspartei Deutschlands* the communist-dominated East German Socialist Unity Party.

"Within this constellation of political forces, let us imagine I align myself with the Polk–Kvertsovsky initiative and I put my hand to the Golden Plough; that, for example, in a speech at a conference at some evangelical academy, one Sunday morning in good time for all the Monday editions, I propose a renunciation of the Pershing II, a limit on the deployment of SS-20s in Europe and, presumably – though, Mr Polk, you did not say this – some cap east of the Urals . . ."

Polk nodded vaguely.

". . . and, though you did not mention this either, some moral or implicit restriction on French or British nuclear forces."

Ritter paused. I wanted to say: At last, the mist burns off and reveals the true relations of power in Europe. Ah, you're a hard one, Polina. Aren't we to have our toys, the affordable mementoes of British world dominion and the glory of France: the boats sliding under Holy Loch and the Vulcans of enamelled cast-iron and the Plateau d'Albion and the nuclear arquebusses in the Vosges? Polina, we cannot live on Shakespeare and Montaigne and Marie-Antoinette's bedroom, at least not in the world: officers carry side arms, if they're officers.

Polk said: "I have no authority to negotiate over third-country systems."

"Of course. As I was saying, in the circumstances I describe, it is possible, or even certain, that my speech would be picked up by the press and television and the organs of my party; and possibly – though let me return to the party later – would become SPD policy. If we prevail in the Bundestag elections on July 5, as I hope and believe, it would become Federal German foreign policy; if not, it would merely be the platform of a party representing some 40 per cent of the electorate.

"Imagine I make this speech. What guarantee do I have that Washington will not repudiate me? That Reagan will not do as Mr Carter did to Helmut Schmidt with the neutron bomb in 1978: expose his ally to a political storm and then frivolously change his mind? As for the Soviet Union, the silence from that quarter is not as grave-like as you suggest. In the course of my visit to Moscow with the shadow chancellor in March, I heard repeatedly from soldiers and civilians that there is not the slightest chance that the Soviet Union would accept such unstable and belligerent NATO deployments. Andropov himself was sceptical and mistrustful of the peaceful intentions of the United States. Gromyko used a graphic formulation: 'You Germans will gape at one another through a thicket of intermediate-range missiles.' I took away the impression of a very serious situation developing if it came to the installation of new NATO weapons in Western Europe in November."

Polk waited a moment before replying. He said: "Thank you for your candour. I'm afraid I can give no guarantees about the Soviet response. I would merely point out that nobody lives forever, not even Yuri Andropov and Andrew Gromyko. On the Washington side, I repeat that an SPD declaration in favour of the initiative, in government or opposition, could not easily be ignored."

"That is not very comforting to me, Mr Polk. What I did not say is that the SPD, this party rich in history and contradiction, this great party in a middling country, is in a most fragile state. The pacifist and neutralist elements that were suppressed during the long era of government under Willy Brandt and Helmut Schmidt have surfaced with augmented vigour. It is theoretically conceivable that, with hard coaxing from Willy Brandt and Herbert Wehner and all the party celebrities, the SPD could be made to endorse the Polk–Kvertsovsky plan, but it would be like the approval of deficit financing for the war in August 1914. Social Democracy in Germany would split, with profound and catastrophic consequences, as a cursory knowledge of German history will tell you. The emergence and rise of the Greens is the first harbinger of this disintegration. Whatever the social unrest in Germany this summer and autumn, the mass demonstrations, violence, the acts of . . ."

". . . your Baader-Meinhof friends . . ."

"Mrs Spratling," I said in German. "I did not bring Dr Ritter here to be insulted. He is, in case you had forgotten, a deputy of the German Bundestag and has a right to basic courtesy" [*mit entsprechender Höflichkeitsanspruch*].

She would not meet my eye. "*Entsprechendem*," she said.

"And don't bloody correct my German."

"Guys, guys," Polk said irritably.

Ritter put his hand on my jacket sleeve and said in English: "I am not so mimosa-sensitive as you think, Mr Fisher. Let me proceed in German. My sources on the extreme Left are not superior — indeed, in many respects they are inferior — to those of the Vfs counter-subversion service. As you know, the Vfs has already warned of the probability of attacks against so-called 'imperialist' installations in the Federal Republic and Berlin which, historically, could mean anything from the US Air Force base at Rhine-Main to the vice-president of a savings bank in the Hunsrück." He collected himself. "In reality, extremism is not my prime concern. My concern is the preservation of the most stable democratic institution in Germany, which is the Social Democratic Party."

"I guess what Mrs Spratling meant is that we are very, very concerned about the security of US personnel in Germany over the next six months to a year."

"Naturally," said Ritter.

There seemed no point in proceeding. With the substance gone, the cordiality had evaporated, too. Polk got up and stretched. He picked up his notepad and mine, laid them on the fire, then crossed the fire irons over them. At that moment, my sense of estrangement from the place and proceedings became unbearable. I wanted to shout: Look, Polina, we'll tell our grandchildren that we saw the last of the great diplomatists, John Chauncey Polk, show how to destroy a document in a country pub in Western Germany in the year of the Euromissiles; and they'll say, Right, that was 1919 or something, we're doing it in school.

"OK, ladies and gentlemen. If you please, we need to be on our way." The place was overrun with men talking into VHF radios, clearing and rearranging tables, hoisting and screwing back the panelling. One handed Ritter his briefcase. Ritter looked, for a moment, quite bewildered.

"Goodbye, young man," said Polk. "What I said just now to Mr Ritter applies equally to you. You are welcome in Geneva at any time convenient to you. Any time."

"I think I gave you my fly-box. There are some . . ."

I reached into the pocket and took it out.

"Mr Fisher? MR FISHER! You and Mr Ritter are leaving now. Now, sir."

Polk was gone, his fishing-vest vanishing through the door. In the crack of the kitchen door, I saw Angelika Simrock's pinched, adenoidal face, like some small mammal's. One of the agents had a steaming dish wrapped in foil, which I realized, some time later, must have been Polk's German fish. (Polina said that he sat, eating it with his fingers, demolished by the meeting, too exhausted to talk.)

Polina stood before me. Her white raincoat was half on. She had her hand out for me to shake. I sensed Polk, the journey to Brussels, her excitement and relief, pulling her away from me. She said: "Mr Fisher, thanks."

"Mrs Spratling, don't you ever do this again." I spoke as quietly as I could. "You're going to have to do some pretty disreputable things with me to make up for this."

"MR FISHER! WE'RE OUT OF HERE!"

"Cut that out," she said. "Go on pulling on that rope, one day I'm going to let go and you'll be on your butt."

She spun round, took a stack of papers from the agent and breasted them, then made for the front door and, as she pushed through it, she kicked up her heel. This arch and elusive gesture meant, I think: first, don't follow me; second, I guess it doesn't look great for you, my going off to the Nuclear Planning Group meeting in Brussels with this famous man in an armoured car with a foil-wrapped penis symbol and a helicopter escort, but a part of me – this foot, in its brand-new, barely scuffed sole – I leave with

57

you as I pass out of sight; and it being a foot and not a more social part of the body such as a hand, it confirms that a state of rudimentary intimacy exists between us.

About Polina Mertz's shoe, a digression. My memory of her has broken up. A shoe, her waist, her bust, her white knickers are scattered about me and I can't remember the colour of her eyes. I recognize that these fractions of her have the character of pornography: they commemorate a being that is indubitably female − see her woman's shape, her woman's underwear! − but one vacated of characteristics that are dispensable to the satisfaction of male desire. I suppose that, in time, Polina will attenuate into a female nude, bent at the waist to retrieve a bar of soap in a hotel shower in Marburg.

Unhappy male! Bombarded every instant of the day by such women without characteristics − in newspapers and advertisements and TV and the top shelves of tobacconists-newsagents − he destroys his own happiness. He is like the repulsive bourgeois in the *Communist Manifesto*, who treats his wife as his property yet longs also to enjoy the wives and daughters of the proletarians. In truth, it is not important that these *Frauen ohne Eigenschaften* are proletarian (though most of them are), but that they, shorn of their names and histories and manacled in lace, are probably no more at liberty than the mesmerized male: whatever Villon says, it is better to give than to sell or buy.

When I said all that to Ritter and Polina, at a picnic we had together at Schloss Brühl in May, in connection with a cigarette advertisement on the gable wall of a redundant barn, he said it was no surprise that I, a British romantic-conservative male, should be drawn to such passages in Marx and Engels: after all, the origins of socialism in horror and disgust have lain bare for some time, and early socialist writings brim with nostalgia for an ideal preindustrial family under the gathering storm of capitalist competition. He, for his part, would pose the problem somewhat differently: How is it

58

that bourgeois marriage has survived the awe-inspiring assaults of capitalism as far as this year of grace 1983?

Don't look at me, said Polina, and laughed a laugh that pierced me, like a shiver of glass.

Die Frau is nicht nur für das Glück der Männer da! I remember in Berlin, during one of those interminable meetings at the time of the Easter Events, that a girl got up and read shyly and furiously from a paper: Irene Jordaens, I think, who was killed at Stockholm. The audience was restless. She wasn't pretty; she kept losing her thread; and at the end, she said that "Woman exists for more than just the delight of man!", which must be a quotation, and there were cries of: On the contrary! and Telling me!

Ritter surprised me. He paused at the microphone, to ensure she had no more to say, though he had the usual mile-long agenda; and then proposed a procedural motion: whether or not to take a vote on the creation of a committee for women's issues. It was defeated in a flurry of hands. At the end of my aisle, seven or eight girls got up – the tallest, Beate Beck, had hennaed hair – and filed out of the Audimax.

About Polina's shoes: Was she obliged, in the social conditions that existed in West Germany in 1983, to satisfy certain masculine sexual requirements just to exercise her intellect? To wear this uniform of a kitsch femininity: hair in her eyes, lipstick, kitchen lace, cripplingly high heels? As if I can stand here, in the office of the British Ambassador to the Federal Republic of Germany, with my view of the Siebengebirge, speaking rapidly, buying time for her, but only if I have on a suit and tie and polished shoes and don't have a hangover, while women's eyes flicker over me like flame?

I tried in 1983 to get Polina to cut her hair, to wear non-vamp clothes from the Königsallee in Düsseldorf, or Italy, to stop dragging Kaufhof into history. I was offended by a contradiction I saw between her looks and her preoccupations. My motives were snobbish-aesthetic, not emancipatory. I know more about the world now. Polina actually wanted to hobble her intelligence, to be

59

helpless and beribboned and sweet as Lübeck marzipan. She dressed in the mirror of a man's eye. I didn't know then who that man was, except that it wasn't me, and it wasn't Bill Spratling.

"Mr Fisher? OK. Red beetle again. Gassed up. Map on dash. Leave it in the parking garage under the Königshof, keys in. Now LET'S GO!"

Ritter sat cramped beside me, briefcase on his knees. With the headlights on full beam, I crept up to sixty kilometres an hour and stopped there. The escort car surged up close, then backed off in a headlit automobile fury.

"I haven't got a driving licence. I hope you don't object."

"Why should I? I also have none."

He opened his briefcase and then shut it again. I thought: She's trying to make an institution of this not-sleeping-together, make it a peculiarity of our friendship, so she can hold her household and career together. Unfortunately, that will not be possible, Mrs Spratling. I'm going to detonate your existence and put it all together again, shapely, sturdy, British-workmanlike: good for our lifetimes and half our children's. I opened the window on icy hill air and the bouncing headlight beams of our escorts, one behind and one in front.

I said: "I must apologize, Mr Ritter, if Mrs Spratling got on your nerves." Stop mentioning her name, you prat!

"Oh, on the contrary. It has been my good fortune often to have to do with legendary females."

"You mean Petra."

"For example. I looked forward with the keenest anticipation to coalition talks with Mrs Kelly after July 5." I imagine he smiled in the darkness.

"Really? Even if you and the Greens can make a Bundestag majority on July 5, which is far from certain, without Professor Lightner you'll never get them to sit down. Imagine going over the Golden Plough with a seven-person rotating leadership, reporting back to a permanent party conference and in the presence of the entire Bonn-based German and international press! And what about the SPD? I can't see all those Helmut Schmidts on the Right sitting down at the same table as . . ."

"It's a good plan," he said. "A serious plan. I never expected a serious plan. A pity, in some respects, that there is no record of it."

I thought: I don't believe this bloke. He's that innocent. You think that lying cow hasn't got you on eighteen tracks, Ritter? Fortunately for you, Richard has his own record, at least of the first sixty minutes, on his little Sony which he took the precaution of slipping under the Hendricksons of his fly-box and placing it in Ambassador Polk's fishing jacket. This may become available to you at a price, if things get mean, which it is more than probable they will.

The trailing car was trying to bump me to the right and up an autobahn ramp. The leading car was halted in a pool of impatient red light on the shoulder. Courtesy had departed with Polk. Ritter either did not notice or chose not to comment.

He said: "I was wrong to lose my temper. False! False!"

"About Mrs Lightner?"

He was silent; and then said: "Why do you use the second-person plural form? It is almost unknown in modern German social usage between friends."

"I don't know the second-person singular forms. I never had occasion to use them."

"How melancholy! To be driven into formality by your exile tongue! England is such a fortunate country, Richard. I discovered happiness in England."

"Excuse me?"

"At the 1966 World Cup."

I am not hearing this. I will not be part of some Anglo-German reconciliation, soothed by the balsam of international sport. Hey-Fritz-Hey-Tommy-Your-Geoff-Hurst-Your-Beckenbauer!

"I absolutely refuse to discuss that goal."

"You've misunderstood me, Richard; although, incidentally and from a juristical-sporting point of view, the referee was correct in endorsing the linesman's judgment and the English victory is safe. My point was other. I have only the most general grasp of British social reality. I had, alas, no Engels to be my guide. I was a tourist. I had left our group and taken the underground to Highgate, to visit Marx's grave, and then walked down through Primrose Hill where Engels had lived, to Hyde Park. I was most anxious to see Apsley House and Rotten Row and the Serpentine and the historical-topographical setting for the 'Agitation against the Sunday Trading Bill' of 1855.

"I had quite misjudged the extent of the Metropolis. It was hot: the sun shone so much in the late Sixties. As I set off, a little wearily, towards our hostel in the southern part of the city, it seemed to me, in my exhaustion, subjectively, that I was hearing music all the time: out of shops, pubs, cars in traffic, at Buckingham Palace and the Houses of Parliament, from buses and in the mouths of tube stations: the music of radios, no doubt, which was by now, on my sixth day in England, somewhat familiar. I recollect I stopped on Vauxhall Bridge and looked down into the Thames, and it occurred to me: Might not happiness be more than subjective but desirable states of consciousness? Might it not be more even than the category of social and political goals presented, for example, in the preamble to the American Constitution? Might not happiness be the very spirit that runs through history and makes it intelligible? I thought, with the most intense excitement, there on Vauxhall Bridge, looking down into the slow river, that I had seen the errors in Hegel and Marx; that I'd found them on their heads and would now proceed to set them upright again; and that, as the shades of summer darkness came down, I had heard the Owl of Minerva beating its wings towards Peckham! Mere sentiment, of course. But here we are in the Federal Capital!"

"Do you want a drink? Something to eat?" My throat bayed for brandy and I wanted to annoy the US Secret Service, which surely had instructions to see Ritter home.

He looked at me. "Eat? You mean: eat in a restaurant or inn? Now?"

"Yes. Now."

"Unfortunately, Richard . . . You see I have a small daughter who goes to bed at this time and if I don't see her now, well then . . . well . . . she'll grow up."

"Another time, then. I'll drop you at the U-Bahn. I have to take this heap to the underground garage."

At the station, Ritter sat for a moment, rigid in his lapels. He said quickly: "Richard, I have a bad conscience on one matter. The sly and fascinating Mrs Spratling attempted to provoke me also on the matter of those insane Red Army Faction people. As you know, there was the view up to Mr Klein's trial in 1977 and even later – a view, incidentally, that I held to be theoretically and juristically false – that the RAF was an internal problem of the German Left, a misbegotten child of our own making that we could not simply disown. Even after the Stockholm fiasco and Mogadishu, some voices were still urging that a bridge be kept open, a bridge into illegality. For all my principled and practical objections to this view, which seems to me sentimental in the extreme, I have received information from an illegal source that I cannot presume to endanger. I am, therefore, not able myself to take this information to the Minister of Interior."

I thought: Jesus, he's going to give me something: a great, big, fat piece of intelligence. Ritter's in contact with Klein or Beck! The villain! I said: "It might be the most secure solution if you . . ."

He pushed hard at his door, which squealed on the raised pavement. I thought:

Shut up, Richard. Don't crowd him. It's hard for him. He's got some sort of problem. Let him say it.

He said it.

"For God's sake, man? When?"

He was walking quickly. In the lighted entrance to the U-Bahn, he turned.

"Please, Sebastian? When?"

He pointed to the ground and vanished down the steps.

Soon.

Now.

I thought at first of going to Klaus von Arnim, Kohl's new security adviser at the Chancellery; but I decided, in the course of the night, that I needed to put some loops in the chain of transmission to protect Sebastian, just as I was protection for his source. Also, I simply did not have the experience to market the information properly on my own. It was of good quality, but imprecise, not very commercial. Polina was in Belgium, barricaded inside NATO headquarters. In the end, I went for safety.

"Not now, Richard." He strode past me like an athlete.

"It's life-threatening, Brian."

He spun gracefully on his heel and shouted: "Doris! Please call Private Office and say Mr Barchard will be three minutes late. On the lawn, Richard."

We stood on the small lawn in front of the British Embassy chancery, while his Mercedes and driver idled. It was as if I'd pulled from my dirty waistcoat a lumpy handkerchief and Brian was picking expertly through dirty copper coins, broken medals, stopped watches, nails and screws.

"NATO-target. Cologne-Bonn district. Assassination. Have I that correct, Richard?"

"Yes."

"Will you tell me your source, please, Richard?"

"No."

"Can you establish your source's access to the RAF?"

"No."

"To the circle of sympathizers?"

"No."

"I see. We're dealing here with a piece of hearsay of some tradeable value." Brian was no longer talking to me: he was off on the wings of his own cleverness. "Clearly, this is not the worst time to move into modest intelligence surplus with the Americans. You can tell Hartig, if you want, Richard. You should get one more wear out of it."

He hopped into the moving car.

The Hartig interview almost didn't come off. The uniformed officer in his anteroom kept looking at me and my business card. I waited fifty-five minutes. From beyond the door came the sound of shouting. At ten to six, Hartig put his handsome head out and said in English: "Do forgive me, Mr Fisher. Policemen! I have, unfortunately, to leave right now."

I stood in his big office while he packed his papers. As I spoke, his suntanned face went suddenly grey, as if a cloud had crossed an August beach. He turned his back; threw off his raincoat; picked up a telephone; spoke quickly, with authority. I thought: This bloke has been promoted to the limit of his ability and a bit beyond. He said, still in English: "I must have your source, Mr Fisher. Otherwise," and here he laughed, "this material is useless, or worse. I mean it."

I said: "What you make of this intelligence is your business, Commissioner Hartig. I've done my duty. You can try and squeeze me, but you might find I'll go elsewhere next time."

I was sitting in the Käfer pub, at a round table by the window overlooking the railway tracks, drinking Cologne beer with Lukas Biermann and Barbara Volle of the Heidelberg Circle, a moderate fundamentalist-ecological discussion group within the Greens. Biermann said:

"The sound of peace!"

This was a fragment of a slogan, devised by the public relations department of the United States Air Force in Germany: Sonic Booms are the Sound of Peace! Teenage girls wore it printed on their T-shirts on blistering open days at air bases. The Inter-City thundered through. Biermann relaxed. It was April 30, 1983. Everything was calm, hung-over, futile, terrified.

I said: "Will you excuse me a moment?"

Inge Mohr, the bar-keeper, had her chin on her cupped hands, not looking particularly at us or at anything. She said: "You haven't got a public transportation licence."

"I haven't got any bloody licence, Inge."

She fished in her apron for the taxi-key.

I think my idea was to go to Reuters at the Tulpenfeld, or better Jim Dole of Radio Free Europe, read the tapes, chew the political fat, exploit my restlessness and hangover. I suppose, in the depths of my dull mind, something was repeating over and over again: That weren't no aircraft, boy! Two police cars raced along the Ollenauerallee towards Godesberg, sirens off. I jumped the light and got in behind an ambulance. A woman stepped out from the Heussallee, waving her shopping bags. Hell, I'd left the taxi-light on! I grabbed at the dashboard. My lap filled with Inge Mohr's change. I passed the British Embassy, car dealerships, the Ministry of Energy, the German Automobile Club, empty lots. Waves of regret broke over me, so sweet and painful I might have been plunged back into infancy: all those things bust and lost and gone to hell: a wetted bed; a broken birthday watch; my father with his yellow legal pad in the American sunshine; my mother in her dirty British grave. The ambulance swerved, reared up on two wheels, ran through a staggered roadblock. Policemen gaped and scattered, their machine pistols bouncing on their slings. You're going to get shot, you imbecile! Dump the car!

I parked across the driveway of a bungalow. I thought: Actually, it is not inevitable. Actually, there are many Americans here. In fact, Plittersdorf is sometimes known as Little America. These streets are bursting with Americans! Look at the tract-houses, the rust buckets in the driveways, the abandoned lawn mowers! Turning on to the Plittersdorfer Strasse, the heat boomed in my face.

"Do not approach! DO NOT MOVE!"

This is a policeman, with his machine pistol level; blond, moustache, cap; very, very frightened. Standing by the crash barriers, barefoot, is a woman in a pink bathrobe and curlers, with cuts on her cheeks; also a girl in a tutu, tears streaking a dirty face.

"Please tell Commissioner Hartig that Mr Fisher has got here. Do you understand that, officer? Mr Fisher. Thank you."

I turn into the heat, which beats at me in gusts. The lawn is snowed with glass. The locust tree has snapped at the bole and the pavement is neck-deep in leaves and branches, green and grey. Through the remains of the downstairs window, Polina's music stand leans at an angle. Above it, thick black smoke – burning bedding? – pours from a gash in the roof. An exercise bicycle hangs from the tangled phone wires.

"Mr Fisher? Please!"

Hartig was leaning into the back of a police van, talking into a telephone. I thought: He only ever wanted the easy life, Number Four or Five on the CDU electoral list for Dibbeldorf or Dumpelstadt, maybe parliamentary spokesman on police affairs, couple of rental houses, stock-market tips, an amenable female secretary.

He said: "Mr Fisher, I cannot . . ."

"You didn't warn the Chancellery, did you, you idiot?"

He put his hand over the receiver. He didn't look at me. He said: "No pathological material, so far. Mr Spratling is definitely uninjured."

Beyond the van, my eyes met somebody's: a civilian, sports coat and tie, athletic, beard, American, crazy: Bill Spratling. He detached himself and vaulted the crash barriers.

"Car bomb? What? Quick, man!"

Hartig shrugged: "A missile, clearly."

"One moment, please, sir."

I had my hand out, but Bill's eyes went straight for mine.

"I'm so sorry, Bill . . ."

He didn't shake my hand. He was looking at my face, recording it. He said: "I don't want you here, Mr Fisher."

I felt his eyes on my back. Over the broken glass, my legs felt so unsteady I kept stumbling. My hands trembled too much to start the taxi. So I held this debate with my soul:

Maybe they weren't after her. Maybe they were after Bill. Maybe she wasn't to them Polina Spratling *née* Mertz, b. Bavaria 1956 or 1957, but a character mask of imperialism, an available American. Maybe, maybe . . .

"Are you for hire, young man?"

"Of course!"

I moved out into the sunny Ollenauerallee. I took the old lady to Bonn station, helped her with her shopping trolley, picked up another fare to Endenich, left the taxi and walked back through the allotments. I got some money at the Dresdner Bank at the station, a bottle of brandy, some wash things and a transistor radio that was on special offer, because the taxi hadn't one. It occurred to me she'd want clothes and underwear and things like that, and I became disheartened. I climbed up to the Kreuzkirche and sat for a while on the marble staircase against the outside wall of the west front and looked numbly through the haze at the Bundestag and the metal Rhine. I thought of waiting at the Mozartstrasse, at my desk, while the window grew dark through the net curtains and a car came softly up the street, without lights, a Dodge Aspen . . . It didn't fit. I thought: She won't go there and she won't touch a phone. She'll go to a place we've been at together, which means the Osteria or the Alte Hirsch in Cologne or . . . I got up, walked through wet orchards into Endenich, where I'd picked up a parking ticket for Inge Mohr. Hartig was on the news at seven o'clock with some imbecile story: still no bodies.

Brühl station was dark and deserted. I parked in a corner of the car park, took a big drink of brandy, and sat down with my back against a tree. Trains roared and hooted. After a while, I fell asleep and dreamed the interior light of the car came on, and went off again. Dazzled, I staggered up and groped my way across the car park by starlight. The car interior smelled of plastic, petrol, air-freshener and the Dutch roll-up tobacco Inge Mohr used, and also of newer things: washroom soap, I think, and wet wool. I was blistered with joy and very pleased with myself: as a poker player when the card in the hole, which he knows by counting just has to be an ace, *is* an ace.

I said: "Bill's at the Ambassador's. Shall I go by there?"

It seemed to me that I shouldn't ask her questions. I should just go: north, south, west or east; somewhere random, unpredictable and safe. My find filled slowly with maddening touristic souvenirs: shrimps in Lübeck, cloudberry brandy in Helsinki, the heaving sea at Norderney, Leicester Forest East motorway services in rain, two quails in a cage in the Cahors Friday market, the warmth of paving stones on bare feet at Anacapri. I crossed the Rhine and followed the signs for Frankfurt and the east.

On the autobahn, Polina Mertz said: "Please stop."

I swung across three lanes and on to the verge. I lifted her out and she was sick. She also peed, helplessly, with her knickers round her ankles. I gave her some brandy but she sicked it up immediately. I put her in the front seat and fixed the belt round her. The traffic swooped and beat at me as I edged round to my side.

I said: "I wasn't followed. I'm pretty sure. I just had to go to the house, Polina."

"It's done. OK? It's done."

"We're going to a town called Marburg, near the GDR border. I've never been there or talked about going there. There's a famous church that I think we should see."

It was three in the morning when we got in to Marburg. I put the taxi in an underground garage, left Polina sleeping and locked in, and walked through the deserted floodlit alleys, carrying my new wash-bag. At the Sternhotel, a Yugoslav porter was reading a comic-book under a pigeonrack of keys. My mind voided of false names, car licence numbers, passport dates and places of issue; but I got the form filled, put a fifty-mark note on top (about £15 in those days) and pushed it across at him with a significant look. He stared back at me, and then took the form and the money. When I hurried Polina in, he was back in his comic, which made me think I might have saved my money or even, much better, given him my Sunday punch. I thought: I was born for this stuff.

We rode in a scuffed lift to a room with flowered wallpaper, an unyielding double bed, and bedside lights that threw a pattern of shade and wire on the mansard ceiling. It smelled of dust and bad wiring and the sadness of small businessmen. It soon filled with Polina's nerves. She was rummaging in her purse.

"Stop that." I took it from her and put it on the bed beside her. I said: "I'm going to take your clothes off, put you in the bath or shower or whatever this palace has, and then we're going to bed."

"Richard." She bunched her shoulders, as if for one last effort. She said: "Look, Richard, a wire-guided TOW missile in your home is not exactly . . ."

"I won't lay a glove on you."

Engels says somewhere that history unfurls twice: once as tragedy and once as wretched farce. I thought, as I unpeeled Polina's trousers to the knee, unhitched her bra, unravelled her wet knickers, that rarely can this historical process have been completed in a single day. Ghosts of self-pity and pained gallantry entered the room and I shooed them away.

A tile was loose on the bathroom floor and she slipped, but I caught her. The water was excruciatingly hot, yet she seemed to like it. I sat on the loose toilet seat. For a long time, she simply stood in the shower holding a bar of soap; then by some effort of will or habit she lathered it in her hands, washed her arms and under her bosom; dropped the soap and bent down, blindly, chasing it; washed between her legs. I thought: This is interesting, this is how a girl takes a shower after her house is destroyed by the RAF. I thought: She can't even bother about her modesty, can't mouth through the falling water: Get out of here, you shit! Delicacy, damn it, got the better of me and I went next door. I filled a toothmug with brandy.

She was trying to tie a towel about her, but it was too small. "No toothbrush," she said. She looked appalled. "I must have a toothbrush."

"In the wash-bag." Mama's got you one.

She said: "We sell those things to anybody who wants them. Saudis, Yemenis, Indonesia, Iraq, for Pete's sake. The idea is you put a guy behind a rock with a TOW, he can disable an armoured

70

personnel carrier, stop a tank if he hits the track or turret. No training. A whole lot cheaper than F-15s. Don't need a fucking Congressional debate."

"We don't have to talk about this now."

Her towel slipped and she clumsily retrieved it.

I said: "OK, Polina. Schiller was killed by a rocket. Special prosecutor in Stuttgart. Twenty-ninth of November 1977."

"From a car or something?"

"Motorbike. Peter Klein and Beate Beck. Or so they say."

"Can't use a TOW from a moving platform."

Don't play games with me, Polina.

She shrugged: "Some guys like rockets."

Good girl.

She gave up with the towel and ran, stooped, for the bed. I turned off the light, kicked off my clothes and got in the other side. The sheets were cold. A streetlight shone in. A clock chimed, medievally, and then a second and a third, which filled the room with ringing metal. I sensed Polina as something rigid, horizontal and cold. I thought: Without doubt, this is the worst moment of my life to date.

She said: "If we could find those guys, then maybe . . ."

You wouldn't have to hide in a hotel room in Marburg.

"I'm history," she said.

I reached across and found the hand at her side. I said: "It's over, Polina. Can't you see? Nobody's going to ask you to stay in Europe, after all this. You did well. Bill'll get his own Embassy. I bet . . ."

I realized she was crying, not really in control. I tried to hug her close, but she spread her knees and pulled me inside her. As I came into her, she seemed to open in a cascade of liquid: the walls of her body seemed to recoil from me. I kissed cheeks streaming with tears. A tear ran down my chest and slithered on to her bosom.

She fell off the bed in a heap. Her wet face brushed my stomach. I reached down to pull her back, but she shook her head in a shiver, scattering tears like a dog on a beach. Her cold breath, as she sobbed, was agony to me. I said:

"Sweetheart, you needn't . . ."

She was shaking uncontrollably.

"It doesn't matter, Polina."

She was trying to speak.

"Your what?"

"MY FUCKING LENS!"

"Well, take them out."

She put her ring finger to her eye, looked round crazily, sat down at the bedside table. I put my arms round her as she took out the other lens. She said: "I can't even . . ."

"Enough!"

"Can't even give a guy . . ."

"SHUT UP!"

I held her, my head against her back, till she stopped trembling.

"I'm OK," she said.

As I lifted her, surprisingly light, and sat her down on me, I had the unworthy thought that while the world sifted the ruins of the Plittersdorfer Strasse by arc light for a fragment of this beautiful woman, she was actually here, two hundred miles to the east, very much in one piece, or rather with that inexplicable compromise in identity that occurs when men and women make love; and also that, while she obviously meant what she said about the explosion putting her right off sex, she also meant the exact opposite. I felt well-designed and -made, old-fashioned Birmingham quality.

Polina let out a breath of air. In the faint streetlight, she was white, tall, liquid; scalloped with shadow and femininity; a column of woman on a male plinth; a set of Russian dolls. Her eyes were shut. I think she was searching for something very deep in her nature, maybe something she hadn't seen for years; shutting me out, heart and head and sex, the drip in the bathroom, her violated house, her sedated husband and her ruined clothes, the missile weaving over the choppy Rhine, the striking quarter-hour . . .

"Sssh," she said.

It was as if, searching through the attics of her affections, she'd found something – I think of a box or an old trunk or something – and rubbed a smear of dust off with her sleeve . . .

"Stop that!"

. . . and still in her gown of streetlight, stepped down the stairs, carrying whatever it was that she'd found . . .

"Please stop. Please."

She tightened about me. I began to reform beneath her: penis, stomach, chest, face, name and nationality. Her fingernails bit into my wrist. She bent down, gasping for breath, and covered my mouth. Her bosom swept my chest: her nipples were hard like gemstones. I broke the grip of her arms and sat up, laying my head against her wet breast.

Polina's eyes opened. She blinked. She said: "You see it's no big deal, making out with me."

"I said: No talking!"

If we were going to sleep, I'd want to turn her round, pull her bottom into the bend of my waist, fit my hands neatly over her breasts; but we aren't going to be sleeping, not with this miracle – this machine for generating happiness – right here in the room with us, in this bed or taking shape in the small morning light; which has abolished hotel rooms and all the people who've ever slept or tried to sleep in this hotel room, wiped out tomorrow and yesterday and the day before, given me her past and her my future:

A busted tile, a dripping shower
Are safe as tum-tum
For an hour
Or however long it takes

To get to the tum-ti-tum.

Polina stirred under my hands. I held her tighter but the desire to speak was building up in her, forcing her up and out against my arms.

"LET ME GO, RICHARD!"

She sat up. She had on clunky, scholarship-girl spectacles. They looked perverse, illegal, nude. She said: "I kind of thought I needed to be out of it for a while. Go someplace. Away. From my job. Bonn. Everything. Take a time-out. Except you're British and you don't know what a time-out is." She gave up. "Look, Richard, I like to cheat on my husband, OK?"

I pulled her back and settled her. I imprisoned her again in my arms. I said into her ear: "You are blessed with an education and the capacity for rational judgment. What you do is you put everything in one scale of the balance – job, husband, all that – and me in the other. See which goes down. Take the one that goes down."

She squirmed with impatience in my arms. This gave me ideas.

"Cut that out," she said, and struggled into a more decorous position. She said: "I'm happy, Richard," and then: "You made me happy, Richard." She lifted my hands co-operatively off her breast and turned round and said: "Look at the guy. A week ago, he'd have paid money to get his hand in my underwear. Now he's talking marriage."

It didn't sound quite right, and I suppose she sensed that because she ran her hands down my sides to my hips. "Come to Mom," she said. "Mom'll fix you up."

"Polina?"

"Yes."

She was irritable; I was tiresome; neither was going to sleep. If I moved away, she reached her arm behind her and pulled me back.

"Why did you say that to Sebastian? At Elmersdorf?"

It was time to get back to work.

"What?"

"About the RAF?" By that I mean: What have they got against you?

She sighed. By now, I knew this meant: I can't be bothered not to tell you. She said: "Jack wanted me to work on it. It's a technique we got into in the Carter Round.* A little needle can be fruitful.

* The first round of theatre-range negotiations in the autumn of 1980.

74

And clearly, it is inappropriate for the delegation leader to act aggressively."

The sweat was cold on my back.

"He wanted to get the message across. Let's keep this thing professional: no bombings, no assassination, no violence against neutral property, no civilians. Kind of optimistic, in retrospect. I guess he thought Sebastian would somehow get the message delivered."

I wasn't listening. I said: "Did you sleep with Jack?"

"None of your fucking business."

I thought: I'd rather have her back in my arms than an answer to this question.

She said: "It's a justifiable assumption that I've slept with all the cabinet-rank males in the Carter and Reagan Administrations, and the Reagan transition team. That's how I've got where I am. And now I've slept with you, my only friend." Then she said: "No. OK? Can we talk about something else?"

I was stupid with happiness: not, of course, because she hadn't slept with Jack Polk, about which I didn't care that much, though he was obviously very, very important to her; but because she was telling me things. It seems inexplicable to me now that I didn't make her tell me things that mattered, like what she'd done to offend Beate. I wanted to chatter, like other loving couples.

Frontier. To get to the front-ee-er. Or however long it takes to get to the frontier.

"Babe?"

"WHAT?"

"Let's go to the GDR. Have some fun."

She was up on her elbow, bare-breasted, bespectacled, furious. "I won't have it, do you hear? Don't even think of it, Richard! Do you hear me?"

75

"I hear."

Polina slid out of bed. In the morning light, I saw her cross the room to her clothes. She seemed to move in a different medium, of woman's light and feminine happiness, naked, indifferent, self-absorbed. She had something in her hand: the new radio. She stooped, pulled out the aerial, which flashed dimly; and this gesture, and the angle at which Polina stood, seemed to me the most beautiful things I'd ever seen. This is my authority; not father or mother, God, government, professors or policemen or ambassadors, but this unmediated beauty, which is a window looking out on eternity, transitory and veritable. The Rathaus clock tinkled. Polina shivered, put her arm across her breast and the radio on her stomach and ran to the bed. As she burrowed into me, she carried a coldness with her: a piece of morning in Marburg, compounded from hard break-fast rolls and the inky *Rundschau*, headaches, black coffee, exhaust.

I said: "Get East Berlin."

Polina stuck out her tongue.

We listened to the seven o'clock GDR news, as I always did if I was up.

"Did you get it, Richard? Did you get it?"

"'The Trade and Industry Minister, Mrs Honecker, has declared that attendance at the XXIst Leipzig Fair has exceeded . . .'"

"NO!"

Calm down, lovey-dove. Richard has it.

I said: "'The Commander of the Warsaw Pact Forces in the German Democratic Republic, Marshall Olgarkov, has informed the three Western air-transport companies serving Berlin (West) that, for the duration of the military exercise, Socialist Solidarity, use of the three corridors over GDR sovereign territory will be, for air-safety reasons, suspended.' Last item. After the young farmers."

Polina relaxed.

I said: "I wanted to stay another night. Rest up. Screw. Be safe."

"I guess."

"Jesus, Polina! An old-fashioned Berlin crisis!"

"I guess."

"We can still see the church."

"Church?"

"The Elisabethkirche."

Her face flashed puzzlement, then irritation; then a tentative pleasure. I think she was genuinely trying to accommodate me. She said: "I need to go to Kaufhof. I need underwear. I need to call Jack."

We breakfasted, cramped by politeness and old clothes. Her high heels clattered on the cobbles of the pedestrian precinct. At the church, a young priest was coming out. He swung round in his cassock and held the door for us. Up slim, brick columns, the church vanished into grey light. I sat down in a pew. Polina hesitated, then sat beside me. I prayed:

> Saint Elisabeth, though I'm unclear about your biography, could you ensure that this young woman is not atomized while I'm visiting with Mrs Lightner in East Germany. Also, just as urgent in its way, can you keep me out of Bautzen gaol?

My prayer rose up through motes of dust and threadbare battle standards. Are you here, sweet saint, in this historic piece of early-Gothic mathematics? Do you exist outside the antiquarian interests of an educated Englishman or the garbled recollections of a lapsed Catholic Pole? This war exhausts us. History has gone on too long. How do we find peace? You don't know, do you? You don't exist, do you? Or we've driven you out, like a headache after paracetamol? All that's here is engineering, and the authentic smell of sex.

By the tombs of the Landgraves, Polina stamped her foot. She was holding a tall white candle, but she'd forgotten what you do with it. I lit it for her, dug into her purse, put a five-mark coin in the wall. I thought: I'm getting into your past, Polina Mertz, you can't stop me now. I find out things nobody else finds out. If I survive, I'll go very deep – to Bayonne, NJ, and Regensburg and Warsaw – and fix what needs to be fixed. Only I can make you happy, Polina Mertz, because only I will put in the time.

She stood, miserable, among the monuments in the churchyard. It was windy. I thought: I should take her back to the hotel, but we'll just go to bed for forty-eight hours and the Sovs will be in Münster and some bloody Leicestershire squirelet will be shooting off Lances.* I said: "Could you or somebody leave the taxi outside the Käfer, the bar by the tracks, keys to Inge the bar-keep? Also seventy-five marks for the parking violation."

"Don't fuck with me, Richard!" She grabbed my hand and then forgot what she wanted it for and pressed it against her breast. "I absolutely forbid you to go to the GDR."

I said: "Polina, if you weren't such a bossy, opinionated and ill-natured cow, you'd listen to me and maybe learn something. One, I know Barchard and he'll already be on his way. If I move now, and I mean now, I can catch him at the Friedrichstrasse. He owes me one. We ride through. Military vehicle. Union Jack. *Jawohl, Herr Fisher!* I hang about listening to Brian and Bob Burnside and Pierre LaFrance tear up some Neanderthal Soviet air general for an hour. Stroll down to the Alexanderplatz. Drop by Platow. Pick up the latest Masur/Schreier pressings. *Sehr kulturell, Herr Fisher!* Hungry, now. Bowl of fat, jar of piss at Zum Stiefel. *Guten Appetit, Herr Fisher!* And I could have sworn Herr Fisher was following a call of nature, but, it appears, he left!" I thought: When we're married, we'll have no secrets. Until that moment, I reserve the right to tell the most transparent lies. Actually, I'm not going to Berlin, or not yet. I'm going to the Leipzig Fair for which, as in each of the past two years, I have a journalist's visa. I'm going to find out about you there. You can't stop me. Not if you want to save your life.

Her shoulders sagged. She said: "You don't even know they're in the GDR."

Blah blah.

"You have no weapon."

Yak yak yak.

---

* Nuclear artillery deployed with the British Army of the Rhine.

"You've given no thought to how you'll get out."

I have, too.

"They'll trace you here. To us."

You bitch. "In fact, sweetest, going to call on Mrs Lightner at her brother's apartment in Leipzig is not wholly the heroic gesture of superannuated chivalry I'm making it out to be. Actually, there isn't a choice. Peter Klein, if you'd forgotten, sent his gun and bullets to the Madrid correspondent of the *Spiegel* in January 1979, and vanished. He is, no doubt, in Aden or somewhere equally convenient of access. I need to have a few words with dear Beate. I do not know where she is, but I am confident her Lightner god-mother does know. If I don't go to the GDR, you can kiss goodbye to your . . ."

Polina took a step back on to the grass, teetered, lost her balance. Her face dissolved. I caught her, hugged her, tried to squeeze the fear out of her, but she fought me.

"You never . . ."

I'm so sorry, Polina.

"You fucking never . . ."

Know when to stop. I know. I promise, Polina, I didn't mean to kill, just to wound.

"I'm . . ."

"I've got you, Polina."

"I'm . . ."

Twenty-six or twenty-seven years old. I know.

"I don't . . ."

"I've got you."

"I . . ."

Don't want to die. I know, sweetie. Nobody does. I don't.

"I've got you."

In fact, I'm going to take a step back myself now, and then another. I'm going, Polina. One part of me is already in Kassel. Another is in Jena. A third in Leipzig, choking in the lignite smog. Other parts consider the nature of pain, imprisonment and execution and the glacial slowness of the Reichsbahn. Yet others concoct faces for my interrogators and stories to mislead them. I feel happy as never before; and fierce and rare and precious, like a tiger. Whatever you've done, Polina, I'll undo it. Trust me.

2

The revolutionary career is not pursued at official
dinners, in senior common rooms or research
laboratories, but in misery, shame, ingratitude and
the penitentiary. The destination is unknowable and
demands an almost superhuman faith. Merely gifted
people need not apply.

HORKHEIMER

Brian Barchard has his eyes on the ceiling. He lets an arm drop to
the carpet.

"Remind us, Richard, if you will, of the nature of the relationship
between the Lightners and Miss Beck."

It is May 21, 1983 and I am back from East Germany, safe and
sound and, God knows, grateful to the British Foreign Office. Sir
Julian Brown, the Ambassador, is at an empty desk, in white
shirt-sleeves, his jacket on the back of his chair. Barchard, Head
of Chancery, lies full-length on a reproduction First Empire sofa.
Seven or eight other people, including Hildegard Hamm-Breuer of
the German Foreign Office, looking discomposed, perch on the
Ambassador's desk or lean against the walls in postures of exaggerated ease. Neither Polina nor her bodyguards are present.

I have my back squarely against the wall and can see over the
Ambassador's curly head and through an armoured-glass window
behind to the misty Siebengebirge. My eyes ache in the watery light.
The room feels tense and under control: we're educated men and
women, mostly but not all from higher social classes, no occasion to
shout or break bones. Not for a little trip to the Soviet Zone.

I'm all right except that I want coffee. After three and a half hours talking, I have a map of Yemen in my chest. I want coffee badly, but there isn't any: no coffee, biscuits, gallantry, unsupported assertion, jokes or smoking. Sir Julian grew up in a boys' home in Romford, Essex. It is his professional predicate, almost an extra surname: I've seen the phrase "Romfordian toughness" [*Romfordsche Härte*] in the *FAZ*. Lady Brown has MS and there's a problem with a son: possibly heroin. Sir Julian sits, islanded in misfortune and a reproduction partner's desk. Barchard, as if in counterpoint to the ambassador's severity, now has his eyes closed.

"Dorothea Beck was a Party member, quit after Hungary, like Mrs Lightner. They were active in the Easter Marches at the end of the Fifties. Gretchen was Beate's godmother: they took Beate in after Dorothea Beck's suicide in 1966, and Frank supervised her doctoral thesis which was — somewhat ironically in the light of her later career — on Hegel's concept of the Rule of Law."

"If there's something you don't know, Richard," Barchard says to the wall, "do say."

Tell me what you want to know, and I'll do my best to say it. I'll tell you everything I know and even some things I don't know. I'll engulf you in information, some of it true. You'll wish you never started these sessions. But something tells me that you don't want to know much, or at least not yet and not here, not in front of the Ambassador and State Secretary Hamm-Breuer and the new bloke from the Chancellery and that little thug Nik Tully and the chappie in the tweed jacket and club tie who's presumably a copper out of London. I said: "Lightner's obituary in *Neues Deutschland* was . . ."

"We have seen his bloody obituary in *Neues Deutschland*."

Nobody says anything. A barge wails from the river. Klaus von Arnim, Kohl's security adviser, unsticks himself from the wall and leaves the room. I feel a ripple of impatience. Somebody peels back a cuff to look at his watch. There's something I can't quite identify and do not like at all: regret, disappointment, even embarrassment.

Sir Julian speaks: "Thank you, Richard. I think we'll have to pick this up again next week. You'll be here? I mean in Bonn."

If you mean: Am I going to get on the next flight to Moscow, the answer is a qualified No. I nod.

Barchard swings his long legs down and yawns. He says: "Richard seems determined to bore us to death."

More people glide to the door. Through their legs, I see Tully is squatting on the carpet, like a football coach at half-time. He says: "When did you last see Polly Spratling?"

"Who?"

"Polina Spratling, that's who."

Barchard guffawed. "Wasn't she at your party, Nik?"

"Yes, I think she was," I said. "Lady Caroline introduced us."

Barchard shut up.

"And since then?" Tully had recovered.

"She was at a picnic Sebastian Ritter gave at Brühl last Saturday. I guess she gets about."

"Might we know more about this young woman?"

"I must have some coffee."

"For God's sake, Richard!"

"I'm so sorry, Richard. You must be thirsty. White? Black? You don't have sugar, do you? Don't wait for me."

"Polina Jadviga Mertz was born in a displaced persons' camp near Regensburg in Bavaria in 1956 or 1957. I'm not sure of the exact date and it's impolite to ask. Her parents married in the camp. They'd been in Germany as forced labour during the war, I don't know why and it's rude to ask. Her mother had been cashier of a resort hotel in Zakopane. Her father was footman in the household of the Schusters, a prominent Jewish family in Warsaw. I don't know what happened to him, because he came out of the war and camp a wreck, never worked in the United States. For some reason, I think he was musical.

"Polina Mertz was brought up in Bayonne, New Jersey, which is just across the Hudson River from New York. She first visited

Manhattan at the age of fourteen. Long before that, Daddy passed out of the family picture, buggered off, died: I'm not clear about this. Mom married a guy called Don Pritzker, who owned a Chrysler dealership in Paramus, New Jersey, and he paid for Polina to go to a diploma factory called Baruch College on 23rd Street in Manhattan, and then to Harvard Business School. Polina married, while at graduate school, Jim Something, but they separated quite soon, though after she'd started on Wall Street. He runs a ski-supply store in Burlington, Vermont. Does New Age therapies.

"Polina's first job was in the capital markets group at Lazard, which is, as you know or possibly don't, Jack Polk's old firm. She disliked investment banking or living in Manhattan or both. She went back to college, to Georgetown, to do a PhD in history. Her thesis was on, wait for it, Robert E. Lee at Chancellorsville. I don't know what exact role Mr Polk played, but she was in the SALT delegation at Geneva, first under Barry Cohen and then, after his dismissal . . ."

"How close was she to Barry?"

"What do you mean, Nik? I don't understand your question."

"Please go on, Richard." Sir Julian had spoken.

"And then, after Cohen's resignation and disgrace, under Polk himself. As you all know, or possibly don't, arms-control theory has borrowed the terminology and some of the approaches of economics, so it wasn't that big a jump for her from business. She married Bill Spratling, the courageous Deputy Chief of Mission at the US Embassy here, five years ago in Washington. No children. She speaks English, French, German, Polish and Russian. She represents all that is great about the United States and its foreign service."

"Bangs like a shit-house door in a gale."

"I will not accept such comments! Do you all understand? Please strike out that last sentence, Eileen."

"Let's take a break, shall we, Julian? Richard can stretch his legs."

*   *   *

"Know anywhere one can knock a little ball about round here?"

"What?" What are you talking about?

Beyond him, Polina was moving away. By various agencies – a glass of Sekt, a wave from Pascale LaFrance, a tray of smoked salmon rolls – she was being taken from me. Her sea-blue jacket vanished sickeningly and then reappeared at the far end of the room, beside Pascale, in the window bay.

Barchard slid between us. "Actually, Denis, there's quite a reasonable course at Coblenz. I could manage a round tomorrow, earlyish, if you like?" He looked at me in contempt.

Somebody touched my elbow, and said: "I invited her, didn't I? What I do for you, Richard Fisher!"

Oh, Caroline, you are the only person in the British ruling elite I can tolerate and sometimes you annoy me so much. What I really hate about you is your patience, your unhappiness, your impenetrable irony, your two or three pieces of good furniture, your bay window over the Rhine which Göring stole from a Jewish family and we stole from Göring, your height and your beautiful face, though I used to like every one of these things, as I'm sure Brian did, once, when he was on the way up.

I said: "Bill's in Washington for consultations."

"Fascinating! You know she brought two guards of her own. Isn't it heavenly? They're all in the kitchen with Marcella, six of the brutes, disabling one another by applying pressure to the back of the knee."

"Look, Caroline, do you want to leave me alone?"

"Of course, if I must. Oh no, they're standing up! Richard, please stop them standing up. She's not the Queen!"

As Margaret Thatcher entered the room, in a long dress of violet chiffon and pierrot-lunaire make-up, with Charles and Carla Powell at each shoulder, she in Chanel, men and women struggled to their feet. Her eyes bounced round the room.

"Lady Mary!" she said. Her voice was like syrup. Behind her, something deep-blue flickered in the hall-light.

85

"It's Caroline, Prime Minister. Just Caroline. May I introduce . . . ?"

"Excuse me, Prime Minister. I'll be back."

Powell raised his right eyebrow. Barchard swooned. I caught Polina in the open doorway. The wind ruffled her hair and blew her cape in. You look a million dollars in those earrings, didn't I tell you, you could trust me in all matters of dress?

"Mrs Spratling?"

Her two bodyguards spun round and put their legs apart. Polina looked puzzled.

I said: "Richard Fisher. I'm . . ."

"Oh yes. You're doing a book."

"I wondered if you could possibly spare a moment to see me."

She said: "In principle, yes. I don't have a problem with you, Richard. Unfortunately, I have to be in Brussels for the Planning Group meeting early tomorrow, and from there I'm flying to Washington. So unless", and here she gave a weak, professional-woman's smile, "you have it in mind to meet in the middle of the night somewhere between here and Brussels, you'll have to wait until I return on the fifteenth."

"That'll be fine for me."

"So you can call Maureen McDowd, my secretary, on Monday. She has my diary."

"I'll look forward to it."

Polina smiled without warmth, turned, pushed between the guards and stepped out into the breeze.

Another digression. At the picnic at Schloss Brühl, Sebastian was out of sorts. I think Polina's attention upset him, though he took out his discomfort on me. He said: "For you, Richard, there is no history, just a nostalgia [*Sehnsucht*] for vanished class privileges. I hold it to be highly unlikely that your class will survive the upheavals of Thatcherism. At present, your heart both thrills and bleeds at the prospect of the coming battle with Scargill; but after

86

the coal miners, who next? The lords on their thrones and acres, the professional interest groups – I understand these matters only in the most general sense – the lawyers, the bowler-hats, the lean and murderous military officers, the alcoholic professors of Greek, the racers of pure-bred horses, the slumberous Clubmen, even the monarchy itself? These are all what Marx called, in his famous article for the *New York Daily Tribune* of 25 August 1852, *faux frais* of production, unproductive social overheads which he believed the British bourgeoisie would eventually tire of paying for. I do not hold it to be excluded, Richard, that the belated bourgeois revolution in England, which Marx so pathetically anticipated all through his London exile, will come to pass under this woman!"

Polina, who was inclined to agree with Sebastian, much to his unease, said: "Political life is always tending towards routine, marked by caution and the perpetuation of institutions regardless of their utility. Margaret Thatcher stands outside the British institutions because she's a woman and they, with maybe insignificant exceptions, are used and operated by men. I believe she has the desire, probably, and the capacity, certainly, to detonate British society."

I said: "I would not underestimate the tenacity of the British male." Particularly not this specimen, my sugar cone; and stop drawing attention to your femininity which is what's causing all the trouble; and, while we're about it, leave Sebastian alone, he's not like us, he's pure in heart, a Parsifal.

At that moment, Nida, the Filipina nurse, in reaching over for Rosa's peanut butter, let her hand rest a moment on mine.

I woke to the click of metal on the glass of the dressing table, then another: earrings. A shoe knocking against a chair-leg. The fall of a skirt. The stretch and pull of nylon stockings. A creaking board. Then, close to my ear: "It's Polly."

Actually, I don't know a whole lot of people who could track me to a remote fishing pub in the Eifel on the strength of a coded message at a cocktail party, at – Jesus! – three in the morning of the fourth of June, negotiate an admittedly forewarned Waltraut Simrock and find my room in the dark, but let me verify. Let me scoop out from the darkness with my lips a long, tense neck and crackly hair smelling of car air-freshener, teeth that taste faintly of chocolate and Coke, a nipple under a new lace bra, a belly-button, a wisp of hair from under cotton knickers . . .

"Hey! Cut that out!"

. . . a cool stomach. With my fingertips, I sketch in two cheeks, a nose where I barely expected it, eyes wet from grit or tiredness; establish two breasts, a waist, two hips in a tangle of knickers, thighs that . . .

"Hello, Polly."

Polly and Richard! Do you know Polly and Richard? Such a delightful couple! She's American, he's normal. She's heaven, he's rather a bore. She's tricky, he's all right. They met in Germany or somewhere like that. He likes a drop, she's a bit of a prude. Everybody was mad about her. Of course, she's a bit of a clever-socks, he's rather messed up his life.

"Ssh!"

She was married to someone, another American, who was the most appalling shit. Richard was there to pick up the pieces. She digs in her fingernails, he thinks about fishing. He's a Leftie, she's a cavalry detachment to the right of Tamburlaine. She's a killer, he doesn't shoot.

Polina switched on the bedside light. She had a red spot on each cheek. Her eyes gleamed.

"Hi!" she said.

"I suppose you think this will burn itself out."

The gleam vanished. Polina sighed. She said: "Do you want to talk about this? Right now?" She cupped her hand under first one breast, then the other. "I thought maybe we could just talk, fool around. I came the long way, Richard. That's three and a half hours driving. Kind of short notice."

I took her hand off her breast. "Let me do that for you," I said.

"I'm paranoid about cancer," she said and stretched to turn off the light. "Did you read that *Spiegel* thing about this AIDS . . . ?"

I said: "Polina, a lot does burn away. I get to not listening to what you say. You get pregnant, snore in bed. I gape at check-out girls, rage when I have to fix the shed door. You're a nag, I'm a boozer. You find out I'm stingy, cheap about some things. But none of this is wasted: it leaves a trace, all this, ashes, a sort of deposit of love, which gathers around us, eventually covers everything. The thing about marriage . . ."

"I guess you've been married a lot."

I glared at her in the darkness. I felt her sarcasm (which I suspect originated not in her childhood but in one of her marriages, perhaps the closing stages of Jim) evaporate. She said: "Why do you want to fight, Richard?"

"Because you're married to another bloke."

"You'd be miles from here if I wasn't."

I didn't answer. Then something splashed me. Her bosom was wet. There were wet lines on her cheeks. I reached out to kiss her eyelashes, but she turned her back to me, shaking. Bravo, I thought. I have now, officially, made Polina Mertz cry.

She said: "I terminated my pregnancy after eight weeks. Is that enough for you?" She leaned over me, sprinkling tears. "When I married Bill, Barry Cohen said I was trading up in the marriage market."

"I don't want to talk, Polina, after all."

"Well I do. I needed a husband, OK? Professionally. I'm a fucking spy, in case you hadn't noticed."

I kissed her mouth. My eye flashed. I caught one wrist, and then the other, and kneeled on her thighs till she became still. Sullenly, she opened her legs.

"Hi!" she said. "Start over."

She got up. I heard her where the dressing table was. I said:

"What are you doing?"

I sensed her half turn in pleasure. "None of your fucking business."

"Go on. Tell me."

"You really like girls, don't you? Are you gay or something?"

"I don't think so. Maybe."

Something fell heavily on the bed by my feet.

"Gift," she said.

"Polina, you shouldn't have. What is it?" My foot told me it was a bottle, probably brandy: a quarter-bottle of brandy. Should last about five minutes, but still it's very, very kind of you.

"Oh no! He hates it!"

"He loves it. But let's finish the old one first."

I found her hand and put my toothmug in it. I said: "They're getting there, Polina. With the best will in the world, I can't stop them. Julian's bright, you know. A week, maybe ten days, they'll have the Plough."

"I guess."

"They'll get to us, eventually. You and me. Us."

"Sure."

"They'll find out about you and Frank, Polina."

She sighed. "I guess you dragged me all the way here to tell me this?"

"No," I said. "I dragged you all the way here so we could go to bed. We won't live for ever, or indeed, if you go on the way you're going, very long. Plus, I need to tell you about Sergei."

"I don't believe this! I simply don't believe this guy!" She leaned right over me, breast in my ear, hair and tears on my face, brandy on her breath. "I'm not listening. I'll fuck you. I won't talk to you."

"We . . ."

"Shut up!"

"I . . ."

"SHUT UP!"

90

Polina swung her legs down and sat with her back to me. I put my cheek against her shoulder, but she shook me off. She said:

"I'm here in the middle of the fucking night in this irreparably compromised location, putting out to some British guy who's been through twenty-five hours of debriefing by MI6 and the Germans for some half-assed trip to the Zone and is now passing diplomatic intelligence to the ranking KGB officer in West Germany and Austria. You know, Richard, that we can never, ever meet again. What do you think you were doing? Tell me. I'm interested."

Have you finished? Can I begin?

"I'm going to fucking Belgium," she said.

"I saw Sergei at Krefeld on May 25, Vice-President Bush's visit. At the demonstration. I knew he'd be there, wearing a suit, vast ancient tape recorder, running after Böll and Petra Kelly. Thousands of police. Hartig got the fighting started early, but he fouled up: the barriers broke and we got separated, by Hertie, with the kids."

"Who else? Richard! Who else was with you?"

"Ulli Kretschmann of the *Tageszeitung*, a stringer for the *Observer* called Annie Barr . . ."

"OK. And then?"

"At the East–West Forum, you know, run by Dole and that old fellow from *Rude Pravo*. Sergei fixed it, invited himself. At the Rheinterrassen on May 27. Heavy, heavy drinking. I thought it'd be best in a crowd . . ."

"Yes. Yes."

"He kept saying: Generation change. He used the word *Generationswechsel*. We were talking German. He was drunk. Pretending to be drunk. No: definitely drunk."

"What are you saying? Yuri Andropov's sixty-one, for Christ's sake. Gromyko's still in there, in his seventies. What do you mean? You're not making sense."

"Don't shoot the messenger, OK? The names he mentioned don't mean anything to me. Romanov . . ."

"OK. Grigorij. Secretary General of the Party in Leningrad . . ."

". . . but there's some kind of dirt on him, to do with his daughter's wedding. A lot of valuable porcelain got smashed . . ."

"What are you talking about? You mean plates and stuff? So what?"

"He got it out of the Hermitage. Look, Polina, shall we come back to him. The other front-runner is a guy called Misha Gorbachev."

"Mikhail Gorbachev, friend and comfort to the Moscow KGB. He's going to the Portuguese CP congress in the fall, first trip abroad. He's on the up."

"He said Andropov is very, very ill. Ninety minutes of dialysis every morning."

"Look, Richard. This is interesting, really quite interesting. But there's nothing you've told me that a diligent and imaginative reading of published sources wouldn't have . . ."

"He said Mr K. didn't take the Plough to the Politburo."

She said nothing.

"Polina."

She was so quiet I reached out to touch her. She had gone from the bed. I imagined her, standing, one arm under her bosom, her fist in her mouth. A board creaked.

"Polina? It seems Kvertsovsky took it to Gromyko, who killed it."

She sat down on the bed. "It was rejected in Washington."

"*What?*"

"Jack presented it to the NSC meeting on June 2. The President said he preferred to stay with the Zero Option. 'We don't want to foul the pond' were his precise words. I guess that's something you should know."

"I'm so sorry."

"Don't be. We simply do our best."

I took her back in my arms. She put her forehead against my chest. She said: "All I do when I see the guy is cry."

"We do our best." Then I said, softly, into her hair: "Sergei kept talking about the manoeuvres."

"Sure."

"About Autumn Forge, Polina. About how it coincides with the

Pershing deployment deadline. What did I know about the exercises? What could I find out about them? Order-of-battle stuff, way over my head."

"Sure."

"POLINA!"

She laughed. "They think we're going to attack. Poor guys."

"Are we? Are you?"

"I hope not. Look, I'll give you some crap for Sergei, OK?"

"No you bloody won't."

"You're crazy, Richard. Do you want to die? I'll get it to you."

"I don't want it. Is that clear?"

My quarter-bottle of brandy was a handgun and two boxes of rounds.

"Listen, we're not talking regional warhead sub-ceilings any more. We're talking about two bullets in the back when you're opening your garage door. I repeat: I am not going to be able to protect you."

"I don't want it. I'm not discussing it any more."

"Oh, I see. You don't know how to use it. I'll fix you up with . . ."

"I said: Just stop. It's no use to me. You have to take it with you. Let's not fight, baby. We haven't enough time."

"I'm crossing a border, in case you forgot."

"You've got plates."

"Wake up, dumb-head! I had to take a car."

"Take?"

"Yes, take. What the fuck was I supposed to do? You come up and harass me at a diplomatic function, say you have to see me without delay. What did you imagine I'd do: bring those Stallones with me?"

The girl's a car thief. As well as everything else.

*   *   *

93

"Polina?"

"What now?"

"Do you love me?"

She turned round and kissed me on the face. She said: "I guess you're in the top quartile."

"That's not what I asked."

"Oh Richard, leave it, won't you?"

"I need you to say it. It'll help me. When it gets hard, I'll manage myself better if you say it. I know I will."

She struggled up on to her elbow. She said: "I do not love you, Richard. I value our relationship because you produce such fine intelligence, really quite outstanding, and I don't have to pay you or baby you or do anything for you except fuck you every now and then and that's not really a problem for me, because I'm a professional. I need you to understand that. Have you understood, Richard, because I can repeat it, if you wish?"

She was trembling. I put my arm round her and lowered her head on to the pillow.

"So how does it end?"

"Richard, please don't."

The birds had started, which filled me with sadness.

"I mean the missiles thing."

"Oh yes. Well, I guess nobody's going to throw Jack into prison, or at least not until the Pershings are at Mutlangen, though I reckon you and me aren't so indispensable."

"There's still the election. Once Ritter's in the Chancellery, in place of that slime von Arnim . . ."

"The SPD isn't going to win."

"You don't know that. The Allensbach opinion poll . . ."

"The SPD will not win."

Her face, in the twilight, was stony.

"Oh Polina," I said. "Oh. Oh. You shouldn't have said that.

This isn't the Fifties. This isn't El Salvador. You'll get a fucking civil war in Germany. You people are mad. Just mad."

"I'm not mad, Richard. Not yet."

"What about the Soviets, for God's sake?"

"What about the Soviets?"

"They could go to war."

"Why would they do that? The war's been fought. They lost. This was their last shot, their Ardennes. They've got nothing else, except a rebellion in Afghanistan they can't put down and a population they can't feed."

"Please, Polina."

She put her head on my chest and said to my knees: "When we finally got a good picture of the SS-20, two of them on the apron of Bela air base in Kazakhstan, during the night of June one and two 1977, Barry Cohen thought it was Christmas. He convinced everybody, from the President down, that the Soviets were trying to bust the SALT limits on intercontinental systems: they'd stockpile a third stage, and, bang, they're in business. But I knew. And Jack knew. And he told Helmut Schmidt, so he knew. You see, Richard, Barry had no experience of Europe. He thought in terms of home-land: Moscow, Washington, Cleveland, Sverdlovsk. He had no feeling for the fringes, for Europe. Hell, he couldn't even speak French. But Jack knew. Jack was on the Midnight Group at the time of Cuba. He'd met Gromyko and knew most guys only have one idea in their lives. He knew the Soviets take insane risks: make these mad dashes for parity. And he understood the weapon, really under-stood it, which Barry never did. OK, it didn't need twelve tractors and twenty guys and forty-eight hours to load and fire or send up clouds of vapour for every fucking satellite to pick up; OK, it had multiple warheads; OK, it was accurate within twelve hundred feet; OK, it was clean, sort of; but it was still the old tin-can blackmail rocket they shipped to Cuba in '62. Except that it wasn't pointed at Fort Lauderdale, but at the Germans. Two hundred and fifty missiles. Seven hundred and fifty independently targetable war-heads. There aren't even seven-fifty capital targets in the world, let alone in West Germany. Jack said Schmidt didn't even flinch. Apparently, Schmidt said: 'Time to engage.' I guess he'd been a soldier or sailor in the war."

"But, maybe it's not going to turn out the way you all thought it would. Maybe if it was fought out, not just imagined: annihilation, terror, chaos beyond description, I haven't got words for it, nobody has. All I can think of is that shadow that was somehow burned into the steps of the Sumitomo Bank in Hiroshima: something out of this world, beyond comprehension. Maybe it would come out differently, maybe even in their favour, or . . ."

Polina came up on her elbow. She said: "Does the name Edmund Fisher mean anything to you?"

"He's a name to me, that's all."

"He was one of my professors at Georgetown: brilliant guy, kind of inspiring."

Did you sleep with him, Polina?

"I think this will help you understand. Ed used to say that the nuclear arms race, far from being the diabolical enterprise of popular imagination, is an appropriate, even benign, form of competition between two great powers. He used to talk like that."

I said: Did you sleep with my daddy?

"The purpose of the Cold War is — I guess you should make that *was* — to save blood, not to spill it, he said. Years from now, it will seem as quaint as harmless as the tournaments of medieval chivalry."

Polina, did you fuck my dad?

Oh, who gives a damn?

"So you won."

"Who won?"

You'd really have got on my nerves, Polina. We'd never have lasted.

"You did. The United States. Democracy. Stockholder capitalism."

"Why do you say that, Richard?"

Annoying bitch.

"Well, who did win?"

I could see her now, taking shape for the last time in the morning light. She turned towards me and said: "Who knows, baby? I guess not the UK: the only thing you guys had were your missiles and now they're not needed. Presumably, the Germans get to unify. How do I know?" She stared at me with huge black eyes. "You know, it's weird, nuclear arms control. Barry simply went crazy, thought he was God or somebody, handing down a new moral order. Jack was very concerned about the proliferation thing. He thought the Soviet nuclear inventory would pass out of central control and the influence of diplomacy. He saw his whole career going up in smoke. Richard, I just felt that nobody had given any thought to the peace. Absolutely nobody had given it any fucking thought anywhere! I felt we just needed to give the Soviets some time, some kind of soft landing. It wasn't an emotional thing: I'm Polish, for Christ's sake, I hate those creeps! I don't give a damn if the Queen rules in England. But what the hell is the use of freedom in Europe if the whole continent is disintegrating? There isn't such a thing as freedom, unless there's security to enjoy it in. Nobody had thought this through. Except me, and I'm just a girl."

She stood in the bedroom doorway, with her white raincoat on. It was six forty-five: time for her to leave for Brussels. She was crying.

Panic engulfed me. I thought: I'm not going to touch or hold her ever again, as long as I live. Quick, here, now, to last me the rest of my life.

Framed by the doorway, she looked quite different. She seemed soft past description, stripped, flayed in her femininity. If I touched her neck or breast, she'd bruise for a month or bleed and bleed and bleed. I thought: She wants to leave, just as I want her to leave, to see if this thing can be done.

There's something she wants to say to me, something important: like "I'll love you for the rest of my life" (though obviously not that, because that's what I want to say, but won't). What we are waiting for now is for her to get through somehow to what she needs to say, and then say it. Then she'll turn and go down the stairs.

She said: "Look for danger. Really seek it out."

"Sure."

Polina ran down the stairs in stockinged feet.

In the old days, when Manfred Köhler and I used to have dinner at the Jagdhütte after fishing the Elmer, little Angelika Simrock would serve us and then sit down on a chair, askew at a table two or three away from us, not saying anything, but just looking and smiling. I believe, for her, company was like a hearth-fire, something to warm herself at.

She brought me my breakfast coffee in the sunny bay window, and also the bottle of *Kirschwasser* we always had. I sensed she was wondering, from her chair fifteen feet away, what was it like to spend half the night in the same room as the *Amerikanerin*? Who was she and why had she given Father twenty thousand marks the time the house was turned upside down? Where was Mr Köhler? I sensed her head aching with these questions. Dear, when they come, which will be quite soon now, just answer truthfully to the best of your ability.

I stared at the run below Manfred's pool, easily the least productive stretch of the river, but the section most clearly visible from the road. After an hour, I climbed out of the water, in obvious frustration, took down my rod, strung my wading boots round my neck and walked to Euskirchen. I knew it was far, but not that far (it is forty-five kilometres): it took all day and a piece of darkness. On the Cologne train, a woman helpfully pointed to my split shoes.

Most of the time, I didn't think or look at the country: I was dazzled with sunshine, Kirsch and sorrow. But something came into my head and stood around, patiently, till I noticed it. It was the certainty that the last thing Polina had said to me, Seek out danger, was the last thing Jacek Mertz had said to her in Bayonne, New Jersey, when he left home in 1964 or 1965.

The thought splintered and sparkled. One fragment ran off into her girlhood: Was Jacek's desertion some wounding experience that she needed to repeat or provoke, as a child touches a bruise, though she knows it'll hurt? I abandoned this line of thought as speculative and intrusive. Instead, I said out loud: "Even in her absence, I am continuing to learn about her."

I had another idea as I was crossing a road in the town of Mirbach: Polina spoke of a sort of Platonic war, imperceptible and bloodless, fought with weapons that are merely ideas; and this – traffic-light red BMW, punk with mongrel outside a REWE supermarket, two ladies in hats and handbags, green prowl-car – is a quiet corner of that ideal battlefield. If so, it will behave like a regular battlefield: opportunities will arise, situations will develop in interesting tactical directions, targets will appear and vanish. The situation, which looks hopeless today, may be full of possibilities in a week. Among these possibilities is that I should see Polina again and touch her lips with mine.

Helmut Kohl was fifty-two in 1983. He belonged to a generation too young to have served in the war, but too old to escape an association with evil and failure. I found him to difficult to judge then and I still do.

He was big: six feet two or three inches and at least two hundred pounds, and he had a habit of wearing sky-blue suits and then fidgeting with the buttons, which made him seem even bigger. He was clumsy. When I interviewed him for my book, on the second or third day after he'd tabled the no-confidence motion against Schmidt, his legs somehow became entangled in the low sofa in the receiving part of his office; and, in extracting them, he kicked over a tray of coffee, cream and sugar packets. He looked aghast.

His secretary, Marie-Luise Möllemann, stood blondely in the door, made soothing, feminine sounds, sorted everything out. My dentist in the Argelanderstrasse repeated putrid gossip about them.

Kohl spoke in platitudes, and certain words and phrases – peace, fatherland, our divided former capital, restitution, Israel, European Community, partnership – caused him to lower his voice, but unconvincingly, like a teenage boy. He liked to dramatize issues of politics: Why, Mr Fisher, should a girl from Dresden not marry a boy from Darmstadt? He used illustrations from his own biography. At the end of the interview, which went on too long, it being about eleven-thirty, Mrs Möllemann came in and, like some German geisha, skilfully poured us glasses of sweet wine, holding the bottle one-handed by its base. The wine came, he explained, undoing his jacket button, from the state of Rhineland-Palatinate where he had been Minister-President for fifteen years.

Yet . . . Yet . . . This was the Kohlian yet, which in Bonn, a city that in those days had nothing better to do than analyse itself to distraction, you heard as often as you heard of his philistine asininities. At the German Foreign Office, sleek and tailored men who in 1945 had lost estates the size of nations in the east, used to shake their heads and say: Yet, Kohl's *schlau* (a smart one), a word used then also to describe foxes and flatter uneducated women. Among journalists such as Hofmeyer of the *Frankfurter Allgemeine*, who had switched professional allegiances from the other Helmut, it was: "Yet I think it would be a mistake to underestimate Helmut Kohl."

Yet Kohl had done well at school in Ludwigshafen, a town on the upper Rhine famous for a dye-stuffs factory that had overrun ten miles of riverbank. He'd been awarded a doctorate in chemical engineering and (unlike Schmidt or Ritter or Polina or Nik Tully or Beate Beck) insisted on his doctor title. I ordered his thesis from the Ludwigshafen University Library, but for some reason, said not to be sinister, it had vanished and Mrs Möllemann also had no copy. Kohl rose quickly through the local Christian Democrats and, at the age of only thirty-four, was running the solidly CDU state of Rhineland-Palatinate. In those years of economic expansion, when West Germans installed washing machines and hobby basements and saw the cliffs of Capri, when the Berlin Wall went up and the cities began to fill with Turkish men, Kohl seemed the natural successor to Adenauer and Erhard; even more so when the generations split asunder in the late Sixties, and Beate Beck read Marcuse and started shrieking about consumer terror and the reification of all desire in this cold and numb republic.

As a challenger to Brandt and Schmidt in the 1970s, Kohl had just one rival, but a formidable one: Franz-Josef Strauss, president of the Bavarian version of the Christian Democrats, a party called the Christian Social Union. My debriefing was, at German request, suspended for the last week of the campaign, and I went down and spent two days with Strauss in the villages of Upper Bavaria. On the stage of the Schongau Wirtshaus, sweating under the television lights, bull neck sunk in his tight Bavarian suit, speaking beautiful German or plunging into the Latin of Cicero, I thought Kaspar Hauser had returned. I felt I might come upon him, the applause still ringing, in a back room slumped in a chair with his collar ripped open, babbling gibberish. After the speech, I asked him how he felt and he said: "Thirsty!" I brought him a jug of white beer and he drank it off, as a child drinks milk, then turned on me his bright eye: "*Non erit pactum,* * Mr Fisher." I sensed that he alone of the Germans had seen the election was a sham; but that his mind was somehow imprisoned in his ugly body, and there was something reckless and dark and mad about him. He scared the wits out of anybody north of Würzburg.

After the rally, we sat in a back room of the pub, with the local and Austrian reporters, and Strauss made fun of Kohl till the lights danced in the room from beer and smoke. I now see that Strauss was frightened of Kohl: that he'd seen (long before anybody else) how Kohl could manipulate not only his party but also those ghosts − Fatherland! Reconciliation! − which had been haunting the

* There'll be no treaty

mansards of West German memory for two generations and now appeared, in his clumsy and philistine hands, to be mere puppets, all plywood and paint, not frightening at all. (It helped a lot with the public that Kohl wasn't a genius like Strauss or a nag and a fuss like Schmidt; that he didn't speak a word of any language except a German you wouldn't find in Duden, liked a good drop, had a pretty wife and a prettier etc.) François Mitterrand also saw that Kohl was somebody and treated him with the greatest courtesy; as did, if in a good humour, Mrs Thatcher.

I don't think Kohl had any ideas in those days, except what he'd learned from Adenauer in the Fifties: that only by burrowing deep into NATO and the new bureaucratic institutions of Western Europe – ah, those white nights of milk quotas and herring tonnages! – would they persuade the Russians they couldn't outlast the West and might as well let the GDR and its seventeen million Germans go. I must emphasize that this idea became ridiculous in the Sixties and Seventies. If there was to be a single German state within the borders of 1938 – that is, before the Hitlerian land grabs – it certainly wasn't going to be the sort of greater Federal Republic that Adenauer and the Basic Law had demanded, but a joint enterprise, in which West Germany became less capitalist and East Germany less communist, till they met in the middle, like tunnelbuilders in the Alps. That, at least, was the theory behind the *Ostpolitik* of Brandt and Egon Bahr, and was summed up in the slogan "Change through Proximity"; though even this vision was too much for the Left of the party, led by Sebastian Ritter, who simply did not believe in German unification or rather thought it would be bad for Germany and humanity in general.

A stopped clock is correct twice a day. History rolled round to vindicate both Adenauer and Kohl, while the tormented theories of Social Democracy now seem but the fossils of extinct ideas.

Helmut Schmidt had two briefings from Polk on the SS-20, both during the Bundestag summer recess of 1977, both in his home in the Hamburg suburb of Blankenese. At the second, Polina sat in the kitchen with Hannelore Schmidt, shelling peas for the first time in her life, and giggling with nerves. Schmidt must have known that the game was up for the SPD and for his administration, at which he was quite as adept as even he thought himself, but he was a trooper. He merely begged Jimmy Carter that before NATO matched the SS-20, a senior diplomat should go back to Geneva and try to negotiate a treaty covering intermediate-range nuclear forces; and, though he would not think to interfere with the Presidential prerogative, he would be grateful if that person could be John Polk.

But even the Zero Option, devised by Sebastian Ritter from across the entire width of the party to try and keep the SPD whole, could not save Schmidt. In September 1982, Schmidt's coalition government of Social Democrats and Liberals collapsed. The Liberals offered themselves to Kohl who, dizzy with excitement and pride, tabled a motion of no confidence in the Bundestag. Schmidt, the Siegfried of this drama, retired to Hamburg. New elections were called for July 5, 1983.

Whatever Polina's masters had intended by way of influencing the outcome, it wasn't needed: the deck was stacked against the SPD. The right-wing newspapers of the *Springer Verlag* seized on the trip by Jochen Vogel, the shadow chancellor, to Moscow and dubbed him "Andropov's Candidate"; that Sebastian had gone with him made the visit all the more sinister, and they dredged their morgues for all they could find on the '68 firebrand and terrorist lawyer. I thought little of Vogel. In that last week before the vote, he saw me in, of all things, a panelled campaign train which had been built by the old Reichsbahn for Göring. The country between Bielefeld and Hanover skidded behind his white hair. He spoke of deploying the Pershings on submarines, way out in the un-enfranchised seas, but this equivocation sounded to the public at best shifty, at worst petrifying. In the restaurant car, Peter Glotz, his campaign manager, sat over a morose whisky: "We might have had Sebastian Ritter as candidate and at least had some fun."

Hans-Dietrich Genscher, the Hagen to Schmidt's Siegfried, *was* having fun. His little party, the Liberals or Free Democrats, had been on the verge of extinction since the foundation of the Federal Republic, but had still managed to be more often in power than out of it: Genscher had habituated himself to life on the edge. In every speech of the campaign, he warned that, if the Liberals were voted out of Parliament, the SPD would ally with the Greens and tip the Republic into neutrality and chaos. In making this threat, he was much helped by the Greens themselves who, at a party congress in Dortmund in March, had, in the name of basis democracy and in the face of a passionate appeal by Pastor Lightner, bound their parliamentary candidates to compulsory retirement after two years and to a total obedience to the party congress – an imperative mandate borrowed intact from Marx's *The Civil War in France*. The same congress, in a despairing attempt to silence the shrieks of a group of runaway children bussed up from a squat in Nuremberg, voted to propose in parliament a repeal of the law banning sex with minors. When, on April 16, Frank Lightner was found dead of a bullet wound at his house in Berlin-Charlottenburg and Petra Kelly made wild and tearful accusations against the Berlin police and public prosecutor, the country – or at least the bourgeois press – threw up its hands. "Weimar Conditions!" was the heading to a leader on the front page of the *Frankfurter Allgemeine*, which argued, in complete solemnity, that small political parties, murder and mayhem always went together and invariably ended in dictatorship and the invasion of Poland. (We'd stopped in Franconia, in a cold lay-by outside Schweinfurt, because we were early for the rally. Genscher worked on his speech by the light of the open Mercedes door. Jim Dole had some Weinbrand and chocolate. Genscher leaned out, his spectacles on his nose, and said: "Our little Red/ Green fiction appears to be working, gentlemen!")

On July 5, which was a Sunday, the result was not long in coming. I'd gone to the CDU/CSU headquarters on the Ollenauer-allee, because I thought Polina might be there: to see, mind, not to talk or touch. Everything I saw that sham-historic evening I saw through a screen of longing and fear, as through a windowpane: the crowds round the TV sets, the wall-clock at 18.15, the arms going up, Kohl clambering, vastly, on to a table and, on Hannelore Kohl's face, a look of inconsolable misery.

"We won, Dick! Our guy won! Way. . . To . . . Go!" Bill Spratling put his arm round me, while his eyes raked the big room.

"Actually, old man, I was rather looking for your wife, if you don't mind." I don't want her here, in front of these sheets of glass, beneath this tonnage of steel and concrete.

"Across the street," Spratling said and was going, going. "Division of labour." He was gone.

Already, the life was draining out of the party. Von Arnim, in a dinner jacket, was making his way to the door. Brian Barchard looked at his watch. He said: "Well done, Richard, you weren't too far off. The Greens have seven per cent on the German TV exit poll."

"Yes. You haven't seen Mrs Spratling, have you?"

"With the SPD over the way." His vanity was pricked. "I wouldn't assume, Richard, whatever that young woman says, that the Western Alliance's problems are over. In a sense, they are just beginning."

Too damn right they are, sir.

Through the Sixties techno-glass of the SPD building, I saw a trestle table covered in mutilated party food. On the stage, men in grey bibs were taking up cable. Ritter stood clutching his briefcase, backed into a corner by reporters. He was saying: "What I said, in fact, Mr Hofmeyer, was that the CDU/CSU and FDP have a working parliamentary majority, but not necessarily a Pershing majority. Still, of course, I am disappointed with the result, bitterly disappointed. Ah, at last . . ."

He pushed gently through the crowd, side on.

"You were held up, Mr Fisher. Excuse me, gentlemen, I have a long-standing appointment." He bustled me back to the door.

"Have you by any chance . . . ?" With a sinking heart, I thought better of it. We took the first taxi on the rank. Ritter got in without saying anything, and he said nothing on the way to the Käfer bar.

"We're shut," said Inge Mohr. She was watching a small TV on the counter.

"Life-and-death, Inge."

Without looking behind her, she picked up a large bound wine list, decorated with embossed grapes and Roman drinking glasses and a map of the wine-growing regions, and tossed it on to the bar by Sebastian. He looked at me.

I said: "Can we have a bottle of Moselle, not too dry, and a bottle of brandy on the side? And some bread and cheese, whatever you've got. And Sebastian, we should watch the news and debate."

He nodded.

Inge said, dropping our bottles on the table (no sip, roll and taste with Inge Mohr, no simpering after the exact, descriptive adjective!): "Cheer up, Mr Ritter. You have your health."

Sebastian made a sound which may have been intended as a laugh. He said: "V. I. Lenin . . ."

"Why not tell me about him another time?"

I thought: Polina will be home by now, safe, in bed even, with that jerk. And I'm here in this maudlin plywood pub, shaken by railway trains and Inge Mohr's progressive tastes in music, about to seal a masculine friendship in a welter of Leftist defeatism. It hadn't occurred to me that a man might make a demand of me: that Sebastian would present a bill of friendship at a moment when I was temporarily embarrassed.

"The wine is sharp," he said. "Don't you find it sharp, Richard?"

"I find it excellent," I said and then pulled myself together. "We'll get Mrs Mohr to bring something sweeter."

Sebastian closed his eyes, and then opened them again. He said: "My father was a Nazi. He was a jurist, like me. An officer in the Reichs Ministry of Justice, under State Secretary Stuckart. They were intimate. Father wrote the commentary on the Nuremberg Race Laws, 1935. Later, after I'd finished school, Mother said he'd taken on this exercise because others would be more severe in their readings." His voice had regained its harshness: *war fasclST, einander gedUTZT, nicht GANZ so mild und zart.* I sensed that his ironical pedantry had originated in descriptions of his father.

"That may have been true, who knows? Fact is that he enlisted in 1943, went missing at Kiev in 1945, a lance corporal. He was a glowing Nazi to the end. Mother gave me his letters from the front." He waved a hand and squinted, as if to dispel a drift of cigarette smoke. "The Bolshevik–Jewish World Peril. Germany's Mission in the East. Et cetera. Et cetera. He was not, it appears, a good soldier. He was a bad soldier."

"How can you know all this?"

"I remember certain things. Nineteen hundred and forty-five, we were living in Bochum, apartment of Mother's cousin. I remember Mother ironing a grey topcoat. I remember a word my mother spoke, as if uncertain of its orthography; and my aunt; as if it were a talisman, Richard, that would keep the roof on the apartment-house, Father alive, beets in the allotment, the Russians at the Oder.

"Where had they heard this word? From Father. And where had Father heard it? From an officer. In my mind's eye, I see my father, stiff and steady and stupid in his topboots, his men all spit-and-polish, except that by now they're the runts of the Great German litter; and the officer saying: 'Men! I have just one word to say! You won't understand it now! But keep it in mind because you will! You will! Very soon!'"

Sebastian put on a face of painful solemnity. *"Atomzertrüm-merung!"** he whispered. "Then the officer salutes, spins round, bounces away in his staff car. And two stupid women and a boy in an apartment in the Ruhr dream of safety under the starshell. Later, of course, when I heard of Hiroshima and Nagasaki and what happened there, I felt the horror and pathos in my own body."

"I thought . . ."

Sebastian waved his hand again. "Correct! By all accounts, the

* Atomic fission!

National Socialists made no serious effort to split the atom. The science was there, but not the industrial capacity or the bureaucratic discipline. The more, Richard, one learns about the Third Reich, the more chaotic, arbitrary and capricious it appears: the very model of an old-fashioned despotism. That was not my point. I related this unimportant personal anecdote simply because it has filled my sad mind this evening; as it did, when I was at gymnasium and went on my first Easter March against nuclear armament, or later, when, under the insistent persuasion of Frank and Gretchen Lightner, I went to the site of the proposed atomic power station at Wyhl in Baden. My father was a very thin man, with poor eyesight. Deep German dream! Deep German illusion!"

"It's not over, Sebastian. Trust me."

He smiled. "I do," he said.

"But you have to endorse the Golden Plough. Now. Force Kohl on the defensive before he's settled in. Embarrass the Americans."

"I have explained, Richard, why I cannot."

Through the schnapps in my head, another idea was struggling to the surface. I tried to scoop it up, but it sank again.

"Mr Ritter!" Inge's head appeared at the partition. "The fatheads are on."

"We should watch," I said.

"Clearly."

The camera was on Vogel. From drink or exhaustion, he was slurring his speech. He was saying: "You have deliberately mis-understood me, Mr Novottny. I meant there is a majority of CDU/CSU and FDP in the House. I very much doubt there is a majority for the Pershing II on the streets of this Republic. I very much doubt there is a majority for doing exactly what the Americans ask, whenever they ask." I glanced at Sebastian, to see if he approved this plagiary, but he was staring at the TV as if it were a famous beauty spot.

Strauss was slumped in the lapels of his Bavarian suit. I suppose he, too, was dejected. He was like a faulty electrical connection, spitting out little sallies in his lovely German. Kohl beside him seemed to have grown. He beamed and fidgeted, like a giant schoolboy, squeezing the others into embarrassing proximity.

". . . an intellectual and moral renewal," he said. Negotiations at Geneva. Ambassadors Polk and Kvertsovsky. Towards a Zero Solution. Strongest efforts. Reliable alliance partner. Fellow Germans on the far side of the Wall and barbed wire.

Genscher was wreathed in smiles.

Among these gentlemen of a certain age, Petra Kelly, one of three rotating chairpeople of the Greens, was a relief to the senses. She wore a brilliant blouse in the colour known in Germany as *Bewegungslila* (Sisters' mauve, perhaps). She was breathless and shrill. She said: "I regard this election with a weeping and a laughing eye. Of course, we are pleased that we have entered parliament; and now all the marginalized of this prosperous society, the poor, women, the sick and handicapped, the land and nature herself will have a voice; but I had hoped that the SPD would be the strongest faction, that in certain restricted areas, we could have tolerated a government of the SPD in the spirit of Frank Lightner and Sebastian Ritter . . ."

Sebastian said: "Without a revolution . . ."

"What?" Inge turned down the volume.

"V. I. Lenin said on 7 March 1918, at the time of the Brest treaty: 'The absolute truth is that without a revolution in Germany, we shall perish.' By that he meant that unless there was a communist uprising in another European state – and Germany was the obvious candidate in 1918 – the Soviet Union would be isolated and could not survive."

I was looking at Inge's breast, when the idea again broke surface and stayed there, bobbing.

"I'd like to see the Kremlin, Sebastian, before I die. We'll work the Russians together."

He wasn't listening. He seemed to be moving between pools of memory or consciousness, as if they were streetlights. Through my fog of drink, I sensed the shape of his soul: thin, pale, shaven-headed, imprisoned. He squinted at me. He said: "Did you ever consider, when you . . ."

The door swung open. Four men tumbled in.

"Shut!" Inge shouted.

They concertinaed to a halt, teetered, made as if to advance, and recognized Sebastian.

"Drowning sorrows, eh?"

"I said: We are shut."

"Sozi crap!"

"Queer!"

"Get over to the Zone!"

"And shut the goddam door!"

He didn't notice. He was still glaring at me. "What possible purpose do you have in bringing a great power to its knees?"

"Look, mate, it's not me." I returned his stare, but he was looking through me: at these inexplicable new Germans, no doubt, or even through them. Oh Jesus, he's talking to Polina!

"I would be grateful if you would tell me what you imagine will happen?"

"I don't know, for God's sake! A pre-emptive attack from the Soviet side?" Would you like me to call her?

"For example! But what if the deployments proceed and the Soviets do not retaliate? What, in the name of heaven, do you imagine will replace the Soviet Union in the East?"

"A greater Germany? How do I know?" I'll wake her up, if you want, and ask her. It's no trouble. I'd like to.

"I will tell you what will happen, Richard. There will be civil war. One, two, a thousand civil wars. Every petty nationalism, from Riga to Tashkent, will have its bloody day. And capitalism, having lost its counter-weight, will spin out of control till . . ."

"I'll drive you guys back," said Inge Mohr. "I can't stand to listen to you."

She turned off the television. Darkness cut off pieces of the bar. Sebastian got up, looked round to thank her, but she was somewhere else, standing in the breezy doorway. I thought: We'll get Sebastian home, then who knows, maybe Inge'll ask me up.

In the taxi, he slid into a corner. When I looked again, he was asleep.

"Römerstrasse 36, Inge."

It was in the north town, between the river and the old Cologne road: a block of glum flats that faced on to the Römerstrasse, built of grey Economic-Miracle concrete with metal window frames. An arched entrance was the only piece of architectural whimsy. Tulips stood in rows on each side of a concrete path that led through the arch to a small guardhouse, where a light was on.

"Fuck! Police," said Inge and drove on.

"Sebastian! Wake up, you dumbhead!" I shook him and then slapped him. The touch of his unshaven face startled me. "You loathsome little Trot, wake up! Do you want to be on the front of *Bild?*"

She'd driven round the block, to a gritty yard lined with garages and trash barrels. Light came from under a corresponding arch.

"Get his door-key?"

"What?"

"In his pocket."

"What? Look in his pocket?"

She tugged at the handbrake; clunked open the door; knelt down, fished in his raincoat and pulled out a bunch of keys attached to a little football. She dragged him out, propping open his door with her hip. Something about us bored her, but I couldn't quite make it out: our being drunk, no doubt.

"See you," she said and drove off.

Damn you, Sebastian Ritter! I tried to make him take a step, but he flopped forward. I tried dragging him sideways, but the sight of his Kaufhof shoes scuffing on the concrete depressed me. I put down his briefcase; leaned over and hitched him onto my left shoulder in a fireman's lift; bent, knees trembling, to retrieve the briefcase, and staggered through the lit arch. Ahead, across a small courtyard, was the sentry box: I could see the back of the officer's head. I crept up and then, in an unbalanced spurt, reached the base of the stairs and rested. The policeman, side on, was looking at the nudes in *Quick* magazine. I thought: Inge Mohr is a lesbian, and I was overwhelmed with sorrow.

The flat, as it turned out, was on the fifth and top floor. In my left shoulder was a pain so sharp that I thought I'd faint. I also thought that, when the pain had gone, I'd have to address the main intellectual problems of the evening which were: Why is Sebastian so eager to show the crummy apartment block where he lives? Why does said crummy apartment block have a 24-hour police guard? And how long would that guard detain Beate?

The flat door gave way into darkness. The orange streetlight revealed a hall with a rack of coats at adult's and then child's height. I staggered into the next room and tipped Sebastian on to a sofa of some artificial material. I groped for a light switch and then thought better of it. The room was small: a sofa, a desk with a telephone, a wall of books, legal-looking, very neat. I thought: Don't look in his desk. I took off one of his shoes, but the nylon sock unsettled me. I pulled gently at his shirt and saw the gaping scar on his side. I walked over to the desk and stood still while it took shape in the darkness. I said in a whisper: "I was there, that day on the Ku'damm, when you were blown through the door of the Society of Socialist Students. The guy with you put both hands on your stomach to stop the blood, while you were yelling: 'My shoe!' and I stood, motionless, in the midst of traffic. It was Klein, that guy, wasn't it? I have to see him now, Sebastian. I have to see little Klein."

Sebastian was quite still. His eyelashes glistened in the street-light. Down each unshaven cheek a drop of liquid gold ran towards his collar. The age of miracles is past, Sebastian, and these tears are not the tears of instant saints, they are shed for me and Klein and the bullet shock that still runs through you; for the nights of *Capital* and Lukacs and Meister Eckhart; for every step – My shoe! My shoe! – of this long march nowhere; for points of order and points of information and newspaper bundles at rainy dawns at shipyard gates; for the women that spat at you in the Stuttgart city centre; for your father sleeping in the Ukraine; for the dog you thought of buying but never did; for the girls you never kissed and the girl you did kiss; for Beate, snatching back her barrister's sleeve on metal and terror; for the guard on your gate; for the injuries of history.

A bar of electric light shot between my feet. In the narrow passage, somebody was standing; small; a little girl in a nightgown with her fist up to her mouth.

"Don't be frightened. Don't cry out."

She didn't move.

"Don't be afraid. I'm your father's friend."

She didn't move.

"I need a blanket for your father."

She didn't move.

"Can you get me a blanket? From your bed? For your dad?"

She ran into her room and came out again, pulling a yellow blanket which snagged on something and tripped her. I made tiptoeing steps. She followed, also on tiptoe.

The blanket was patterned with ducks. I put it over Sebastian. She tucked it in, then changed her mind, and untucked it. I shooed her from the room. I said: "Your dad's very tired and you must go to bed."

"I want a drink."

Like hell you do, I thought. "I'll get you a drink, darling, but then you must go to bed. Your dad's very tired."

"Because of the Bundestag election?"

"Yes."

"You're Richard."

"I'm Richard."

The kitchen was too small to hold a table. It had a sort of counter, with stools to sit on, a gas ring and a formica cupboard. The little girl climbed on to a stool. She said: "I'm hungry."

In the cupboard were packet soups, tinned food, potato crisps, Cheez Whiz, chocolate bars, marshmallows, peanut butter, eggs.

"Do you want a boiled egg?"

I was sure she wouldn't eat it. She just wanted to see if this man would really cook one for her in the middle of the night. She swivelled a full revolution on her stool and said:

"Will you be my boyfriend?"

"I'm your father's friend. That makes me your friend."

"Father had to work late."

"Father had to work late."

Rosa Luxemburg Ritter, I'm not going to ask you any questions. I'm going to get your egg out of the boiling water, put it in the base of the egg box because there are no egg cups, make you bread soldiers, pour you a cup of this toothrot, what is it, Kool-Aid. I am not going to ask you any questions.

"Nida's not my mum," she said. "My mum's my mum."

I know, my darling. I met her in Leipzig. "Do you like school?"

"My mum's all right, but she's not here." She looked at me with ludicrous solemnity and pushed up her chin: the remains of an adult gesture, a gesture unique to the Germanies: a vestige, fragmentary and imitative, of the word *drüben*, which means "over there". Beyond her, in the doorway, I saw a pair of brown legs, blue knickers, a sleepy face, pretty breasts disappearing into a patterned silk dressing gown.

"Rosa! What are you doing here!"

At that moment, I thought, not necessarily in this order: she's an idle bitch, not even bothering to cover her tits in front of the child; she doesn't like the child, who has put her face straight down into her hands, pretending to cry and now crying; something about her breasts – Jesus, how do I know this? – tells me she once had a child of her own, presumably back in the Philippines; she's a bad hat, but then so am I and she knows it, two bad hats in this good house. Quits.

"It's not her fault, Nida. It is Nida, isn't it?" I spoke English. "Mr Ritter's asleep, and I thought we'd have a midnight feast."

Rosa lifted her head, her red cheeks beaming. "I speak English," she said in German.

"You were at the picnic," said Nida. There was something whorish in her accent. Hell, I thought, she's been around US marines since she was ten, poor thing. Fear and frustrated desire had made a sort of ball in my guts. I thought: Intellectual problem number three, who is this girl?

"Richard's my boyfriend," said Rosa.

"Got to go, my love."

I kissed Rosa on the hair, which smelled sweet. Nida didn't see me to the door, no bad thing, but regretted at the time.

Crossing the floodlit Oxfordplatz, I remembered. Oh yes, the picnic at Schloss Brühl. Silly me.

Nida, in reaching across for Rosa's peanut butter, had touched my hand. When I looked up, Polina was still looking at me: her eyes were, if this is possible, black.

After lunch, we walked in the park. She said: "I'm not messing up my fucking career so you can make out with some oriental bimbo."

"So what about you and Sebastian Ritter, madam? 'Or perhaps the view is somewhat too absolutist for Dr Ritter.' Flutter."

"She's working for the Germans."

Her eyes slithered away, like soap in a bath.

I thought: Polina's getting talkative. Not like Polina. She must care for me.

I should have said, Oh yes? And how do you know, my treasure? For the Germans, you say? And who else, my dove? Look at me, Polina.

The Oxfordplatz yawed beneath me. So you've put an agent in his house, a gaoler on his child. What do you want him for? You and Beate? Can't you leave the poor man alone? And his daughter.

At the British Embassy later that morning, I was not at my best.

Von Arnim looked up from his papers: "Perhaps I might

intervene here, Brian?" He spoke good, slightly American English: he'd probably done graduate studies there. He said: "Under the Basic Law of the Federal Republic, telephone surveillance is legal in individual cases, personally approved by the Minister of Interior and endorsed within fourteen days by the Interior Affairs Committee of the Bundestag. A strong application might be made now, Mr Fisher, with the evidence arising from your visit to the GDR on May 1-2. But this charming conversation was recorded on April 27. There can be no question that your phone was bugged."

I see. What excellent German logic: what isn't permitted, cannot be! It's not *my* phone that bothers me, you Baltic scum. It's the phone of the recipient of these tendernesses. I said: "So where, if I might ask, did you get that tape we've just heard?"

Arnim's eyes flickered.

"Let's just say it was in the market," said Tully.

Barchard groaned and turned to the wall.

"In the market, Nik? Did you say 'market'? There's a secondary market in my phone calls?"

Barchard pulled himself together. He said: "Shall we calm down? Richard, nobody's remotely interested in the romantic material. As far as I'm concerned, you can run after every married woman in the diplomatic corps, excepting only my wife. Actually," and now he had decided he would be angry, "I'm so bored with your fucking biography and opinions I could scream. I have one or two things I would rather do than listen to you, notably represent the interests of Her Majesty's Government in a tense and trying situation. Nobody asked you to go to Leipzig or seek diplomatic assistance in returning. You must take the consequences of your actions, and one of these consequences is the examination of your recent career in the light of that visit. You are here, crudely expressed, retrospectively to earn your passage home. Meanwhile, yes: your friend's analysis of the UK independent deterrent was characteristically penetrating, but certain cardinal elements of British policy appear to have gone right over her lovely head. First . . ."

"One moment, please, Brian." Sir Julian was standing in the

doorway of his secretary's office. He looked desolated; or perhaps it was simply that he wasn't smiling. I realized that he always smiled: it was his politeness. Stay out of this, Julian, it's nothing to do with you.

He said: "What is the Golden Plough?"

"The golden what?"

"What is the Golden Plough, Richard?"

The Golden Plough is a place. The Golden Plough is an idea. A late and inordinately difficult novel by Henry James. A work of amateur 19th-century anthropology. An icily snobbish hotel in Salzburg, Austria.

The Golden Plough is a diplomatic enterprise. The first and best of all eras of the world, in which, according to the Greek and Latin poets, mankind lived in a state of ideal prosperity. The division of a line into two such parts that the area of the rectangle contained by the smaller segment and the whole line equals the square of the larger segment.

The Golden Plough is a breathtaking exercise in feminine manipulation. The Golden Plough is a late and desperate project to preserve the peace of Europe. A pro-Axis secret society in wartime Iraq. The inlet of the Bosphorus around which Istanbul (formerly Constantinople) is situated. Whore's slang for pissing. The strait forming the entrance to San Francisco Bay. A Hapsburg order of chivalry.

My father, the famous strategic theoretician Edmund Fisher, once said to me on Deer Isle, Maine: "Julian's like a trial lawyer, never asks a question unless he knows the answer."

"To sum up," Barchard said. "An Englishman, professionally and emotionally on the make, meets a young American woman intellectually active in his father's academic speciality, that is to say, the strategic analysis of nuclear weapons. As presented by Fisher in often cloying terms and at excessive length, this young woman would beggar Eleanor of Aquitaine for beauty, intelligence and ambition. Her company I always found peculiarly wearisome, but I have learned over many years not to underestimate the potential of this combination of intellectual rivalry and sexual intoxication.

"What is the Golden Plough? Stripped of its frills and bows, the Golden Plough is a mildly ingenious mechanism to stabilize conditions in the Soviet lands of Eastern Europe and Asia and the remaining satellites in the Third World. If ever incorporated into a ratified and verifiable treaty, the Golden Plough would probably release the Soviet Union – for ten years, perhaps for a generation – from the ineluctable pressure of military competition with the United States which we have reason to believe is destroying its economy, the will of its elite and its popular legitimacy. During this interregnum, it is possible or more than possible that the centrifugal forces already evident in Poland, Romania, the Balkans, the Baltic States, the Caucasus and parts of Muslim Central Asia could either be held in check by force or channelled into reformist directions that would, none the less, leave the authority of the Soviet Communist Party intact. That this project has been devised not by the ideologues and tacticians of the CPSU but by a young American woman of irregular habits and an elderly East Coast Brahmin lends Fisher's account a perverse and granular authenticity.

"After sixty hours of excruciatingly tedious discussion, we are now reasonably confident of the engineering of the Geneva back channel as it existed on May 1, 1983, the day of the Four-Power Meeting in East Berlin and Fisher's visit to Leipzig. What we are not at all sure of, ladies and gentlemen, is, first, the two ends of this channel: Has the Golden Plough been presented in any coherent form to the President and Andropov, or merely to the staff of the National Security Council in Washington and the terrorized and devious cold warriors around Gromyko at the Foreign Ministry in Moscow? Second, we keenly need to know on what authority Polk and this girl believe they can bargain away the nuclear forces of the United Kingdom and our French allies. Third, we have to establish whether there existed or still exist other back channels, possibly through Bonn and Leipzig, as the SIS has surmised, and again who the Soviet and US interlocutors might be. Fourth, assuming this channel or channels to be whole and unclogged, can we feed our concerns and interests into them?

"As a subordinate matter: at Fisher's repeated and shrill insistence, I sought hypothetical advice from Her Majesty's Government's law officers. This advice is purely hypothetical, but I am informed that there is a *prima facie* criminal case against Fisher of immense gravity and he should be aware of it.

"Does that all sound fair to you, Richard?"

"Yes. That sounds fine."

"Thank you, Eileen."

Among the telephone intercepts, delivered in fat packets by courier from the UK Government communications intelligence centre at Cheltenham, was this gem from July 23, 1983:

"Patty! Darling!"

"You don't know what trouble I've been through . . ."

"You're on a recorded line, Patty."

"You sound like Kidder Peabody! I'm going to say what I called to say, and damn everybody else. Two creeps from Chuck's old shop in Washington . . ."

"I know."

". . . came up from Mexico City. Asked a lot of damn fool questions about you and some girl. Chuck saw them off the property. Are you all right, sweetie? Do you need . . . ?"

"I love you, Patty Livingston."

"I'm getting old. Chuck's got an enlarged prostate. We have to go to Houston."

"I'm so sorry, Patty."

"Don't get old, Richard. It ain't worth it."

"Goodbye, Patty."
"Goodbye, sweetie."

On August 1, a bank holiday in Germany so the Embassy was shut, Manfred Köhler took me to his gun club.

I fired twenty-eight rounds at a target. She'd given me seventy-two.

"I think I'd be safer without this thing."

The instructor at the *Troisdorfer Schützenverein* looked relieved.

"But not your foes," said Manfred Köhler.

Dr Horst Tümmers, who specialized in disorders of the urinary tract but was also my general practitioner, prescribed for my insomnia a drug called Halcion in ten-milligram doses. This medicine, which was sold in Germany under a licence from Upjohn, a pharmaceuticals company with its headquarters in Kalamazoo, Michigan, was removed from sale in Germany and the United Kingdom in 1991 because of clinical evidence of side effects in long-term patients. The most alarming of these symptoms was memory loss.

I laughed when I read of this in the *Financial Times*. For it was precisely the amnemonic or Lethean qualities of Halcion that endeared this fine product to me in the summer of 1983. I woke in delight, without thought of the night that had flowed through my bedroom. In the afternoon, I could remember nothing of the morning. Nightfall brought not dread but excitement that I soon might be swallowing one or two or three of the light blue, ovoid drugs. When mixed with brandy, they made for me a veil of sorrow and elation, which is the defining characteristic of that summer and permits me to date these next episodes to August and September, 1983.

Mornings dazzled me. Beyond Sir Julian's curly head, the Rhine glittered. Mrs Hamm-Breuer's coat and skirt seemed drenched with madder and indigo and other mild and brilliant antique dyes. When somebody moved to my left or right, my eyes sparked.

The room was full. It was one of those occasions on which I went over quite stale material for an expanded audience. Barchard, who seems to me in retrospect the archetypal high official of the last years of British power – imaginative, flexible, dishonourable, parsimonious – liked to wear things until they fell apart.

I recollect an Italian brigadier was there, and against the wall a young man, fidgeting in his handmade suit, who clearly did not understand a word, and was probably from Downing Street.

These meetings were bizarre. The excitement, the consciousness of selection and ceremony among the newcomers, could not disguise the distinct impatience of the regulars at Barchard's vanity and love of theatre. Pierre LaFrance, who I believe always thought I was lying, had a look of permanent Gallic amusement. Tully made fists of his hands. Von Arnim worked at his despatch case. Only Sir Julian, seated at his desk or with his jacket-draped chair standing proxy for him, kept his thoughts to himself.

At these larger meetings, it was agreed that I should not introduce new matter; also, though Barchard and the others never said as much, I need not keep strictly to my notion of the truth. This was obviously less than ideal, from Brian's point of view; if I might tell lies here, why not in the *kleiner Kreis*, or little circle, as the regular group was known. The other risk, of which he was less aware than I, was that I'd smash a table through the British Safety Standard glass and plunge to the esurient Rhine.

"Would you read the next paragraph, please?"

"From the *Times* or the *Post?*"

"From the *Times*, please."

"Of August 3?"

"Of August 3."

I read:

> "In a second series of meetings in Switzerland, Austria and West Germany, Ambassador Polk promoted the initiative to a key group of German politicians and opinion-formers. This series was known to US officials as the Fishing Party, because of the remote, rural locations selected for the meetings.

"Shall I go on?"

"Please."

> "'Jack has got it into his head that Russia is going to blow up
> if deployment goes ahead,' said a senior Administration official
> who spoke on condition that he not be identified. 'The man's an
> inveterate problem-solver,' he said."

"More?"

"That's enough, I think. Julian, you were asking?"

Sir Julian was smiling. He said: "Did you talk to the *New York
Times?*"

"Why should I?"

Between you and me, Julian: I did not speak to the *New York
Times* or the *Washington Post.* I leaked the Golden Plough to Jim
Dole of Radio Free Europe. When his report ran at nine p.m.,
Middle European Time, the evening before last, the US State
Department panicked and called in Karen Erlanger and Bernard
Stills for separate but substantially identical briefings. It being
afternoon in Washington, there was ample time for these experi-
enced diplomatic correspondents to ring round their sources for
confirmation.

I leaked the Plough, Julian, after prolonged if incoherent
thought, because its secrecy had ceased to be an asset and was
becoming a liability. There seemed to me a danger that either Jack
or Mr K. would be fired or, immeasurably more important, Polina
chucked in the slammer. I can't imagine US public opinion allowing
any of that now. Also, this crowd here couldn't keep a secret to
save their lives and the thing will be public in a fortnight anyway.

It also seemed to me a good way of prising that elderly thespian
who is President of the Great Republic, and the stunned and immo-
bile functionaries of the Kremlin, off diplomatic positions that are
patently doomed. This is a good example of how, in a blocked and
brittle situation such as we have now, a small action can blow the
game open and send the grandmasters gabbling to the elevators.

I wanted to stop all this before you get anywhere near Sebastian
and his daughter. Above all, I wanted to help Polina, which is by

some distance the chief interest in my life. Unfortunately, since I have not seen her for six weeks and she is apparently lecturing in Aspen, Colorado, I can do this only at long distance. I feel sure she would approve my action, though she might not express that approval.

I leaked it to Dole, Julian, because I promised it to him that afternoon in his office at the Tulpenfeld and I keep my promises. He grew up in a heroic era of American journalism and would let you slice his liver before he betrayed a confidential source. Which is why, though everybody in Washington knows she is the ultimate or teleological leaker, before they cart her off to Attica they'll consider: weird, that the story appears in Europe while the girl's in goddam Aspen. This is the virtue of an old-fashioned espionage technique called, I believe, the Cutout; which she used, for example, when she had me set up the Fishing Party for her. She's a model spy, you know: never does anything herself that someone else can do for her; and in delegating tasks, she is much aided by her interesting shape and winning personality. She's bright, that girl, Julian. And she doesn't quit. I'm not sure you've fully grasped that.

All this you know, so I won't say it out loud. I note that you've rumbled me, as you were bound to; and that I get just one warning. I believe it is now time to end this nonsense. I need to see my friend Sergei. Some people have got to work.

"May I make a personal declaration?"

"Must you?"

"Of course you may, Richard. You should have said."

I said: "I am grateful to the UK Foreign Office and to SIS for giving me a lift back from East Germany and saving certain time-consuming formalities."

There is a knowing titter. Even State Secretary Hamm-Breuer wears a temporary smile.

I said: "I believe I have now substantially extinguished this debt of gratitude. Without prompting or complaint, I have taken you deep into the draft treaty known as the Golden Plough. But for my intervention, you would have been helpless to prevent the

Americans bargaining away Britain's nuclear deterrent and the *force de frappe* for their own diplomatic advantage. I first revealed to you the existence of the Geneva back channel on July 8. On July 16, the Special Consultative Group, which comprises representatives of the UK, French and West German governments alongside the US Under-Secretaries of State and Defense, convened for the first time at Leeds Castle. I rather think this cosy little sewing circle is my creation."

"Get on with it."

"Patience, Brian! I've told you everything I know. I've given up so many mornings to these meetings I cannot count them. I can't work or reproduce myself. My phone has been tapped. I've been tailed in the street. I've been threatened with treason charges. I've been obliged to listen to Dr Tully make offensive remarks about a young woman he would not dare to confront in person. If you want me to go on fighting the Cold War for you, you will have to let me go. Or you can arrest and charge me. I am leaving now and I shall not be coming back. Thank you for your patience."

Sir Julian said: "Klaus?"

Von Arnim nodded from his papers.

"Pierre?"

LaFrance shrugged. Barchard looked dazed. Tully's eyes seemed to say: Can you run, boy? Can you hide?

"Thank you, Richard," Sir Julian said. "Thank you very much."

3

While to himself he seemed to be acting of his own
free will, he had never been more in the grip of those
inevitable laws which compelled him to perform for
the world – for history – what was destined to be
accomplished.

TOLSTOY

It had been my desire, ever since coming to Germany, to visit the
United States Air Force base at Mutlangen in Swabia, so I might
see where history is made. With my debriefing in Bonn ended, I
now had leisure for such a project; and planned a tour of southern
Germany to include the opera in Stuttgart, a certain volume of
Spätzle, the air base which was under blockade from the German
peace movement, and, if there should be time, a view of the Veit
Stoss crucifix in Nuremberg Cathedral.

"We worked for peace!" he said suddenly.

I didn't know if Sergei meant peace in the Soviet sense – that
is, security for the USSR and the rest of the world can go to hell
– or in the commoner sense of absence of war or in the sense of
some ravishing Lightnerian utopia. I never got the measure of
Sergei, either as the devious and paranoiac cynic of the Cold War
or the glowing Russian patriot of the 1990s.

Nor do I know why the KGB had so espoused the Golden Plough;
but that day at Mutlangen, I sensed behind Sergei the shadow of
a bureaucracy so vast and self-absorbed that it believed it could
make and unmake reality; and this process I needed to encourage.
When I showed Sergei what I had, his inattention hardened like

cooling wax; there was fear in there, real *bureaucratic* fear, and fear of death which I also wanted. He didn't know that I'd multiplied Polina's figures for Autumn Forge by a coefficient of one and three quarters (two in aircraft) and, in a sense, it wouldn't have mattered to him if he had known: all that mattered is that he could say that the material came, by the usual channels, from his best intelligence source. The policy had to be supported. Truth didn't come into it.

"I'm sure," I said.

Sergei looked at me under his eyelids. He said: "May I be of any service to you, Mr Fisher?" He seemed at once to regret the offer, which was presumably of protection not money, because he immediately laughed: "Not that we can do much for you."

I thought: Try not to kill me, if you can avoid it. "Thanks, old boy. You're a gentleman. Look after yourself."

He bristled at the suggestion he needed any looking after. The circle around Petra Kelly had opened a little. Sergei said: "*Schöne Mädel*" [Fair maid] and hurried off. I suppose he meant Polina, but he might just as likely have meant Mrs Kelly, who was doing TV interviews against the outer fence of the air force base. I haven't seen Sergei since, except on television, of course.

It was August 5.

The sun had burnt my neck and my shirt collar chafed it. I walked across the meadow, past the celebrity groups and the picnicking Christians, to the main gate where the blockade was already in place. Groups of young people were sitting or squatting in ranks thirty or forty deep, hugging their knees or singing; tense, expectant, self-righteous. I thought: How strange is the end of the Cold War! All these thousands of people, the smell of warm grass and cattle, the police in their stiff green uniforms, Sergei and his villains, the Americans imprisoned on their station, the writers and politicians, the fulminating Jesuits, my own overstimulated watchers and, ah!, I know that man, there, in the second row: cap, checked shirt, jeans and boots, eternally American and youthful, talking to an eager ring of listeners with their chins on their knees.

"Mr Cohen?"

"Barry," he said. Scores of eyes looked up at me.

"I'm Richard Fisher. I believe you knew my dad, Edmund Fisher."

"Sure did," he said. "And every word he said or wrote was wrong, including *and* and *the*. Hi! Are you blockading?"

"What about Her Majesty?"

There was merry laughter. Eyes sparkled at me. Cohen moved generously to make a space for me. "She won't mind," he said.

I sat down on the warm road. There was light applause. I thought: You can all hear this, if you care to and can understand English.

Cohen said: "Don't get me wrong. Ed was a gifted thinker. He was just always wrong."

Polina once told me that Cohen had been smashed by Vietnam. He'd been at the Saigon Embassy, running the US Information Agency, and had become a friend of the famous soldier John Vann. She said they used to ride reconnaissance missions in the Mekong Delta in an open jeep when nobody else dared stir, save in helicopters. I sensed that Cohen could sit here, blockading the chief overseas base of the Sixth Air Cavalry with their 108 Pershing missile-launchers, because he didn't doubt his own courage in war, and neither did other Americans; or he was still fighting the war, though the enemy was no longer the North Vietnamese Army but his own, the one that had sacrificed two countries and his friend; or maybe – one last time, and then I'll give up – he slept each night shaded by green leaves.

Look, he wasn't part of my tour.

When the SALT treaty he'd negotiated was rejected by the US Senate in 1979, he wrote an incendiary article in *Foreign Affairs*. He resigned before he was fired, by about an hour. I thought this fallen bureaucratic angel, this Lucifer in L. L. Bean, might, in his descent from the celestial heights of power, have brought with him not only his pride and anger – He would never go back! The Administration must come to him! – but also something valuable; that as he was ferried by night across the Stygian Beltway, he had something hidden that he could sell or spend.

127

I said: "Why did he reject it?" It was a start: flattering and unimportant. I imagine Lucifer made a poor living in Hell as a God-watcher.

"Good," he said. "I was just telling these folks about how Ambassador Polk got into the Plough and that kind of fits in nicely." There was a woman in green beside him, with a lilac scarf, who looked like a sixty-eighter. She seemed to own Cohen or thought she did: trouble. "Jack made a profound error if he thought he could end-run the Department of Defense – that's Dick Perle, basically – and go straight to the President. It's an egregiously high-risk strategy that can only succeed if, one, you have a simple, clear and plastic proposal that'll catch the President's imagination – really dramatize the issue for him – and, two, you simultaneously cover all the institutional bases in town: State, Defense, the NSC, Central Intelligence. If only Jack had come to me!" He looked round at his hearers.

"Can Polk survive?"

Cohen turned to me in surprise. "Oh sure. He won't work again, which'll hurt, but, hell! he's seventy-something. Look, he doesn't matter. Jack's a nice guy, but he's no rocket scientist." He tailed off. Quietly, he said: "She matters. Massively."

I've changed my mind, Mr Cohen. I don't want to hear this.

"Central Intelligence went right down the limb for a treaty. Far too far, in a Washington context. Say what you like about George Bush, when he was at Langley he really had a feel for government. That girl was just out of control."

"I don't believe I've met her."

A cock crowed from somewhere. Thrice.

"Married to that horse's ass Bill Spratling. Central Intelligence had been fantasizing about her since she was in eighth grade. Jack found her someplace on Wall Street, sent her down to me in Geneva. She was raw, sure, but smart: her work on CBMs* was just out of this world. And pretty! Holy smoke! Sure, I looked at her

* Confidence-Building Measures, a verification category in SALT

clearances. She was clean as new snow. They're just going to eat that girl up!" He giggled at the unintended impropriety.

"What makes you thinks she's bad? From all I hear, the KGB has no particular commitment to the Plough."

He looked at me sharply. "You tell them that at Langley, Virginia or at the White House! You tell that to Dick Perle! She had most of Washington running after her. Slept with half the NSC, including Jeane Kirkpatrick, I wouldn't doubt. Christ, she sat in with Jack at NSC meetings, six feet from the President! Man, we're not talking about Europe here. Nobody gives a damn that you guys have been an outstation of Moscow Directorate since 1935. Nobody cares about the West Germans. We've never had anything like this. They are going to crucify her!"

"Excuse me." The green woman leaned over Cohen, who pulled in his chest politely – evidently he didn't know he was private property. "We just heard the police are on their way. To clear the road to the base. I think you must go now." It's Thyra Pohl, isn't it? Still at it, are we, after fifteen years? (Though if she'd taken me up in Berlin in 1968, seventeen and never been kissed, I would have been her slave.)

"Come on, Thyra! Let him have his day in court!"

"Actually, I'd better be going. I really appreciate talking to you, Barry." Then in German: "Take it easy, friends." There were one or two jeers. Cohen seemed to wake from a dream.

As I threaded my way between the seated people and out of the blockade, I sensed him behind me, disentangling himself from Thyra, stumbling, apologizing. He caught me on the grass, out of breath.

"Look, Richard. This –" he waved at the base's ring fence, the advancing German police, the stone-faced American MPs – "this insanity must be fought both democratically *and* bureaucratically."

I see. You have fallen so low as to be scrambling for intelligence from infatuated British freelances. You, who survived the ambush at Ap Noi and dismantled the radar station at Kraznodvarsk! Let me look and see if I have anything for under a quid. Oh yes, this is nice. How about this?

"I can tell you who hired Klein to kill Lightner." I believe you know her.

"Don't even think of that stuff! You're out of your mind. They'll eat my balls and spit them out again. And you," he looked at me in blank astonishment, "you're a bright guy, keep out of that shit! It's real messy. Fucks your head."

I thought: I dug this trench, I poured this wine and honey, to repose your soul, Ulysses, not to torment it. In you, Mr Cohen, I see the second half of my life. We are like gymnasts, we spies. We age and grow heavy and timid. We live off charity.

"Barry, what I know is this. It's going to go to the wire. The KGB is very, very interested in the Plough. If Andropov dies – start again – *when* Andropov dies, the KGB can deliver a secretary-general who will sign a treaty on the basis of the Plough. The man's name is Gorbachev."

"Name and patronymic?"

"Mikhail Sergeyevich. Born 1931, Stavropol. Attended Stavropol Agricultural Institute, 1949. Bachelor's in law, Moscow State, 1951. Joined Party 1952. Married 1953 – Raisa Yvona Somebody. Stavropol Komsomol City Committee 1956. First Secretary City Committee 1966. Central Committee of CPSU 1971. Member Political Bureau 1980. He's travelling abroad, for the first time, to the Congress of the Portuguese party in early October, six weeks before the Bundestag votes on the Pershings. Also he has a birth-mark on his forehead."

"And Romanov?"

"The dinner service was Gardner. Francis Gardner: Irishman, set up a factory in Moscow for Catherine, 1743. Three hundred and eighty-nine pieces. The whole lot, every single damn piece. There're these jokes in Leningrad, This guy, he's . . ."

Barry Cohen was gone.

I got drunk in the restaurant car on the way back to Bonn and was overcharged by the waiter. The next day, I didn't leave the apartment, or the day after that. When Caroline Barchard called, to invite me to dinner, I said I was in bed.

She said: "I was so worried that you might not have enough to drink, poor fellow. How are you feeling, anyway?" She was carrying one bottle of brandy, two of German champagne and a gaudily decorated box of the Italian cake called *panettone*. "Don't worry," she said. "I won't stay."

I heard her washing up in the kitchen, opening the window. She came into the sitting room, carrying the brandy and two glasses. She had on a floral dress. The tall *Jugendstil* room suited her. I felt acutely the unmade bed at my back, my dressing gown and stubbled face. She fished into her leather handbag, I supposed for cigarettes, then lost her balance: her legs scissored, like a thoroughbred foal.

She had out a little leather notebook and a propelling pencil. She looked away and held it out to me. I'd never noticed her beautiful hands. On the block she'd written, in girlish handwriting:

MRS S. HAS BEEN ARRESTED

I said: "Help me, Caroline."

I want those three words back. Caroline shivered in her summer dress. I saw, in an insomniac flash, that she could not bear to write Polina's name; that it'd made her sick to read her husband's cables, and yet she'd done it; and I was overwhelmed by the sadness of things.

She looked at me in what must have been horror, shivered again, and took a step away: from me, from Brian, from the world and her children, from Kate at Jesus and Hugo at the *Economist* and the water-garden she made with her own hands at Highclere, her Lutyens house in Devon.

I said: "Thank you. For this. Thank you."

Her face blurred and then came into focus. I know that if I'd reached out and touched her, gently, in the way the dead on Attic grave monuments touch one another, she would have stepped towards me, dazzled with tears. It was as if the clouds had blown open to show a ridge, a tip of a mountain of affection, which I hadn't seen and now wouldn't see. Or as if Death had appeared from somewhere and was leaning against the bookcase with the *Aufbau* Marx and Engels, an hourglass resting on his bent hip, smiling, *farouche*, not unkind.

Caroline turned and walked into the kitchen. I heard her rinsing the brandy glasses. The window clunked.

I came out in my dressing gown and stood on the path to the gate. I felt that my experiment in German small-bourgeois living was now formally at an end; also that I was becoming crazier than I quite wanted to be. Caroline said quietly: "The plan is to interrogate you separately. The only thing I can think of is that you ask Pierre, who likes you and cares for me, but you must go now, this moment."

I waved my hand. I meant: Don't do it for me, Caroline. Don't do anything for me. She was looking at me, in her clever way, straight into my traitor heart. I took her hand and put it to my cheek, I suppose so that the world – or rather MI6–SIS and the *Bundesnachrichtendienst* – would know I had a kindness for her.

She turned and got into her car. I went back in, dressed, unwrapped the gun and walked out, leaving both doors open.

The railway to Cologne runs over farmland. There are small fields under beets or cabbages, with no fences between them, just a new crop or plough to mark where one field ends and another begins. On the horizon is an abandoned office block, the Wesseling gas-cracker, the towers of Cologne cathedral; as if, on this tedious plain, scale and history had disintegrated. Transmission lines lope out of sight. Somewhere, parallel to the tracks, is a slabby 1930s autobahn. Also the phlegmatic Rhine.

Halfway to Cologne, a line of trees swings in from a wood on the left, stops at the track, then reappears on the right side, running backwards towards another wood. If you turn on the moving train, you'll see between the trees a gravel path and, suddenly, an 18th-century house. That's on the left, going towards Cologne. On the right, the path races out of sight, but, that evening at least, something flashed back a crimson sun.

I went to Schloss Brühl on August 8, 1983, the day I last saw Caroline Barchard. In my dank, amnesic daze, in the thick summer fog, I felt as if I were dissolving.

In the carriage, a man dozed like an infant, reeking of brandy. He stirred. I heard him shift heavily, start up the carriage. I filled with panic, stood up, put my hand in my coat pocket on the rack and touched the cold metal of the gun. He passed by, muttering, as we moved into Brühl station. Nobody else got down, though I stood on the platform, listening, while the train pulled away, and then for some time after. Fog drenched me.

I could not see the house, only a sort of heaviness in the fog. Crossing wet grass, I found a giant gate, with the initials of the Prince-Elector and a mitre worked in gilded iron. I used the hinges as footholds to scramble on to a high wall. On the other side, I jumped into mist, shins a-tingle. I landed in a rose bush.

A gravel path led away at a diagonal. I crossed another, and then something colossal came up at me out of the fog: a tank that should have been a fountain, but was dry, with a stone merman or sea-god, his chest discoloured by centuries of falling water, and monsters and tritons blowing conches. I sat down on the stone edge and let Polina come into my thoughts. But vertigo swooped at me, and I pushed her away. I saw her, for an instant, shoulders dropped, at a boardroom table, while a question was repeated over and over and over again: in one picture, a female Captain was seated in a corner, in another she wasn't. A regret for the damaged rose gnawed at me.

I thought: I have come to this place, because it was the place of my happiness. I remember, particularly, on the day of the picnic, how the spray of the fountain blew in our faces; also how Polina, having followed Sebastian around rejecting picnic sites, looked up at the Elector's palace and said: "Or perhaps the view is somewhat too absolutist for Dr Ritter?" I remember Polina was plaiting the little girl's hair; and I realized that children are doors into the past as well as the future, for I saw Polina herself on a wooden stoop and her mother biting on a ribbon in her teeth.

I thought: A man needs a wife, a child, a friend. This is my share of bourgeois happiness. This is my family: a killer and adulteress, a resting whore, an innocent man imprisoned and corrupted and you, little Rosa Luxemburg,

> you, my darling,
> mutely elided
> by all the sweetest joys. Perhaps
> your frills are happy for you

and she jumped up, hair unbundling, Polina astonished, and said, You hold hands, the game . . . This little girl, this repository of risk and power, this infanta, this baby shrieking in the ghetto of Lodz:

> Minds of murderers
> are easy to fathom. But this: death,
> all of it!, before life's even started,
> to hold it so gently and without throwing a tantrum,
> is indescribable.

These bits of verse, Rilke's, swim in and out of me on surges of Halcion. I have come here for the fog and the *Sonntagsruhe* and the temporary security and the silence, to get going, out of the world.

You see, after lunch, Sebastian and I went for a walk. The sun off the gravel was blistering. From time to time, I looked back and saw the others — two women, a child, a picnic, a fountain, the bodyguards — diminishing in scale before the palace, as if I were composing a photograph.

Sebastian said: "This garden with these arrow-straight paths, topiary, imported statues and so on and so on, is all that remains of a German society that is hateful to me: autocratic, ignorant, violent, frivolous. And yet, this place appears to be beautiful. I think of it often, even in my constituency."

"Art is long, Sebastian."

He looked at me, a little uncertainly. "Correct! I mean, in the sense that I take you to intend, which is that art is not an inevitable production of an unjust society but appears, as it were, even in an unjust society, where certain conditions that I do not understand are fulfilled; and lives on long after that society has fallen prey to its social contradictions. What these conditions are . . ."

"Genius, for example . . ."

"No, no, because that replaces an abstruse term − art − by one even more so − genius. I don't understand. I don't understand."

"Why are you hiding Beate?"

He continued looking at the gravel, as if we were still talking aesthetics. He said: "That is a matter of which you know nothing. Don't touch, Richard. [*Lass die Finger davon!*] But, merely for your information, I am not concealing Miss Beck. I do not know where she is. If I did, I would seek to persuade her to return and stand trial."

Sebastian had turned round. Polina, at a great distance, was walking towards us down the path, holding Rosa's hand. Nida was smoking a cigarette by the fountain. The two agents were eating *Rippenspeeren* on the terrace. Couples and families crossed in front of them.

I said: "She's in the GDR."

I felt a movement in him: as if his abraded spirit had touched something and recoiled. He said: "How pleasant, for the German patriot," and here his voice became harsh, "that there is not one Germany to love, but two! Ah, Mrs Spratling!"

Polina stood, holding the little girl's hand. Her smile seemed to come, not out of her own happiness only, but up and through Rosa Luxemburg's arm. I, too, was baffled by happiness. Loving Polina, I couldn't conceive how Sebastian could hate her; or see, in this brilliant Holy Family, a malignant and corrupt maternity; or feel, in the touch of her hand round his daughter's, pain as if from a scald. Blinded by sunshine and geometry, I couldn't see that Sebastian was signalling, through veils of inhibition and panic, an agony beyond my ability to comprehend. He'd shown me his home and his daughter, the scar on his sternum and the wound in his heart, given me Lightner's papers, the photographs — all that, not for my help or love, but for my understanding: as if with Luther to say, Here I stand. I can do no other.

Back to today. I was walking. I came to a place where four paths converged. I took one of them. It passed over a bridge, where the water was black and greasy, and then into brightness. On each side were pleached lime trees, evenly spaced. Beyond them was a plough. I heard geese or swans overhead. The trees mesmerized me. I went through a tunnel under the railway lines, the walls crazy with neo-Nazi messages, *Pershings weg!*, and love stories, and on between the trees.

The summer house was octagonal. It was white and blue. French windows rose to the roof. I pushed at a pair, which opened enough for me to reach in and lift a catch of bent wire. It was so bright. Between each french window were mirrors, floor to ceiling, framed in silver. I touched silver quivers, muskets, hares and pheasants intertwined, women in hooped skirts playing blind-man's-buff, a stove tiled with baying dogs. There was a sofa, covered in rotted blue silk. I took out from my raincoat the handgun Polina had given me, checked the chambers as Manfred had shown me at the *Schützenverein*, and sat down.

I said, "I've come to this place, which I've never seen before, with the gun she gave me, to consider, as rationally as my regime of alcohol and sleeping pills will permit, certain courses of action, including suicide. I include suicide not because I'm going mad or out of self-pity or to please Polina, or because the possibility of happiness has been replaced by the certainty of unhappiness, but because they are going to dismantle me, memory by memory, when they find me. They will take even her name, and then expel me, like a time-served prisoner on a city pavement, wearing a too-large suit and carrying a paper parcel: shorn, washed, pale, hungry, terrified, ignorant, free.

"Second, my suicide has certain advantages for her (as she no doubt realized long ago, but then I'm always some way behind her: that, alas, is the story of our love affair). They'll think, of course, that I couldn't face the ordeal ahead of me, but deep down, there'll be a durable nugget of doubt. Polina has a talent for sowing uncertainty. Look at the way she handled the Lightner assassination!

"Third, all my running is vain, like Lee's generalship after Gettysburg. It cannot prevent defeat, merely delay it at an unspeakable cost in blood and misery. Fourth, I may not survive the interrogation. To satisfy themselves she isn't a Soviet agent, they'll need to take us to the absolute extremity, where precise judgment becomes near impossible: that is the perverse logic of torture. Unlike Polina, I, at least, thanks to Caroline, have the power to dispose of my own life."

I picked up the gun and put it in my mouth. I thought I'd cleaned it well at the club, but there was a taste of saltpetre under the oil I'd used. I rested it on my lap and said: "Set against such arguments, which have merit, are these. First and trivially, I don't want to mess up with blood and brains this irreplaceable room. Second, even after firing twenty-eight rounds at the gun club, I am inept with this weapon and may well only blow off my jaw. Third, although I always seem to be a couple of steps behind her, I'm a good deal closer than anyone else. Fourth, after they pick me up, I will have a unique ability to influence events: it is they, after all, who want to torture me, not I them. Fifth, though we will be interrogated apart, we will, in some submerged sense, be together: to leave Polina to endure this on her own would be taking contempt for the chivalrous ideals of the English high bourgeoisie too far. Sixth, the Berlin Wall, bless it, is still, as far as I know, standing. Seventh, and decisively, anything can happen. Do not underestimate the contingent in human affairs!"

I looked round me for adjudication. The gun in my mouth repeated itself in the mirrors, retreating down vistas of silver and illusionary space. I got up and opened the door. At full extent, I fired a round at the blurred bole of a lime. There was barely a crack

137

in the fog. I walked to the tree and found, high up, splinters of lead embedded in the bark over an area of a square foot. It would have done its business with my head. A sound made me jump. It was the whistle of a train, repeated over and over. I put the warm gun in my coat and ran down the avenue, sucking fog, so the Inter-City would pass over me and bring me luck.

At Cologne station, I bought two bottles of Asbach Uralt and some cigarettes. We drank the brandy by the Schnell-Imbiss snack bar till the police moved us on. Then we sat round a burning trash can on some sort of building site. I tried to get the skirt off a woman called Zara or Zarna, but I or she kept falling down. This may have been the night when two junkies were doing each other up in the toilet of the Bahnhofsmission, or when I woke to the Moroccan running through my pockets and I stuck the gun in his ear and he backed off, smiling sweetly. Night and day, as I lowered my bearded face on wool or polythene, I touched with my fingers the stone-cold pistol in my groin. Behind me, the bushes whipped back together. The grass stood up again. The waste engulfed me.

I caught up with Jack Polk at a pedestrian crossing on the Paradeplatz. Among the well-fed people – in Zürich, pedestrians are dressed as if for weddings – he didn't stand out. He didn't turn his head when I spoke.

"Are you armed, Richard?"

"Your colleagues will be intrigued by your banking arrangements." I spoke to the point between the shoulder blades where his tailor had eliminated even the suggestion of a ruck. "I also have a handgun."

The shoulders shrugged as the light changed and he strode over the tramlines into the heart of the square. He said: "You can't beat death or taxes, they say. Where are we going?"

"The Volkspark."

"Goddam, Richard!" He spun round and saw me. "Is that where you're living? With those . . ."

"Yes, sir."

"We'll go to Sprüngli, if you don't mind."

In the café, the smell of chocolate and scent made me swoon. The head waiter bustled up, unperturbed by my beard and lichened teeth: Swiss don't bother with the small things of life. The room fluttered, femalely, with Polk's celebrity.

"And perhaps the young man would like . . ."

"Have the *Torte*, for God's sake, Richard. It's world famous."

"Just coffee, please, *Ober*."

"I'm sorry about Geneva. In the circumstances . . ."

Yes, much better to set up a phoney rendezvous and try and get me killed.

"It's fine. I like junkies."

"You're on the wrong horse, boy. There's nothing in that bank account that would interest anybody, except the IRS."

"I didn't come to talk about your tax returns. I need you to go to the President."

He frowned. The word was, at best, inappropriate in this setting. His eyes went distant: Even diplomatists, he seemed to say, sometimes have real feelings. "We missed her father, you understand? It was my decision." He smiled like a wise old *roué*. "She was just too good to vet."

"He was a domestic servant, for pity's sake, . . ."

"We looked every place for him, even goddam Canada . . ."

". . . came out of Dachau in pieces . . ."

Polk stopped, as if to say: There's no margin in talking to people who won't listen.

I said: "You're going to see him alone and tell him the truth. He'll listen to you, because Kennedy did, in '62."

He said, more to himself than me: "The essence of diplomacy is control. She was just out of control." The repeated phrase chilled me: Who'd used it first and given it such currency that even Cohen had heard it? Polk? Perle? Casey? The President? Not the President. He said: "Richard, there are folks in Washington who want to win this damn war. Mr Perle's word, to be exactly precise, is 'prevail'. The Plough just won't lie down and die decently. So its author must be discredited. That's the silver bullet, the stake in the heart. You and I will not . . ."

"*Dürfen wir bezahlen* [The bill, please], *Herr Ober*."

As he pushed through the doors, he said over his shoulder: "You don't care about money, do you? Like your father!"

"No. Please walk on. I'll follow."

He tried again: "Margaret is coming to the Davos conference. I could . . ."

"Please do that."

He gave up. He was somebody, Jack Polk, I never said he wasn't. He could take his medicine, even at the Zürcher Volkspark.

He said: "May I ask how you knew?"

"Knew what?"

"About the account?"

"I didn't, sir. I needed a place you'd go without your detail. I couldn't think of anything else."

"I might have had a girlfriend!"

"That didn't occur to me."

That's a hard thing to say to a man at the end of his life, especially if it isn't true. Ahead of me, his shoulders quivered, then straightened. He strode on, two steps ahead of me, towards the rattling trams in the Paradeplatz, while I turned into the Bahnhofstrasse. Perhaps he thinks I'm still two steps behind him, but I can't do anything about that now.

Peter Klein had his back to me: cropped hair, T-shirt, Indian pyjama trousers, bare feet, a rectangular tattoo on the right ankle. He seemed to be holding something. The room was clean and neat: a thick grey carpet, a glass-topped table and department-store prints of autumn woods and sea birds.

He coughed bronchially. He said, still with his back to me: "How did you get here, Mr Fisher?"

"I don't know where here is."

His back was muscular under the red T-shirt. I thought: Stop trembling, you prick. It's the most dangerous moment in his life, too.

"How did you get here, Mr Fisher?" Frankfurt accent, incidentally.

Aim low, you poltroon, so you at least hit something. I said, so quietly it rattled in my throat: "Polina."

He turned and I saw he was holding a cigarette and plain book-matches. His eyes were clouded, perhaps with hangover. I couldn't look at his jaw. I thought: The court officer that Beate killed at Stammheim – what's his name? Kurras – really did get a shot off. This is very interesting, if I get out of here.

Klein said: "The gossip!"

I said: "I have a piece of information for you which I give freely. It will buy you a commuted sentence in the Federal Republic and a new identity in . . ."

Klein smiled with his floating jaw. He said, "I stand by my identity."

"In return, and since I heard you were a gentleman, I have two favours to ask."

"Only two?"

"First, you don't bloody shoot me. Or let any of those weekenders [*Wochenendterroristen*] outside do it."

"And second?"

"Jesus! I know you!"

"One does enjoy a certain notoriety."

"I mean, I know you. From Berlin. Cutting down the coat of arms."

He lit his cigarette. "An infantile folly," he said and then: "You are aware by now that for us Terror was not simply the famous Liberation of the Act from the Prison of Theory. It was also a Liberation from the interminable hectoring of Sebastian Ritter," and here his voice took on, with uncanny precision, Sebastian's pedantic rasp, "and the crazy, mystifying, insipid, illiterate and nauseating maunderings of Pastor Lightner. Ah, Mr Fisher, the fathomless boredom of legality! I used to read like an ox: two-thirds through *Phenomenology of Spirit*, did not understand one word, not even the definite article, so start again!" He shook his head urbanely. "Do you like morphine?"

"Yes, anything."

He extended the cigarette for me to take. I thought: It makes no difference whether I'm legless with morphine, I can't stop him killing me if he wants to; also the faith, assuming it ever existed in him, is gone. What sustains him, it seems, is dandyism.

He watched the cigarette through turbid eyes. He said: "And second?"

"I need you to spring her."

My chest filled with sweetness. As the drug scurried about me, into my heart and legs and groin, I saw, for an instant, the shape of his violent and romantic soul.

"I have no quarrel with your lady-friend, Mr Fisher. Rather the contrary, in fact. However, I don't do US mainland. No USA. No nuclear. No East. Otherwise," he said ruminatively, "one would always be travelling." He took the cigarette from my fingers.

"I'll help you."

"Thank you!" He shivered with impatience. "I'm afraid your friend must take her chance."

"And the little girl, too? Without Polina, she's history. You think the German police and a Filipino tart will protect her?"

For the first time, he looked at me. He said: "Objectively, of course, the child belongs to the anti-imperialist struggle. In practice, you should know that when the ideology dies, what remains is merely a way of doing things. The maternal instinct beats in Beate Beck's bosom. She does not, I believe, feel that the GDR will last for ever or indeed very long. She wishes to spend some time with her daughter. I'd keep out of her way, if I were you."

I said, "This has to stop somewhere: the German misery, passed like some hellish baton across each generation . . ." I stopped, embarrassed at the junkie emotion. Klein looked amused.

He coughed. "You should be aware, Mr Fisher, that I owe Miss Beck a debt of gratitude, in allowing me to exchange Stuttgart-Stammheim for this more sociable prison. Solitary confinement is wearing to the spirit."

"You paid it — with the Plittersdorfer Strasse!"

His eyes narrowed. "How admirably informed you are. I assume you also know Chatila Camp in Beirut?"

"Yes."

"Well, you no doubt will have visited a hospital there by the name of the Gaza Clinic which Beate selected, after some thought, for the delivery. (They also did the carpentry work with my face, made necessary not, in fact, by Warrant Officer Kurras's bullet itself, but by splinters of granite from the courtroom floor.) The child was delivered by a Palestinian doctor called Fatima Hallaj, who for some reason omitted to tell us that she had trained at the Karl Marx UniKlinik in Dresden; or that she was in regular and affectionate correspondence with the Dean of Medicine there, a certain Dr Tertsch. Evidently, this young woman wanted to broaden her experience beyond the occasional treatment of German terrorists and cluster-mine paediatrics . . . Please say if I'm boring you."

"I came a long way to learn this."

"One hears! Your progress through the undergrounds of Hamburg and Berlin was, forgive me saying so, elephant-loud! This Dr Tertsch, rather than immediately inform the State Security like a good citizen of the GDR, chose instead to tell old Lightner for whom he harboured an irrational admiration and felt might be interested in his god- and doctor-daughter's whereabouts. Frank told Sebastian. Now I owe a debt to Beate, but I have a fondness for Sebastian. I couldn't have him wandering about South Beirut, lugging his briefcase, demented with fatherly anxiety, could I? Anyway, I believed it was theoretically desirable and practically possible to pursue the armed struggle in the metropolises of late capitalism, or rather I was utterly arsed off with camelburgers,

143

Palestine-good-very-good and the gallant Israeli Air Force. Being from the working class, Mr Fisher, I never shared Beate's cosmopolitan interests. I know nothing of athletics, but I felt, on balance, that the child had a more solid future with her father, even in the historical area of capitalist accumulation. I delivered little Rosa, if I recollect, to Basel."

"Jesus! But Beate, how did . . ."

"She was a little sour at first, but was eventually reconciled. And Frank, too, after I'd patiently explained the situation. The difficulty with Sebastian is that he is a German patriot of prehistoric character, and is blind to the achievements of Existing Socialism. As a Stasi operative, he lacks both vigour and imagination. He must be persuaded by means other than historical materialist analysis. Little Rosa's value as a hostage could not but increase in proportion to her proximity to her father and his accumulating love and distress. And, though I didn't labour this point to my friends, or indeed mention it at all, one had earned the undying gratitude of the next Federal Chancellor but two, just in case one opted for early retirement."

I said, in genuine curiosity and utter impotence: "You'll work for anybody!"

He smiled his ruined smile. "One must live, Marx says, to be able to enter history. Also, being outside the social net, one needs health insurance from as many providers as possible. Now, if you'll excuse me, I have visitors." I noticed he had a Blancpain wristwatch.

"You have nothing to gain from killing me."

"Are you sure? For a young man, you are quite unpopular." He smiled sympathetically.

"Who'll protect the child, if you kill me?"

Klein coughed. He said: "We were rather intrigued by your weapon. I assume your girlfriend gave it to you. From Langley, no? I could find a use for it."

"It's yours. But I need something as good, and also clean. I mean . . ."

"No gun is clean, old chap," he said in English. "You'll catch on fairly quickly. The weekenders will sort it out. Oh, and a piece of advice, if you need it: History is made not in individual heroics, or refined diplomacy, but by exasperated people acting in mass. The war will only end when there is insurrection, on the streets of Leipzig and Warsaw and Bucharest and Königsberg. You'll see that, too, in due course."

Courteously, he walked me to the door.

They pushed me out at a place called Lindau on Lake Constance. It was September 25. I knew I should return to Bonn: I'd done as much as I could on the outside, and I wanted my arrest to happen on ground of my choosing, to prevent a cockup. I knew Bonn and its people. If Tully or the Americans turned out a whole crowd to get me, I'd sense it, I was sure. I knew nothing of this pretty lakeside town. I couldn't see what didn't fit.

Also I was running out of money, having thought it wise to distribute tips among the weekenders. Polina would simply have robbed a Mühlenseipen – "I had to go to the liquor store" – but that was not my style.

Even so, I thought I'd stay a couple of days in Lindau. Wash and brush up. Get clean. I liked the way the lake glittered in the sunshine, and the gleam of the baroque church domes. Pieces of sky had embedded themselves in my heart. Walking along the esplanade, or drawing down my small change for coffee and Kirsch, I felt light as air. I thought: How strange to be thirty-two and to have no money, property or securities, no wife or child, just a handgun of Bulgarian manufacture and, I imagine, 19th-century technology.

I had overestimated their caution. Walking through the town centre – pedestrians only – I saw a boy of about sixteen or seventeen, in a green jumper and black jeans, but no shirt or socks, and with lank, dirty hair. He looked injured and interesting, like a runaway or prostitute. I was thinking: Funny, these German small towns, when I woke from my dream of sunshine. Superimposed on this shopping morning, on the lines of women queuing up at the *Metzgerei*, the smell of coffee, the striking of eleven, is a faint and shifting pattern of activity. The green-jumper boy. A man in his twenties sitting on a sheet of cardboard, a black mongrel beside him, and a sign saying MY DOG AND I ARE HUNGRY! propped against its chest. A fashion shoot of a girl in a fur coat, tossing up her hair over and over again in and out of a shop doorway, while technicians lounge or chatter into portable telephones. And, decisively, because this is the third time, a man with a short leather jacket, white trousers that showed his big bottom, a bald head and a single steel earring.

I plunged into Kaufhof and up the escalator. I think I wanted to be where people were, where they'd need to keep calm and act with circumspection; but I saw, in a foam of horror, that I'd run into a crowd of women, in separates and suits – God damn you for eternity, Peter Klein! – and in the flurry of arms and shoulders and hangers and new cloth, between the racks and signboards decorated with brown leaves and the legend GERMANY IN AUTUMN! AMAZING REDUCTIONS!, coming towards me with his hand in the flap of his leather jacket, was the bald young man with the earring. There was no recognition. It was as if he would just walk past me, heading for menswear.

He drew his arm out and I fired through my coat. I thought I'd missed him, because there was no mark on his black chest and his gun continued to rise; but there was blood on the racks and the ceiling and on a shrieking woman's face and I saw, as he fell backwards, a gusher of blood from his right eye. I felt a curious, warm pain in my neck and saw, in the mirrored column holding up the ceiling, that my hair and collar on the left side were on fire, though I'd never heard his shot. I screamed and put my hand to my neck and burned that as well.

In front of me, the women were quite still, one poised to replace a blouse on a rack. I said, "Who's the buyer on this floor?"

A young woman in blue uniform, her black hair streaked prematurely with grey, stepped forward courageously. "Breuer," she said. She was in control of herself.

"Mrs Breuer, please would you kindly get me ten thousand marks from the tills. The uniformed officers will give you a receipt. Also I want to ensure that nobody touches this man, who is quite dead, or his weapon until the uniformed police arrive."

She spun on her heel. I thought: So I'm the law round here, is that it? I have gathered to my person all the impulses of respect and subordination in German small-town society! And all because of this Bulgarian musket in my coat pocket!

Mrs Breuer placed the money, still in its bank wrappers, on the till. I could see that she was anxious that I should now leave, if that were convenient for me. I turned my back and walked towards an open lift. I didn't think it likely that anybody would take a shot at me or, indeed, do anything to restrain me at under brigade strength. I said to myself, I'm on my way now. I'm coming to do the hostile. I do it of my own free will and on my own time.

I was weeping, though not out of Oedipal panic or for the man I'd killed, about whom I didn't care a toss, though I'm sure somebody somewhere would mourn him. (It turned out he was a Croat called Milli Cetin, who did intimidation work for the Austrians and had been dug up off the bottom of the barrel when Central Intelligence started to panic about not finding me. He also did work for Sergei when he could get it and, presumably, Peter. Peter insists that he was not interested in the instruction and says, on the contrary, he saved my life at least once, back in April 1983, when he overruled Beate about hitting the Fishing Party. He also says that he passed Polina a warning, through me, of the Plittersdorfer Strasse attack and if I was too idle to act on it, that was not his fault. Maybe a department in Moscow changed its mind about the Plough. I have been meaning to write to Sergei, but I haven't got round to it. Hell, it may even have been Polina. Who cares?)

I was weeping because I'd passed out of the world I'd been born into, and lived in more or less at peace, and into outlawry, a windy and depopulated region where I'd scrape a hard living for the rest of an abbreviated life. I'd hoped to capture Polina for my world, or at least what remained of it; instead, she'd captured me for hers. In time, I thought, I'll be adequate with this machine in my pocket. I'll learn how to use people and how far. Railway stations, airports and street intersections will be my glamour and peril. I'll be crazy, like Polina.

4

A fundamental prerequisite is the shortening of the
labour day.

MARX

After the whole business with the Golden Plough, Polina was pen-
sioned off and her distinguished service medal returned to her.
Lazard in New York took her back to head a new department of
mergers and acquisitions. My book on the RAF had done reasonably,
and I'd started on a history of the 1983 events for a decent advance,
though this was depleting rapidly in a suit to extract from the CIA,
under the freedom of information legislation, transcripts of our
interrogation sessions.

We had a gruesome apartment in a new block in the East 80s
and also rented a place at Woodstock, New York, to go to at
weekends. I generally went upstate on Friday morning and then
picked her up, in the late afternoon, at Rhinecliff station. From
the footbridge, I'd see her drag her briefcase from the rack, scratchy
with heat and exhaustion, then step up the platform while the
commuters scattered like mercury. She'd sit, slumped into torn
upholstery. As I tugged and pulled the Impala up on to the Hudson
bridge, I sensed her wake to the billion-acre sky and the oceanic
river flowing beneath us, and New York City begin to fall off her.
She'd say something like: "I hate that fucking Milken guy."

The place was a decrepit 18th-century farmhouse, with the ceiling
fallen in in the living room, a yard overrun by strippy sugar maples,
and an owner called Jake who always seemed to be doing things in

149

the barns. Fifteen yards away on the highway, Dylan ("Who?" said Polina) had famously crashed his motorbike. Polina slept much of the weekend on an orange sofa which must have come from the Montgomery Ward catalogue *c*.1904, ate cold cereal, drank Coke. I used to fish if there was any water in the Sawkill, or climbed up a hill behind the house called Overlook Mountain, up wood roads past fire towers and the concrete ruins of a burned Depression-era hotel, and a dusty lake now turning to swamp where wild Indians had camped before vanishing westwards. From the high, cool top, I could see for miles and miles: to the east, past broken farms and failed subdivisions, the beautiful river funnelling hot air to Canada, the cities of New England and, way out there in the hot purple morning, the tumbling Atlantic and our European history. To the west, wooded hills rose and fell and rose and fell all the way to Pennsylvania. Below me, in the thick shade of second-growth sugar maples, beside a ruined tennis court, I could see Polina lying on a flaking swing-seat, asleep in drifts of partially corrected tender offer documents.

Last year, which was 1986, Polina was one of three managing directors at Lazard who received bonuses of a million dollars. (The story, which was repeated in the *Institutional Investor* profile of her, that she told David-Weill, the Lazard chairman: "That, Michel, is a fucking insult," and strode out of his office, is neither true nor particularly discouraged.) In truth, Polina's money bores me, and not just because she is so reluctant to spend it. What I want her to do is buy the Platte Kill Farm, which is also what Jake wants and why he's always hanging round the barns pretending to fix his truck. He's mentioned a million. He's also mentioned $750,000. I know he'd take a third of that in cash. He's being crucified by interest payments and real-estate taxes.

When I said to her, "Look, we can keep 150 acres and subdivide the rest, it's self-financing, can't you see?", she looked at me sharply, suspiciously. I suppose I've become sly in my love. I also think there's something freakish about the money she's getting on Wall Street: it'll all go to hell and we might as well have something of substance – a beautiful house in a beautiful town – to show for it. Sometimes, when she's talking about her job and she sees I'm not listening and her lip hardens, I say: "But what if the Delaware Chancery Court *does* throw out the General Brands poison pill?" And she says: "OK, first, that'll trigger the flip-in provisions of the tender offer and, second, it will so incense the arbitrage community that . . ." I've grown clever. After toil, rest.

And in the hot afternoon, when she's calmed down enough from the city, I shoo her up the creaking stairs and into a bedroom with red wallpaper invaded by green trees: to slip and slither on her stomach or catch at her laughing mouth, her humid hair, old sheets that are tangled at her neck and smell of damp laundry; or to watch her rise in the abandoned light, bend, scoop up her clothes and underwear and run, bent double, for the stentorian bathroom. I think that the worst is over, and that, even though Bill is being a real pain, we're going to be all right. History has stopped and she's sat down in my lap.

I also know that she had the test on Friday, because Connie Brucker, her secretary at Irving Street, called me at the farm to say that Doctor Steen was fine with five o'clock. As she comes back to the bed, through the light that is losing its greenness and starting to teem with real darkness, a white towel knotted at the bust, my heart trembles with a premonition of winter: me splitting cordwood in a workshirt in the snow, she through the fogged-up kitchen window, nursing, out of the world.

"Are you ready, boy?"

"No! I don't want to hear anything!"

"She said it's already eight weeks."

"I don't believe it!"

"Why not? You're controlling this thing, Richard. You could give me triplets. It's a dream, for Pete's sake!"

"Oh Polina, I don't want to wake up. I don't want to go back in there. I'm so scared."

"I know, baby. Nobody does. I don't."

*   *   *

151

"Can we do Leipzig again?"

Leipzig again.

"Richard? Leipzig, mate! We're doing Leipzig."

Doing Leipzig.

Leipzig.

"I went to the Fair."

It was just Tully. He said: "Did you write this?"

He pushed a newspaper cutting to me. The table was of scuffed formica, which means we were probably in the place I think of as the cafeteria. There was a counter, upturned to reveal shelves, and, beside it, on the floor, a perspex cabinet that might once, hours or years ago, have held sandwiches. He said: "It says: 'By Richard Fisher in Leipzig, East Germany', doesn't it?"

"Would you like me to read it?"

"Yes, please."

"*US Journal of Commerce*, May 4, 1983. The headline is: Missile Furor Set Not to Impede E–W Trade. Shall I read the text?"

"Do."

"Leipzig, East Germany, May 2. Tensions between the United States and the Soviet Union over nuclear forces in Europe should not be allowed to hinder trade across the Iron Curtain, say leading exhibitors at the XXIst Leipzig Fair, the annual showcase of . . ."

"Go on, please."

"Nik, I went over in 1982 and also in 1981. It's an OK story, just about. More to the point, it's the easiest way for a western writer to get a visa for the GDR. You turn up, move about, peer at some antediluvian machine tools, file lengthily at the telex office at the Fairgrounds and then vanish. Everybody does it. The Stasi know all about it. They tolerate it. Otherwise nobody would cover the Fair."

"Have I understood you right? You had another purpose in going to Leipzig than covering the Leipzig Fair for the *US Journal of Commerce?*"

"Yes, Nik. I'm writing a book on the Red Army Faction."

"You didn't mention it."

"Didn't I? Are you sure?"

Such exchanges had become ritual, highly abbreviated, schematic. Tully made to reach, with infinite patience and good humour, for the stenographic reports of the interrogation while I lifted my hand as if to slap my head in amazement. We could, of course, have gone through our last discussion of Leipzig, but it scarcely seemed worth it. We were in for a long haul. Letting this bit go would not, I believed, cause my entire position to collapse: that is, provided I'd done my preparation. (At this early stage, I thought of the interrogation in the metaphorical language of chess.)

I said, "Can we take a break?"

"If you don't mind, let's get on."

"The other correspondents were all looking for dissidents: specifically, some kind of East German peace movement independent of the SED and Moscow. They had this idea that a new German nationalism was coming to birth, in which Germans would be united across their fence in a common disgust at the war-mongering of both big powers. There was the group in Berlin round Bärbel Böhley, which was pretty much done, and also something going on in the youth wing of the East German Evangelical Church. There was a pastor in Leipzig that everybody had got plugged into through the West German Bishops' Conference."

"Name?"

"Udo Paschke."

"Actually, it's Paske."

"So don't ask, if you know."

"Did you see Pastor Paske?"

"I did not."

Tully showed no irritation, not a flicker. I assume that these sessions, between just him and me, were largely maintenance and recreation, like cutting the grass at the weekend. Everything he did and said was designed to show me he had lots of time; and that, in the end, I'd be better off telling him rather than anybody else.

"Can I have a glass of water?"

"Certainly. Can we just get this out of the way?"

"I have a $50,000 advance to earn out. I went to see a defector for my book. Do you know who I mean by Gretchen Piotrowska?"

Tully thought this beneath his notice.

"Stasi agent from way back when?"

Tully said nothing.

"Do you?"

"I do, Richard."

"Good. So that's what I did. I guessed she might be at her brother's apartment in one of those Potemkin blocks on the Lenin-strasse. I made a mistake."

"A mistake?"

"The place was crawling with coppers. I had trouble."

Tully reached over for the stenographic reports.

Gretchen Lightner put down the photograph of Sebastian Ritter and his daughter skating. Manfred Piotrowsky got up slowly and went into another room.

She was smiling.

"What's so bloody funny?"

Gretchen Lightner sighed. "You want to know why we left her over there, so far from her mother's love?" She lifted her chin, abruptly, to indicate West Germany: *drüben*. She said: "How else would we control him?"

"Mrs Lightner, I do not have much time. More to the point, neither do you."

She looked up at me. "Has it never occurred to you, young man, why Sebastian Ritter is so hostile to the noble ideal of German unification? Your girlfriend is much cleverer than you: she under-stands why."

"You're a liar, Mrs Lightner."

"Why should I lie, Mr Fisher? Listen. I've come here to die, in the city where I was born, with my only surviving relation, and

I'll die soon; and you'll die not long after; and that woman will choke on my husband's blood . . ."

"Shut up, or I really might kill you."

"He doesn't believe me! The brave British gentleman! The fine British gentleman! What do I care if you kill me? It's all coming to an end. It is the force of history: neither you nor Sebastian nor Makhaev nor that whore can arrest it. The evil that you thought to wall up in this little prison-state is already swimming the Elbe. At the very moment of your triumph, we will consume your prosperity and rob you of your peace of mind. At the moment you are declaring history has ended in your favour, a new chapter is being written. Your cities will be bomb sites, your castles orphanages, your seaside hotels stinking refugee hostels, your factories and offices empty ruins. Everything you have will be taken from you and spoiled and squandered. We shall bury you."

I saw that my arm was raised to strike her.

Somebody, not Manfred Piotrowsky, was standing in the door to the next room. I thought: Of course, silly me, what a pity. I don't know if I looked at the person in the door or just constructed her, with complete fidelity, in my imagination: a woman, very thin, in old blue jeans, hair cropped and brown with grey streaks, not hennaed – definitely, not hennaed. A malicious picture from my Berlin daydreams – a girl soft as swans' feathers – appeared and vanished. I saw her in her barrister's cap and gown, a pistol in her sleeve and morning sickness in her belly. I saw the misery of German females, Rosa Luxemburg and Ulrike Meinhof and Petra Karin Kelly. I felt crushed by the accumulation of years and the fatality of things.

The woman had a handgun raised to my head, which she was about to fire. I thought: She's all right, old Gretchen, she tried to save my life, though it was nothing to her. What a damn pity!

With difficulty, I opened my hands to show I had no weapon. I opened my mouth to speak, but I couldn't make words, and certainly not, Why are you afraid, girl? I knew that if I spoke, she'd shoot me in the face. I saw that every part of her body was concentrated on saving her life; or rather that part of her life which was not messed up for all time and which was, perversely, embodied for her in a little girl three hundred miles away. The gun she was about to fire was aimed at my mouth and said this: Go tell that woman what you've seen here, messenger boy.

I turned my back on Gretchen Lightner and walked – all right, strode – to the apartment door.

"I said: I need counsel."

"I heard you, pal."

Across the table, Spratling was wearing a green-and-white striped polo shirt which showed the breadth of his chest.

"I have a right to call Ritter."

"I think you and I should get some ground rules straight. You're not a United States citizen, and we ain't bothered by what bothers Sir Julian. I don't greatly care to use severe procedures with you, but I have the authority to do so. You should understand that. I'm a good Foreign Service officer, a damn good one, and you have compromised my career and abused my home; but I'm going to take that as read. What concerns me is what that deceiving bitch, in the intervals between . . ."

I had my feet resting on the stretcher of my chair, which gave me excellent spring. I felt, in the moment of crossing the table with my hands outstretched, widening circles of regret and happiness, as if a stone had been thrown into a pool. My head and belly erupted with anticipated pain; but, in the functioning circuits of my intelligence, I knew it was good the violence was now in the open and I'd started it; and, in gusts of aerial pleasure, I was glad at this conjunction with Polina (though not in the vulgar sense of leaping to the defence of her good name like some clapped-out English gent, but rather as if I'd smashed through a door into where, through a fence of men in shirtsleeves and uniforms, she's saying something she's obviously said before and turns at the noise and, for a moment, our eyes meet).

Once, as a child in Portobello, a seaside town near Edinburgh, I ran into the lintel of a coalshed. The bricks were rotten with damp. I remember, in the midst of the pain in my forehead, the feel of crumbling brick. I felt this now, in the same part of my forehead and temple, but the crumbling must have been bone. The shock was indescribable. It meant: These nerds are going to kill you, boy! And: What's eating them? Then I fell asleep.

It gets harder. I cannot use words descriptive of time, because I didn't know night from day or Monday from Thursday or October from September. I cannot use words of place. I remember some red plastic chairs from somewhere, because they reminded me of Weingut Zons; also a room which had billowing net blast curtains of the kind used in official buildings in London to catch flying glass; a bed that smelled tormentingly of scent; a sudden view of mountains. I remember the words "mud pie", which I tentatively attribute to Brian: perhaps, "I'll leave you to your mud pie". Also the French word *"illustre"* which caused me an inexplicable pleasure and was probably Pierre formally distancing himself from the procedure: "Ça ne nous illustre."* Even with Tully and Spratling, I remember less of what they said or did than the longing, when I was with one, to be with the other. Presumably they divided the work unequally between them. I imagine I had been stolen by the Americans but that Tully had been permitted to hang on – the Special Relationship! A Place at Table! – like some dim and scrupulous family shareholder on a reconstituted, growth-oriented board of directors.

I thought I had an advantage over my interrogators: I knew more. It was also clear to me that I should try, provided I could keep control, to withhold my meetings with Sergei, Lightner's murder, the tussle over Rosa, etc., as long as I could; not that these things

* This does not exactly give us lustre.

mattered in themselves, but so that my questioners felt, when they at last prised them out of me, that they were getting value. As I've said, torture is worse than useless as a method of inquiry because, in destroying the will of the prisoner, it tells you only what he thinks you want to know: in this case, that Polina was an agent of the KGB. In antiquity, I believe, the evidence of slaves was admissible only under torture, which scarcely recommends the system of criminal justice we experience in Cicero's forensic speeches.

I saw my role as a control for Polina's testimony, a confirmation of her value and veracity. I thought I would have problems with fear of violence; then with Bill, that uneasy complex of pity, guilt and contempt one feels towards a man one has cuckolded; and with Nik, a sort of British solidarity and subordination. I also felt oppressed by their masculinity: I'd never been much around men. As weapons, I had my arrogance and a sense of heroic community with Polina. Which didn't amount to much. I would have preferred my Bulgarian howitzer. But sometimes one must make do.

I thought there were limits: that the Americans had no particular interest in really messing me up; and that my survival as Richard Fisher, two eyes, two rows of teeth, two testicles, a double-lobed brain, etc., was not in question. It was only in the course of the hostile interrogation – time, place, personnel, God knows! – that I realized even Nik didn't mind killing me. Which meant he was more frightened than I'd thought.

It was not the agony, or not only. It was the efficiency, the soft commands and feeble jokes as my arm was swabbed and the IV went in, or my knees were tapped for reflex: the cleanliness and quiet despatch of it all as if this shock, this insult to my body, the invasion of all that I had thought was mine, was somehow benign and conscientious and ill-remunerated, as at the casualty department of Edinburgh University Hospital, and I should really just lie back and rest and let them get on with their work. The drugs they gave me, while they peeled away the laminations of memory, replaced them with images of the future of a breathtaking precision, that left in the mind the sense only of an unbearable relief, as if I'd got up on a hot night and plunged my arms in water to the elbow.

I therefore decided that I needed to come out of my defensive posture; to sit up, and try, curious as this sounds, to turn the interrogation on my questioners and find out something for myself. Something that would save my precious life. But if that was not on, something that would help Polina save hers. And, if that too was out of the question, something that could injure these men and England and the United States in general.

I said: "Nik, you've got to stop that bloke hitting me. I'll just tell him lies. I'm not good at being hit."

"We noticed. You will tell lies for a bit. Then you'll stop. It's not an issue."

For some time, we talked of Patty Livingston.

Tully had grasped that both Polina and I had American step-parents. He looked both shy and eager, like a TV game-show contestant on a roll. I said that it wasn't similarities that drew me to Polina Mertz but differences: in gender, of course, but also in nationality, education, habits, language, political allegiances. These polarities were magnetic to me. Tully appeared to have understood.

Yet he was on to something. There isn't, as far as I know, any historical affinity between Anglo-Scottish strivers and the Polish servant class. I imagine if, say, in Warsaw in late 1981 when Jaruzelski declared martial law, I'd come out of my room at the Gdynia and seen, at the end of the dim corridor, her brown overalls and dingy hair under a scarf, the bags under her eyes and the Marlboros on her desk, I'd have passed on to the elevator, thinking of food and drink, though she calls in good English to my back, "Your key!" America gave Polina her health, her perfect teeth, her freight of degrees, her elegance, her mobility. God bless America!

America gave me Patty Livingston: a lady on a house-porch, in pink shorts and a checked shirt tied at the waist, smoking a mentholated cigarette. She said, Just call me Patty, dear, you'll need a beer after all that, it's in the ice-box, he's old enough, Ed, hell, what am I going to give him, sarsaparilla? That last word, and particularly the double l at the end, and the way her voice fell rather than rose with the question, also this nickname for my father, transfixed me; or rather, if my sense of myself was raw, they were like salt and lemon.

The house was on Deer Isle, Maine, near the town of Castine, but I would have to go back to situate it exactly. It was just one-storey high, with grey wooden siding and a spiky lawn that ran down to the granite shore. All around were spruce woods and Patty's relations: Livingstons, Chaunceys, Stillmans. Patty said to me one morning, You don't have to go to the cookout, sweetie, if you don't want, I'm taking the truck for crab, let's see you drive on the right side of the road, God's side, there ain't been a trooper here since 1941.

I was fourteen. My world had fallen in. If I leaned against its walls, I thought I'd plummet into emptiness, which was a piece of wet churchyard, a rectangle, dirt on fake grass matting, the sound of a bouquet of flowers dropping on wood. Somewhere nearby was my father, who'd left my Ma in 1960 or earlier. He was sitting in the sunshine – which, in my memory, is hard and crystalline – with a yellow legal pad on his knees (presumably, a draft of *The Balance of Terror in Europe*) and saying: "I think it would be a mistake if you left school," and Patty shouting from the kitchen – I see her stooped, her right leg back, maybe taking something from a low oven – "Ed, give the guy a break, he can go to Cornell like everybody else, amortize those damn books nobody reads."

I felt I would go mad. The world tasted and smelled of Patty Livingston: the hot spruces, the kraftpaper in the supermarket, the bloom on blueberries, the clamshell under the rake, the nylon of her white bathing dress drying on the deck, the flake of paint and creosote, the cool air on my legs as I jumped up in my shorts in the morning, the hot granite rip-rap and the icy sea, the yellow warblers flickering through the woods; tobacco, menthol, cornbread, Budweiser, lobster claws, hot dogs, kerosene and, Hey, guys make great cooks, don't you believe that crap! – and you can get your bad stepmother a drink, bourbon and branch, just like my mammy used to drink; or rather, I was in some sensorial chaos in which I couldn't distinguish my bounding appetites.

What did she make of this gaping British teenager? What did my father? At one point, I think at table, he lost his temper. He said: "For the last time, Patricia, he is not going to New Mexico (Alaska, Oregon). Ranching (roustabouting, harvesting cherries) is no education for him. He has no money and can expect none. He is going to read history and a hard European language and engage, and I mean engage, with his times. There is also, if he stays in the United States, a not insignificant possibility of his being drafted, which can hardly be your intention for him." Patty said "Phooey", which she often did, but looked at him as if to say: Don't push your luck, Ed Fisher.

She took me to Bangor airport in the truck. As she kissed me, she said, "You'll do those damn A-things for your daddy, won't you?" Then she waved and drove off. She may have known, as I didn't, that we wouldn't meet again.

Patty Livingston fascinated Tully. What he wanted to know – and I suppose it was worth knowing – was where my main loyalty lay: with the United States or Britain. Unfortunately, I could not satisfy him. I could never do what my father did and select between Patty and my mother; or rather I felt at fourteen that if I tried it would blow me apart.

Once, on Deer Isle, Patty said: "I'm so sorry about your ma, sweetie. She was a nice lady, everybody said. Oh blow, I wish I hadn't got into this."

I was educated at British boarding schools and barely remember my mother. I have a picture of us walking together in autumn beech woods. I remember the lope of the dog ahead of me, the chink of his name disc on his collar, but not the tall woman beside me. Trivially, I can say my mother loved places unchanged from her girlhood, which more or less confined her to Scotland; she sought authority in the past, the nobility and the throne, in her great-uncle the general and his great-grandfather who, as a child held up to a casement window, had seen the Highlanders stream in terror into Inverness; she thought my holding a knife in a particular way would help me in life; who didn't know or didn't want to know that the society she admired was history. I think it was hard for her not to have a man: at airports, she affected an excruciating helplessness. I thought I could be her man, but throat cancer beat me to it.

At the picnic with Polina and Sebastian at Brühl, when we were talking about political influences, I said I stood in the tradition of the homosexual English traitors of the 1930s, combining a hatred of my country with a passionate love for some of its old amenities: in my case, small racecourses, the looks and conversation of aristocratic Englishwomen, churches standing in fields, and so on. Sebastian looked at me in horror. It was not just incomprehensible to him that anybody could hold so irresponsible a position, but he also looked anxious: as if he'd been mistaken in me, I was a chatterer, unserious. Polina leaned over and said: "I believe he's teasing you, Dr Ritter," at which he noticeably lightened.

In contrast to my mother, Patty Livingston had an ironical view of the past. It was a source of bad habits (on her mother's side, drink; on her father's, extravagance) and large amounts of money. She liked men but didn't need them. There was nothing Patty didn't think she could do: go to China, eat alone at Lutece in New York, short the stock market. She'd drive the truck right to the end of the dock and swing down in her shorts and sneakers, door open, engine idling, and plunge her hands into the twitching snow-crab. The fishermen looked away or dickered with the boat, as if they wanted a picture of her, not now but to take away and examine at home.

Once that summer, when we'd gone up for land-locked salmon in the Restigouche, I stopped and sat on a rock to smoke a cigarette (my father hadn't come) and watch Patty cast a long line, forgetful of me, lost in concentration, bare-legged in the warm stream, her hair in a ponytail out of the back of her cap. A purist would condemn her casting action. She moved her shoulders and hips. On the back-cast, her rod went past the perpendicular. But she was relaxed, and her timing so exact that her cast looped out in tiny bumps behind her and, coming forward, shot through the rings and hung in air for an age, before sinking on to the water. There have been times in Scotland and Germany, at the end of the day, when I, too, could sense my cast hang weightlessly over the water and I'd say, I'm fishing like Patty Livingston, and touch the shreds of a dreadful longing and anxiety.

This then, Nik, was my first notion of liberty: a beautiful woman in a beautiful country, free of the prisons of embattled social class or female subordination, unobtrusive, as likely to be a cocktail waitress in her shorts and vest as the chief stockholder in American Brands. A sentimental notion, of course: in truth, Patty was one-third Jack Daniels, one-third preference dividends and the rest adultery, but these things never interested me. Perhaps there were times later, living with my sister in London or at the Free University, Berlin, when I wished she'd given me some of her money. I think what she gave was better: a sliver of love which, husbanded through school days then staked and leveraged on the affections of young women, has accumulated into a substantial sum: enough to do something with, including sit here and say all this.

My father died in 1976, when his Northwest Airlines DC-8 crashed on landing at Toronto. He was buried at Arlington National Cemetery. I couldn't get there, though President Ford did. At his Memorial Lecture, at the International Institute for Strategic Studies in Bloomsbury, London, Helmut Schmidt revealed the existence of the SS-20 to an astonished public. I got postcards from Paris, Samoa, Bali. But I suppose Patty was too rich and pretty to be a merry widow long and she married, in 1980, a Texan called Chuck Pierce, who'd just retired from the CIA and was in the process of liquidating, with a small group of other ex-officers, a front company called Arabian Metals and Mining. According to *Barrons* magazine (November 7, 1980), this returned sixty-four million dollars on just $150,000 in equity in twenty-four months, but then money just seemed to rain on Patty Livingston. They moved to Tepotzlan, Mexico, which looked, from her postcards, a pretty place.

The summer I was in Maine, this also happened. I can't imagine Bayonne, New Jersey; or rather, I can all too easily, in images delivered down the IV which, for all that I fight them, overrun and capture my imagination. I see low GI-Bill houses in pink brick cladding, cookie-cutter, with young men shouting from stoops; a guy in a singlet fishing in the bonnet of a Lincoln Town Car; the towers of the World Trade Center at one end of the street [anachronism?], at the other a tank farm or marshes. Gusts of wind blow down paper and grit, or maybe it's methane, or some intense pharmaceutical emotion. Polina has on a dress with nylon frills, none too clean, and round her neck, a sign saying: "This child is for sale!" Jacek Mertz is standing back to admire it, or maybe already walking backwards up the street, losing shape, vanishing into this forgiving continent or some other helpless metaphor for death.

I don't understand it any more than I understand the Bayonne Junior High yearbook, We're doing the '67 yearbook, Richard. Yes, Richard, again. First the photograph (bunches, braces) and now the entry: "America has fulfilled all my wishes such as: Eighth grade majorette . . . Valentine queen . . . math honor student . . . and meeting a wonderful entertainer 'Dion' this summer." Or the letter to Bobby Kennedy, in which she writes: "Europe left me with strong impressions: thunder, sunshine, unforgettable people and memories that will form me in later life. Here in the States, I have 'found' myself. I have to try to develop my capabilities and go for the top."(*Letters to Bobby: America's Schoolchildren Mourn Robert F. Kennedy*, Houghton Mifflin, 1968, pp. 98–99)

Jacek shatters and reforms in the American sunlight. Sometimes, he's Billy the Kid on the balcony of Lincoln County gaol, hacking at his chains, skimming pleasantries over the cowering house fences; or Tombee, snoring by the Niagara Falls, the year that cotton was high; or Lincoln in Springfield, lopsided in his suit of stiff blue jeans; or Bobby Lee at Appomattox, walking Traveler down the broken files of butternut-grey; or St Luc Lacorne, upright in his birch-bark canoe on the brilliant expanse of the Bras d'Or.

These American heroes come between me and the images on the monitor: of Jacek and briefcase beneath gantries, so that even I can see it's Gdansk; or this street-name, and, which now, here, refigured and enlarged, is, yes, has to be, Le-nin-grad-sky-Pros-pekt!

There is one picture I ask for, again and again, and not just because it's genuine. He's in a Bavarian suit, she in dirndl, and the studio stamp says it was posed at Hoffmann u. Braun, Mommsen-strasse 47, Regensburg. Before the studio backdrop (castle, two swans on lake), Jacek stands adrift in his hire suit, cheeks fallen in, eyes shy with corpses, but he rests his hand on her shoulder-ruffle so lightly; and she, seated on something her apron hides, looks back up at him. Through my slitted eyes, their faces dissolve and merge. A child takes shape, becomes articulate and vanishes.

During this second period, I saw the interrogation as a siege, in which certain outlying bastions of my position – viewed from the air, in sunshine and wisps of smoke and tattered shouting, messengers riding up on prize horses – were to be given up, allowing an orderly retreat of the defending forces. Since my interrogators still knew next to nothing, I couldn't predict where they'd attack: and so I fortified each of these bastions equally and also mined them.

I think the first to fall was the attack on the Spratling house. The numbers had swollen. I sensed people closing round the table. There was an air of relief, as if a project, doubtful in conception and repellent in execution, had suddenly produced a return.

"You said: 'A GDR-based unit of the Red Army Faction'?"

"Yes."

"Expand on this, please, Richard." Tully said this.

"What more do you want? It was Peter Klein, using a wire-guided missile, fired from the car park of the Rheinische Hof in Königswinter at 11.05 a.m., three hours after schedule, on April 30, 1983. Jesus! Am I the only person fighting the Cold War round here? The missile – Klein already had the launcher, which he'd used in the attack on Schiller in 1977 – was smuggled into Bonn in the diplomatic bag by that fat anus Hashim abu Hashim, the Ambassador Plenipotentiary of the Republic of Iraq to the Federal Republic of Germany, with whom Klein was then on good terms, though he isn't now."

"Why the hell didn't you tell somebody, you little creep?"

"I did."

Nobody said anything. I thought: Don't touch it. It's going to blow up in your face. You're going to find it hard to trust one another from now on. And suddenly, in a jagged flash, I saw that this, too, would be Polina's strategy three thousand miles away: that she'd start detonating the bureaucratic secrets she'd amassed during headlit nights in Chesapeake Bay motels or drunken gropings at Geneva cocktail parties, and I brimmed with such pleasure that my eyes swam.

Tully leaned forward and said: "I understand you told Mr Barchard."

A vast column of earth and smoke. Its dark sides showering sparks of fire. Flushing to an angry crimson as it floats away to meet the morning sun. The rain of stones and timbers.

I saw Barchard's face again, tight with rage. He looked murderous. He said: "I don't fucking want to hear. As soon as we reach the American Sector, you will be put in the charge of the Military Police, who will take you to Brunswick by train."

"You don't even want to hear?"

"I do not. You'll learn – or rather, you would have learned – that some information is so corrosive as to be without value."

He pulled an unfolded telex out of his briefcase and tried to read it. East German border guards stared through the windscreen, leering at us and then at our passport photographs, first one way, then another. I thought of deep-sea fishes pressing their noses against the bathyscape of the military Daimler. I thought also that, at some point, Barchard's curiosity would get the better of his fury and fear; but this might take time; and so, do us a favour, you *Vopos*, Guardians of Socialism against the Plots of the Imperialists, hold us up for another fifteen minutes!

The telex began to flutter in Barchard's hand. I decided it was time. I said, quickly, so he couldn't interrupt: "The attack on Bill Spratling's house was conducted by a unit of the Red Army Faction operating out of the GDR."

"I'm simply not interested."

This was patently untrue.

"Klein, acting on contract for the GDR Government and, through it, organs of the CPSU."

"Source?"

"A reliable source with established access to the senior levels of the East German Party."

"Don't be an infant, Richard."

Shall I kill you now, Mrs Lightner? Shall I crush your chicken-wing wrists or smash your swollen ankles? Tear out your concentration-camp hair? Shall I give your name? There are so many Stasi agents in the Bonn Chancellery, somebody'll be round in half an hour to lace you up.

"I'm waiting."

"Do you want to fuck off, Brian?"

He laughed. He said: "Of course, as long ago as Mogadishu, it was clear to anybody of even moderate insight that the RAF would not be able to survive as a functioning organization except under some form of national sponsorship."

Barchard wasn't talking to me. He was talking past me, and Julian, and the Secretary of State, to the Prime Minister herself! "I myself saw them increasingly acting as mercenaries, somewhat on the model of the Palestinian resistance groups after the Rabat Summit of 1974. In a sense," and he didn't actually say, Margaret, but the name danced on his lips, "once terror becomes insti-tutionalized in this fashion, it becomes amenable to the operations of classical diplomacy. You are aware, of course," and again the

167

phantom vocative took shape and disappeared, "that the Federal Republic has rather substantial economic leverage over the GDR: intra-German trade, the so-called Swing Credit which is a form of extremely generous import finance, personal remittances and so on. I think that an Exchange of Notes between the Permanent Representatives in Berlin should put paid to the mischief of Mr Klein and Ms Beck at least until after the Pershings are in, when nobody minds any more."

Barchard came out of his reverie. We were moving very slowly forward. He said, staring straight ahead into the Friedrichstrasse, and the limp stars-and-stripes of the American Sector: "This is a piece of intelligence of outstanding value and interest and worth taking substantial risks to gather, but not including the demolition of all the diplomatic advantage achieved at yesterday's Four-Power Meeting. Why do you take these insane risks? What's the benefit to you, Richard?"

Begins with L. Four letters. L-blank-V-blank. Not your thing at all, Brian. "I'm writing a book."

He looked at me. "I'm warning you, Richard. I shan't again." I sensed him scanning my story a second time, rapidly, professionally, for inconsistencies. He said: "Curious that it should be Bill Spratling. Not one's first choice of assassination target – or rather, very much one's first."

I panicked. I said: "There'll be reporters at Checkpoint Charlie. Waiting for you. Armies of reporters."

"There will, as you say, be reporters at the Friedrichstrasse crossing. What are you going to tell the reporters? You are going to tell the reporters: Representatives of the three Western signatories to the Four-Power Agreement – Barchard, LaFrance, Burnside – held two meetings lasting respectively six and a half hours, and thirty-five minutes at the Kommandatura. For the Soviet side, Marshals Olgarkov and Akromeyev, who stated that parcels of the international air space over Berlin would be pre-empted for Soviet military use for the duration of the Warsaw Pact exercises, Socialist Solidarity, May 1–4. UK representative – No, make that NATO

168

representatives as the others will also be briefing – argued forcefully that the Four-Power Agreement, which has regulated the affairs of Berlin in relative peace and stability for blah blah blah, did not exist purely for the convenience of the Soviet military. *Background*: Western powers are not willing to tolerate even the smallest compromise over the Berlin air corridors, memories of 1948 Berlin Blockade blah blah blah. Olgarkov and Akromeyev agree to report back to WP High Command. Meanwhile, situation frozen at *status quo ante*. *Analysis*: Seem to have stabilized situation. Sovs clearly surprised by vigour and energy of NATO response. Their execution somewhat haphazard: as Pierre put it with his usual precision, *un mélange bizarre de frivolité et folklore*, which is obviously off-the-record in French but all right in English as NATO source. The UK view is that the Soviets are genuinely anxious about some form of Western aggression to coincide with the Bundestag vote and the Pershing deployment and the utmost military and political restraint must be observed blah blah. At some stage, we will need to hear all about your trip. Now get out, you repulsive youth."

"Thanks for the lift."

"You know, one does rather love a Berlin crisis, once in a while."

This remark was not a confession or a signal for intimacy between us. Barchard was again talking through me: to the newspapers, biographers, history itself. He was handing me a trowel for his pyramid. I did my job. I told somebody, I can't remember who; and the sentence surfaced, more or less intact, in the profile of Her Majesty's Man on the Spot that appeared in the *Independent* in August 1991, at the time of the *coup d'état* in Moscow. It said: "What everybody remarks on is Sir Brian's zest for diplomacy. He once remarked, after personally defusing a dangerous dispute with the old Soviet Union over air access to Berlin: 'I do love a Berlin crisis, once in a while.'"

"She's just a cunt, Dick. There are half a billion in the world. I'm sure one'll suit you."

"You don't understand, Bill. Do you? At all. It's not who you love, it's that you love."

"Bullshit!"

"'You have to love to be able to enter history.' K. Marx. *Eighteenth Brumaire of Louis Bonaparte.*"

He looked unconvinced, as well he might.

What I meant, I think, was this. Just as Polina, with her femininity, could bring my dull and useless body to life; so my longing for her had woken parts of my nature that had fallen asleep so long ago I did not know they existed: courage, stubbornness, humility, sympathy. All right, not humility. I didn't feel I could say this to Spratling. I said:

"The Plough would have bought time for you guys, too, Bill. For the US."

He said, so quietly I might have imagined it: "Let her go, Dick."

"Can we stop?"

"Let her go."

Oh do shut up! "I've told you already that nothing I say will stop them questioning Polina. I explained that to you."

He had his head in his hands. "I don't need it, Dick. You and Poll. Those fucking RAFs." He looked at me, eyes glistening. "I get a lot of enquiries from business, Dick. I never intended to be a Foreign Service officer all my life."

I said: "Wall Street?"

"Wall Street! Who wants to work on Wall Street?"

"I'm sorry about your career, Bill."

"SHE'S MY GODDAMMED WIFE!"

I thought: I'm sorry that she doesn't love you, but then she doesn't love me, and there has to be some question whether she is capable of love in the conventional sense. I think you should take a break, old thing.

I said: "Excuse me, I have to lie down."

*　　　*　　　*

Then a lighted door appears, some way off, and standing in it, a small woman drying her hands on an apron. The room is full of people, all standing and talking, and queuing to embrace Polina and shake my hands. It is hot and smells of drink and sugar. In the corner is a vast television set – Polina says they've all bought television sets – on full blast.

In my right hand, I have a *Linzertorte* and some cherries airfreighted from Oregon; in my left, a bottle of Kirsch, a box of Lübeck marzipan and an expensive new spinning reel. Polina's grandmother takes these things off me, and then pushes me down on a chair beside Polina, at a table with small plates of sausage, unfilleted carp, rye bread, pickled beetroot. Polina's two young uncles pour me vodka from bottles they keep in their armpit pockets. Polina herself does not drink, for obvious reasons, though it offends them.

She seems shy. She has a way, when speaking or when her uncles prod her stomach or when her grandmother makes a dirty joke, of lowering her eyes, her right arm crossed under her vast bosom. I suspect this is because she's speaking Polish, the language of her early girlhood, and memories of her father and mother keep coming into her head and going out again.

A Christmas Carol is bellowing from the TV, dubbed into Polish. I watch the screen or Polina flirting with her uncles. I talk a bit to her grandmother, who speaks good German and hates it. I do bridge problems with Uncle Leszek, who was Warsaw junior champion, but I keep losing track of the Polish numbers and suits till he gets impatient and writes them down for me on a piece of cardboard. Uncle Roman shows me a photograph of his job site in Iraq. He stands, ludicrously erect, shirtless, in front of the unclad reinforced steel frame of a very large building. When I ask him what the building's for, he puts his finger stagily to his lips, then plunges into his coat for his bottle. I ask, Could I perhaps have the picture, as a souvenir of him and this afternoon? and he says, But yes, he's already said so to Posia! I think: Polina, you may be Walesa's specialist foreign adviser on the privatization of state enterprises and about to enter your third trimester, but you're still a better spy than I will ever be. I doze off in a welter of boredom, drink and guilt.

It's dark when we leave and Polina trips on the unlighted outside staircase. Terrified, I take her arm. There are no streetlights, though occasionally an old Mercedes bounces past, still with its German plates. We stand at a bus stop and Polina leans her heavy hip against mine, or rests her head on my arm. She gets cold and sets off, picking her way down the middle of the road because of the pot-holes, saying she remembers the way from 1988, but the road ends in another construction site or a place where streets are laid out around overgrown vacant lots. Headlights – one bright, one dim – appear and scuttle by.

I hug Polina tight. I love the way her stomach and bust stick in to me. I even like the way her hair has lost its silkiness, the dimples in her bottom, her unbelievable scratchiness. I say: "Didn't I say you could trust me?"

She struggles in my arms. She says: "I've got to go. They're hurting me."

"Don't go! For God's sake, don't go!"

"I don't want to live, Richard. I need to die."

I squeeze her, but she evaporates in my arms.

I must have water.

"Then who did order the Plittersdorfer Strasse?"

Water.

"What are you saying? I can't hear."

"May I have a glass of water?"

"Yes, later."

"If you give me water, I'll tell you about Lightner."

"Who? About who?"

Water.

*   *   *

172

"Nicky, I can't. I can't. Please let me be."

"Just one more time, Richard. Take it from: Criticized by Göbbels 1936, banned from preaching and so on."

"Will you let me have a drink?"

"Yes, after."

"Criticized by name by Göbbels 1936. Banned from preaching 1937; publishing 1938; 1940, conscripted. Medical orderly on Eastern Front. Bad head and neck wound at Stalingrad. Prisoner of war camp in Yakutsk. Returns, after Adenauer's second Moscow trip, 1949."

"Now: Anderson."

"In Tulagai, seen by George Anderson, Sunderland fitter and British CP member (emigrated 1931; imprisoned 1938) in summer of 1947 but not later. Anderson confirms (*Daily Worker* interview, 1957), that all prisoners received Lenin's *What Is To Be done?* and a Marx–Engels compendium. Active opponent of German rearmament . . ."

"Where was Frank between '47 and '49?"

"No evidence."

"All right, go on."

"Active opponent of German rearmament. Speaks at Paulskirche, Frankfurt, 1955 January. Marries, 1956, Gretchen *née* Piotrowska, Thälmann's niece, ex-Ravensbrück. She quits German CP, ostensibly over XXth Party Congress and Hungary. First and all subsequent Easter Marches. 1961, on one-vote majority in Berlin Senate, elected to chair of Evangelical Theology at Free University. Holds till retirement, 1979. In 1968 is only faculty member with confidence of students. After Ritter's shooting, appeals for calm among students, evidently in consultation with Moscow. Develops, in conjunction with [Valentin] Suslov and [Leonid] Zamyatin, concept of Long March through the Institutions, with the aim of fitting the sixty-eighters for eventual power in Bonn. Moves into squat in Berlin-Kreuzberg, 1970. Publishes, 1972, *The Faith Principle* (*Prinzip Glaube*), swansong of Western Marxism.

"Various diversionary activities in the Seventies. After open letter to Beate Beck, *Letter to a God-daughter*, 1977, calls by the CDU for his prosecution as 'friend and helper' of the RAF, which calls are blocked in Genscher's Justice Ministry. Motion to pension off, 1978, narrowly defeated in Berlin Legislature. Also 1978, successfully sues Hofmeyer and *Frankfurter Allgemeine* over 1978 article: 'Serving not God, but Terrorism.'

"Persuades Sebastian Ritter to rejoin SPD 1978–9.

"Active against atomic power. Wyhl, Brokdorf I and Brokdrof II, where arrested. Observer-delegate at Greens' founding party congress, Offenbach, 1980, where coins phrase: 'Not Left, not Right, but out in Front!' Chief speaker with Heinrich Böll and Petra Kelly at Bonn peace demonstration, 1981. Composes with Gretchen Lightner the Tübingen Appeal against the Pershings, but both resign from organizing committee, 1982 July, over alleged German CP infiltration. Drafted, 1983, as chief candidate on Green Bundestag lists for Bavaria, Schleswig-Holstein and North Rhine-Westphalia and the Green/Alternative List in Berlin. Found . . ."

"I can't hear you, Richard."

"Found shot, 1983, April 16, in garden writing-room, Berlin-Charlottenburg."

"I still can't hear you. Take a drink. It's all right."

Stand back. It's going up.

"Who?"

It'll take your head off.

"Who shot Frank?"

My baby.

"Virginia who?"

Langley, Virginia.

Spratling was shaking his head. "You say, Klein took two million Swiss Francs from Polina for the Lightner assassination, then goes crying to Mrs Lightner and gets a third million from the Stasi to hit Plittersdorfer Strasse! That guy is something else! What a whore! I don't know why anybody uses him."

He's supposed to be quite good, though dear, of course.

"What? What are you saying?"

"Just one more, Richard. Then you can take a rest."

"I need to rest now."

"Come on, mate. Give it your best shot."

"The Soviets followed a twin-track strategy. The SS-20 build up *and* Lightner's Long March. Makhaev utterly misanalysed the election campaign. He was telling Moscow there'd be an SPD/Green coalition, paralysed under a nonentity chancellor; Ritter running arms control from the Chancellery, a hostage to his daughter's security; Lightner himself the unopposed candidate for the Presidency of the Republic; and nothing at Mutlangen but beer and potato chips. Kvertsovsky had instructions to stonewall at Geneva. To get the Soviets to negotiate at all, she had to get Lightner out of the way. She killed Lightner, as if she'd shot him herself. She killed him."

"All right, Richard, calm down. We'll take a break."

What I think of as the third stage of the hostile interrogation is not clearly marked off. This block of memories is labelled by the presence in the room or rooms of Jack Krauskopf, the chatter of some electronic monitoring equipment, and by the horror of waking from sleep. This is guesswork, but I date the beginning of this phase to October 25 or 26, 1983, for the following reasons.

On the 25th, as I later learned from Valentina Roques (now Head of Station in Guatemala), Spratling lost his clearance for the edited transcripts of Polina's questioning. He may still have been present at my interrogation, but I only remember taking questions from Tully, with occasional supplementaries from Krauskopf. Ms Roques believes that it was on the 25th that Polina was moved by air to a military facility at Columbus, Georgia, where she also lost the use of soap, toothpaste, tampons, etc. This move may or may not have precipitated her first suicide attempt.

Also on the 25th, at 3.30 a.m. Eastern Standard Time, a Soviet air-defence interceptor aircraft shot down a Korean Air Lines jumbo jet which was crossing Soviet airspace, killing all 269 people on board. Nobody thought to tell me about it or that, as we now know, Reagan at first thought the Soviets were offering war. The National Security Council convened in emergency session. For the Pentagon, Richard Perle argued that the Soviets were now cracking, as was clear from such callous, jumpy, irrational behaviour, and one more push would bring them crashing down. The State Department agreed with the characterization of the Soviet action, but they interpreted it differently: that the Soviets were now so frightened of Western attack that they might just do something really crazy and incinerate us all. In this view they were supported in the course of the Washington morning by all the Western European governments, above all by the West German, which called for the firmest restraint. Perle's proposal to withdraw Ambassador Polk from Geneva was rejected by the President himself, who on television that evening condemned the Soviet action as a crime, but said towards the end of his fireside address that it was important to keep the arms-control process open and that the next few weeks might yet yield up a treaty. In this atmosphere, which some Washington old-timers said made the Cuba facedown of 1962 seem positively routine, the French Note of the 26th, written by LaFrance* and requesting information on Polina's and my whereabouts, must have rattled like gravel on a windowpane.

Sir Geoffrey Howe sought enlightenment from SIS, which

---

* After Pierre's death in 1992, Pascale LaFrance sent me a letter which, she said, Pierre had wanted me to have. It was written in good French by T. E. Lawrence to Louis Massignon, the great orientalist who was Pierre's uncle and had served with the French Military Mission to Syria. Dated July 6, 1917, it described the capture of Akaba in terms quite at variance with the account in *Seven Pillars of Wisdom*. It was valuable in financial terms, but I don't think that's why Pierre left it to me or not just. I think it was an offer of posthumous friendship, from a French to an English romantic. It was to this gesture – generous, impulsive, flashy, futile, in the great traditions of French diplomacy – that I responded. I sold the letter at Christie's New York and sent the proceeds, which came to $32,000 less commission and premium, to Pascale.

replied, after a day's delay, that I was at a secure location co-operating voluntarily with a US investigation into one of its foreign-service officers, all of which was true. At that, for the time being, the matter rested; but I suspect everybody involved with us now wanted the interrogations accelerated, even if that risked comprom-ising mandatory margins of safety. With Polina, it appears, the situation was deteriorating: she wept uncontrollably and for much of the time could not be made to make any sense at all. At around this time, I believe, she attempted to take the Fifth* – a move that, while futile and time-consuming, stripped away the last pretence of legal procedure. In my case, they appear to have decided to concentrate everything on reconstructing the period known as *"Das verlorene Wochenende"* [the Lost Weekend], which comprised the days and nights from the time I lost my tail in the fog on August 8 to my surrender on the Prince-Elector's steps on the Kreuzberg above Bonn on October 4.

My last grenade.

Krauskopf said: "You just didn't think it worth telling us Dick was your agent? All this time? That kind of surprises me, Nik." Krauskopf was a calm individual, in marked contrast to Bill Spratling.

I'd never before seen Tully put out. He said: "Richard's lying again, can't you see? I went to Berlin myself to interview him, in the summer of 1971. You have the report. Didn't you read it, for heaven's sake? Reasonable German . . . excellent memory . . . access to Lightner- and Ritter-circles . . . openly admits use of Class I and Class 2 narcotics . . . unpleasant manner . . . unreliable . . . disturbed relation to male authority . . ."

"I'm not familiar with this Special Research Group. What is the Special Research Group, Nik?"

---

* Invoking her right, under the Fifth Amendment to the US Constitution, to remain silent.

Tully didn't know.

I said: "I want a cup of coffee."

The room we used at King Charles Street had a steeply pitched roof. Julian liked to wear a white pullover, of the kind German submarine commanders wore in British war films. A two-bar electric fire spat and crackled between our desks.

He would hold a document in two hands, looking at it steadily for minutes and minutes on end, as if it must yield up its meaning to the force of his concentration; then he'd lower it – a speech, let us say, by Mrs Ceauŝescu on Bucharest Radio, monitored at Caversham – smile at me and say something like: "I believe she wants a bomb of her own." Even languages he didn't know – Arabic, Magyar, a scrambled telex message, a murdered photostat from the archive of some bankrupt Midlands engineer – were eventually intelligible to him, because he saw into the very nature of language and through it to the rituals of secret bureaucracies. I never knew what error or indiscretion had brought him to this graveyard room, up tottering housemaid's stairways, past miles of rotten dado and weathered rainspouts, through hecatombs of dead houseflies, and it didn't matter. From him I learned the value of concentration, of plugging away at published sources, day in, day out. He once said that almost everything of interest is published somewhere at some time. You don't need to rob or bug or murder. You read and listen, listen and read.

Once, returning from Colindale while he was still out getting his sandwich, I saw on his desk my *Islamicist Opposition to the Regime in Syria*, on which he'd minuted to the Secretary of State (then David Owen): You might like this to while away the flight, J.B. This was, ridiculous as it now sounds, a pleasant moment: as good in its way as that other, just after the Tories took power, when I came in late, almost weeping with hangover, and heard him say: "Your father's old editor at Random House is in London, staying at the Connaught." I stared at him, as if a curtain had opened an inch and revealed a bastard affection.

He said: "You are not made for institutions, Richard, even for an institution as nebulous as this one. Our new Prime Minister, as it turns out, has an ungrounded admiration for me and wants me to go to Bonn to manage the theatre-weapons issue for her. I shall be," and here he laughed at the sheer folly of it, "KCMG, though not, I hope, to you. Joe was very interested in a book about your Berlin *Kommilitonen* [fellow-students], and there should be some money somewhere, rather a lot of money, in fact. We might do something together, perhaps. In Germany. And Joy will be pleased."

"Have you come to kill us, Richard?"

They were eating their supper in front of the ZDF news. The microwaved pies on the Minton Ambassadorware, the dirt inside his shirt collar, the track of her wheelchair across a Kerman rug – the pathos and helplessness of it – fingered at my heart. She spoke with a Yorkshire accent. Barnsley, I think.

Julian stood up: "If you've brought a weapon in here, I will not exchange one word with you."

I shook my head. The gun was in the safe-deposit at Godesberg station, locked in galvanized steel and shrouded with fog. The key was in my trouser pocket. My tail, fascinated by Caroline Barchard's visit to my flat, had taken just twenty minutes, one cab ride and two U-Bahn stops to lose. The Rhineland fogs have their advantages.

Julian smiled. He said: "I'll get you some whisky."

I panicked. "You'll hear me out, won't you?"

"I'll hear you out, Richard, *and* get you some whisky."

Lady Brown leaned forward over her tray table. She said: "Are you all right, Richard?"

I said: "Do you want to be here for this, Joy?"

"I think, for your sake, I'd better be."

As he brought me my whisky in a vast Waterford tumbler, he

placed on her tray a glass of yellow wine, and touched her on her white hair; and I thought: Perhaps we should all be around sick women and junkie boys, to learn such restraint in our ways with people.

I said, "I must have time, Julian. Not long. Just till Gorbachev's in place. That could be two or three months: Andropov has not appeared in public for six weeks. If we can only push out the deployment deadline – an additional Geneva round, explore all diplomatic avenues, conscious of responsibility to whole world, gesture of goodwill and so on – the kind of thing Sebastian Ritter's been working on – we'll get a treaty, I know we will."

"Why are you telling me this?"

"She'll listen to you, Julian. She can have her mind changed. That's why she's so good. And the President will listen to her."

Julian raised his hand a fraction. He said: "You appear to be on another planet. That young woman has deranged you. You know Gromyko said to Senator Pell in Moscow that she was their agent. If you are innocent, lad . . ."

"He would, wouldn't he? That bloke's been lying since Yalta."

On Julian's face, I saw a tremor of his old kindness for me. I plunged on:

"And anyway, even if she were, it wouldn't matter. What matters is the plan. What matters is the Golden Plough. Look, please. What do you think will become of the UK in this brave new world? Sitting twenty miles off the coast of a continent dominated by a united Germany; a Britain divided, class-ridden, unproductive, polluted, poor; a sort of Mexico. You must see, don't you?"

Julian said: "Have you finished?"

The curtain flapped shut.

"I suppose so."

"With respect, this is mere speculation. I've just had a call from General Guthrie in Rheindahlen to confirm to me, as a courtesy, that Rhine Army has successfully deployed on to Launch-on-Warning. Do you know what that means, Richard? He reminded me that the armed forces had not attempted, let alone completed, this manoeuvre since 1948, and never with nuclear weapons. Do you understand that? While you and your friend are constructing woolly, irresponsible and evidently treasonous diplomatic fantasies, we are trying to contain the most dangerous crisis since the war. Let me repeat: If you are innocent, you have nothing to fear. Will you stay with us here, Richard, or shall I call the chancery guards?"

I looked at him. I said, "I worked with you three years at King Charles Street."

"I'm sorry, Richard. My duty could not be clearer."

Beneath his shirt and fifty-shilling suit, he was iron, unmalleable.

"Duty? Duty, Julian? People talk about duty when they have no other reason to act."

"I'll call the guards, then."

He turned, but it was too late. Duty hung a moment in the air, and then took shape: a sick Yorkshirewoman in a wheelchair. In his eyes, I thought I saw a flicker of despair; as if he were drowning in her demands on him, day in and day out, taking all his vitality and affection and respect, and terminable only at her agonizing death.

I couldn't look at them. I ran out of the room and into the friendly fog.

"Pick it up, Dick."

No.

"Pick up the phone, Dick."

I can't.

"Here. Take it."

I think I'd like to die, if I may.

"Hi," a woman's voice says.

"Hello."

"Bad line."

"Frightful!"

"About that thing we talked about in the hotel . . ."

"Oh yes."

"I've thought about it."

"Yes."

"I'm thinking about it."

"Good!"

"It's hard."

"I bet!"

"Catch you later."

"'Bye."

Can you decipher this conversation? If, say, it were playing out of a tape deck on a big desk, in a room with 1950s furniture and men lounging against the walls, listening and frowning, and a view of wet or sunny city streets? Or if the streetlight had suddenly dimmed in Cheltenham, Gloucestershire? Would you have noticed the absence of proper names and the unidiomatic use, by the woman, of *bad* in the sense of public or overheard? Of course, you would! But would you have known what she was talking about? Unless you'd been in love or Marburg or seen the famous Elisabethkirche there and heard him ask her to lay her life in the balance? Or heard the silences on the tape and realized that these were not the silences of indifference or inhibition but of his stopped-up mouth, his hijacked heart, his breath racing down the telephone, over cold fields and dusky city suburbs, and streets jostling with banners and rockets sleeping on their launchers, and the tumbling, merciful Atlantic? And would you have guessed that she'd hung up, not out of completed business, or because something had happened near her – a man standing up, say, putting his hand on the phone cradle – but in a hurricane of tears?

Fine spy you'd make!

I told him all about Sergei. Sergei at Mutlangen. Sergei at Krefeld. Sergei drunk. Even Sergei sober. I told him about Sebastian and Beate and their daughter and about Nida and Caroline and the Moroccan at the Bahnhofsmission. I gave him Beck's address in Leipzig and Klein's in Ascona. I told him how to get the tape of the Fishing Party from the Dresdner Bank in the Heussallee, and my gun from Inge Mohr's flat above the Käfer. I told him about Mikhail Gorbachev. I told him about Eduard Shevardnadze. I told him about at least one attempt to speed Andropov on his way. I told Tully everything I knew, and some things I did not know I knew, and some things I did not know.

"I'm sorry. I really am, mate."

Through closing eyelids, I could see a patch of fear in him, spreading like a flame catching paper.

"I'll leave you on your own for a bit. I'll get you a coffee. Milk? Two sugars? Three? He'll give you some Panbutane. Why not lie down for a bit?"

He seemed to want to say something in addition.

"She was . . ."

He tried again.

"She was . . ."

He gave up.

"She went and fucking died on Ed Cogswell! Jesus, what a mess!"

I told him how once, when she kissed me, she lifted her knee to my hip as if I were a tree she was climbing. I told him how, another time, she touched my teeth with hers. I explained to him how the contradiction in Marx between his determinist and libertarian views of human activities – between the Realm of Necessity and the Realm of Freedom – is more apparent than real and anyway can be resolved through application of the insights of psychoanalysis. I told him how men and women make their own history, but not of their own free will; and how the traditions of dead generations squat like nightmares on the breasts of the living. I told him how once, at the Alte Hirsch in Cologne, when I asked her if she'd ever searched for her father, she'd said, He can find me, Richard, if he wants to, I'm getting pretty well known now. I said there's no simple reason for why she did what she did, but fame is as good as any.

I wanted to tell him other things, but the words ran away from me. My mind began to slide. When he moved, it was with a maddening, pettifogging slowness. Things went liquid in the tails of my eyes. I wanted to tell him that that bit about the heaviness of death is not, after all, mere rhetoric.

I said, "Nicky, it's different now. With the best will in the world, I can't answer you."

"He'll give you some more Panbutane. Hang in there, boy."

My body was dismantling. My chest and legs had broken off relations. My nerves passed out of central control. Grim little wars erupted, unreported, in my hands and feet. Muscles starved or hoarded. One by one, the great organs of my body shut down.

"I checked New York."

Good.

"And Warsaw."

Excellent.

"Why are you lying again?"

Don't know.

"And the meeting at Brühl of September 16 didn't take place as described?"

No.

"Or at all?"

No.

"And the detail – the fog in the mirrors, Sergei's face repeated over and over, those bloody wild geese squawking— all that . . ."

No.

"For pity's sake, Richard, why have you gone back to lying?"

Forgotten.

I heard the word *Schildgedächtnis*, which is a term from classical psychoanalysis. I think what the speaker, who may for all I know have been von Arnim, wanted to say was: Let's get to the actual memory which is concealed beneath this screen. I know I felt: It won't be long now.

A face came up close. It said: "Richard, please, if you did not meet Sergei at Brühl, how did you communicate with Gorbachev?"

I opened my eyes and saw the movement of Tully's mind. It was ponderous and regular, like a medieval clock.

"Jesus! He went to fucking Lisbon for the Portuguese Party Congress!"

The Convention of Cintra.

"Did you meet Mike in Lisbon, Dick?"

The lines of Torres Vedras.

"Let's take a break, gentlemen."

"Did you, Richard?"

The earthquake that destroyed Voltaire's optimism.

"SHIT! The monitor's out of paper!"

A green and fizzy wine.

"Did you go to Moscow to see him?"

Moscow?

"All right, Richard, say it into my ear."

How long have I been here?

"What? Try again?"

How long have we been doing this?

"How long have we been here? Long enough, mate!"

I want to know how long we've been here because it interests me, in the way that circumstantial facts and statistics interest lovers of sport. I want to know, very roughly, how long it has taken us to see the scale of Polina's enterprise. How many days or weeks? How many men? How many man- and woman-weeks of how many counter-intelligence and -subversion services to comprehend her ingenuity which now begins to take shape before me, to assume the attributes of a hallucinated femininity? It took all this time; and I, who am not fit, as it were, to latch her terrible shoe-straps, have got here at last, a little before you and my death, in the beam of her posthumous intelligence which still travels through time like light from an exploded star.

"OK, let's get him back on the IV."

How could she know we'd all do as she wanted: Jack, me and Makhaev, then Sebastian and Mikhail Sergeyevich? She's not a Soviet agent, you poor saps: they are her agents. Leave it, Richard. Leave it. Leave it wrapped in its last layer of obscurity. For if you take it out, in these last moments, these men who led you here – through trodden grass and busted thickets, in bevies of whimpering dogs – will have it off you. Leave it, Richard. Without you . . .

"Hey, man! Wake up!"

. . . they'll not find it. They're lost. They're history.

"JESUS CHRIST!"

How could she know Sebastian would do it for her? Leave it, Richard. Label it with this agony, and if you save your life – Who knows the mind of God? I sure don't – you'll come on it one day and unravel this last and best secret. Or take it with you where you're going.

"Hang on, Richard! For God's sake!"

Crowds invade the squares of my heart. In my guts, a graffiti-covered wall begins to shudder, buckles, bursts; and there, against the tide of streaming people and two-stroke automobiles, a school-girl stomps towards her mother. Leave it be.

"Don't you fucking die on us!"

Sunlight flickers off the Kremlin domes. Ritter sets his briefcase down on the long table, and sits down. The man with the strawberry birthmark is speaking. On the green baize, Yuri Andropov's hand trembles with the premonition of his own and his country's extinction. Men in uniform lean forward as Sebastian runs through his rigmarole: equal warhead totals on each side, a cap on third-country systems and in Asia, confidence-building measures, a hundred-kilometre demilitarized zone on each side of the Inner-German border, annual joint exercises. It is too late, of course. Above his grating drone, and the gabble of the interpreter, you hear a crash and roar, like an ice-shelf in spring; and then it breaks, an immense, flat, frozen slab of history, and topples slowly into the sea. The real history of humanity begins.

Oh my poor friend, my only friend, sweet Sebastian: you are all alone now against futurity. Against your back, that wall shakes and crumbles. You cry out: The freedom that you seek is not here! Rosa stands in the traffic before her downcast mother.

"He's going, you asshole!"

Death, I can reveal, is indescribable in the language of appearances. Here is a metaphor. Imagine a high mountain pass, blind with snow. A figure turns into the wind and soldiers on through hip-deep snow. The wind whines in the binder-twine that holds his pack. The air is too thin to breathe. Nothing of the world can live up here: not greed or ambition or bravery or envy or hatred. Only love, because it came from here. Love is the figure that steps on through the drifts. That is the last secret and the only thing worth knowing in this world below.

It was for love, Polina, that you drew these men and weapons into your hands and wrote your will across Europe, that something of this tumult might reach into the spaces of eternity; and there, among the orders of angels, your father will stir and listen and say, in Polish (which is the language some angels use): "Ah, that's my girl."

Philosophy comes too late to teach the world what it
should be. The Owl of Minerva begins its flight when
the shades of night have already fallen.

HEGEL

In a long interrogation, such as I went through in Germany in the
summer and autumn of 1983, a prisoner will go very deep into
himself, like a diver. Then he comes up fast, and the pain is in-
supportable: he begs and whimpers for death. I kept thinking I
heard Death, coming down the rubber corridor on squeaky soles,
or peering, unsmiling, through the porthole of my door. Once, I
woke with a woman's sweet arms on my shoulders, my teeth clink-
ing against glass, a drink of something tasting of iron and sugar,
the reassembling room.

"So who's this Nick-fella?" she said.

Another time, I woke up and felt next to my feet the warmth
of where he'd been sitting, the print of his weight; thought that
was his raincoat, hanging from the screen because there was no
hook on the door. "Cheer up, lad," she said, wiping my eyes with
a warm washcloth.

I didn't understand. I didn't understand the doctor, who smelled
of soap and cigar-smoke, and laughed, and flashed and clicked his
oculoscope while I followed his finger round the dizzy room; who
laughed and said, I think we'll keep you with us a bit longer. I
didn't understand what this meant or if he was talking to me. What
I knew was that Tully would soon be back, to continue the discussion we'd been having. I thought this discussion had been broken

off, accidentally in some way, and the broken-off piece was like a splinter in my heart.

When Sebastian was shot and badly wounded in 1968, Lightner found him a speech therapist. He was a just-promoted graduate psychologist named Thomas Ehleiter. The report of the treatment, which took place that August at a summer house the Lightners had rented at Århus in Denmark, was among the documents Sebastian gave me on the train from Herder to Bonn. Ehleiter must have shown him some kind of ABC with pictures, because, in the ring-binder I took off the train, on a sheet of squared paper, I found a column of words in laboured and shaky handwriting:

The tractor
The strawberries
The salad
The scissors
The sheep

Next there is a word which has been carefully crossed out. Then, with a determination that brought tears to my eyes when I first saw it, he plunges back into his beloved dialectic:

Immanent/transcendent
Totality/singularity
Analysis/synthesis

I suppose women were my dialectic: I mean that men and women are the antithetical pairs that combine to make history. I remember, early one morning when the hospital seemed to hiss and rumble and spark like a factory, the nurse coming in on her flat heels and, as she pulled me forward to put up my pillows, I laid my arms on her back and felt, through the stiff nylon, the warmth of her skin. I said: "Will you kiss me, Kathleen?"

She turned and shouted to the door: "We can knock off here, guys!" She finished the pillows, shook the little cup with my pills before my eyes, slapped me on the cheek, hard, and wheeled my tray out.

So I knew I was not dead; or rather, to get some precision in here, I thought there was nothing to stop eternity resembling a British military hospital in western Germany, but this was multiplying the metaphysical possibilities beyond necessity. It was quiet, which was unusual in Germany in those days: no cars or aircraft or building noise, just the chirrup of heels from the corridor, the burly shouts of the male doctors, the nurses' paradisial accents: Liverpool, Cork, Speightstown. I ate big meals of British food, with curious German interventions: paprika in the hotpot, strong coffee. Through the window on the left of my bed, through the metal 1960s frame, I looked across swept tarmac, a row of white-painted, crenellated flettons marking off a lawn round a vacant flagstaff, and beyond it a wall of windy pines. It reminded me of the Royal Air Force base at Lossiemouth, near Inverness, which I'd been to for air displays as a child. I was looking into the pines one day when Polina stepped into my mind; and I realized my loss was not Nik Tully.

"Oh, don't you be doing that all over again."

"I'm so sorry, Kathleen. I'm OK. I'll be OK."

On her round face, which was pretty enough to hide her hard upbringing (but for how long?), there was a look of sly recognition. I suppose she'd heard something about me and Polina, just a little. When Dr Mason – Clive to me – said, "Have you arranged to be picked up?", I trembled and, for an instant, Nik was standing in front of me. I closed my eyes to shut him out.

I said: "Could somebody call a taxi?"

Kathleen McConaghy drove me to Neuss station in a pool car. She was all dressed up, with her hair moussed and piled about her head, a short skirt showing her thighs. She seemed pleased with herself, above all with her hair and the clouds of Opium by Yves St Laurent, but also by the way, when she shifted through the gears of the Ford Corsair, her skirt rode up and drew my eyes to her as if they were on silk line.

She said: "Are you a civilian, Rick?"

"Yes."

"I like civilians."

Off duty, she in her gladrags, me in Clive's third-best Next for Men suit, we were moving on formal repetitive lines, as in a well-known chess opening. I didn't think we'd progress to the middle game, to Schnapps-and-Coke in a Cologne bar, a raucous, tactile stumble through the glistening Old Town. Something, perhaps her mother's stinging wet hand in a Co. Armagh kitchen, had taught Kathleen McConaghy prudence. She was looking at me and then the road, happy yet suspicious: what sort of civilian anyway, severe bruising, opioid intoxication, weight loss, dehydration, bed rest, 5 mg Vitamin B anticoagulant on the IV, fishy, leave it.

I said: "Going out tonight?"

"Going clubbing, ain't I? With the lads from VII Squadron."

"Don't do anything I wouldn't do."

She turned on me a smile of emerald sweetness. I thought: I'm going to write to Air Marshal Daft-Bottomley about you, Kathleen, recommending promotion. You've made me whole again. That's what I call nursing.

At Neuss station, I bought a *Kölner Zeitung* dated November 22, 1983.

Jacek Mertz's theory that in danger is safety is not, I now see, a piece of rhetoric but a brilliant intuition that I have managed partially, but persuasively, to verify.

After surrendering the army, Lee rode at a walk past the courthouse and back to the lines, where he supervised the distribution of the thirty thousand rations Grant had offered and he'd accepted. Then he spoke two sentences to the army. For a long time, nothing happened; then one by one, at first, then in groups, then the whole army pressed up close to touch Traveler's mane and bridle and withers, before turning and walking southwards in the direction of where their homes had been.

I imagined Polina descending like the Archangel Gabriel, scat-

191

tering tourists in terror. Instead, I felt a head being laid lightly on my shoulder, her Polina-breath on my cheek. I felt acutely the church at my back, the gilded wrought-iron screen, the staircase vanishing into a heaven of clouds and angels and translated princes.

She said, "We lost! We had fun!"

There was a slowness about her.

"Are you OK?"

She said: "I never believed you were dead."

I put my arm round her and pulled her tight. Her bust and hips had been replaced by bone. But living, not dead.

She said: "Chuck Pierce hunts dove with the President, for Christ's sake. You didn't say."

"He married Patty."

"Patty?"

"My stepmother."

"Oh, that Patty."

She said: "The President was incredibly distressed. I've been authorized to offer you permanent residence and also an income: not a whole lot, but a good middle-manager's income; after federal, state and local taxes, that'd be, I guess, $35–40,000 and . . ."

"Polina?"

"What?"

"Do you want to shut up?"

I felt her shoulders slump. I looked at her, at last. Her hair was cut short. She was wearing dark glasses. Her face had gained lines and texture. I thought: She's aged a decade, but she'll be beautiful at every stage of her life.

She took off her glasses and blinked from bruised eyes. She said, "What are you thinking?"

"I'm thinking: I want to remember you. Not what I think about you or what you've done or my sorrow or wanting to go to bed with you for the rest of my life; but what you look like: your face, your eyes, your hair, this awful coat . . ."

Polina yelped. She knelt on my thighs and hugged me, as if she wanted to get into me, to hide her flayed person in my skin.

Through her hair, I saw the Inter-City appear, noiselessly, against the green of the Poppelsdorfer Allee. The storm of tears slowed to a drizzle.

I said: "Leave Sebastian alone."

She flapped her sleeves, which slipped to reveal the American lint and tape on her emaciated wrists. "I'm out of it, can't you see? I'm history."

"He must be allowed to make his speech in the House tonight."

She said into my chest: "Not make his speech. Definitely not make his speech. Baby, they're here. They're at Upper Heyford USAF base in England. Two missiles. Two bodies [sets of spares]. The avionics are still a fucking zoo, but nobody needs to know that. The plan is for Kohl to call the Secretary of Defense as soon as the vote is read off."

Lights had come on in the valley. Scraps of traffic noise and rustling trees blew past me. I stood up. I thought: Let's do our tenses now, Herr Fisher. I have taken a step: perfect. I am going: present continuous. I shall take two steps more: future.

"You must get them off me. Just for this evening."

She waved her arms again. "Can't you see? They're not mine. I guess they're Nik's or the Germans'."

"It's Grand Central in the rush hour."

"Richard, it's got to be. It's not safe for you. You have to let me protect you."

"I have to be free. Just for this evening."

"Stop it! I don't want to hear any more about it, OK?" She looked at me in the twilight. "Oh baby, I never meant you to be hurt, you of all people. What have I done?"

I said: "Everything washes away in time, Polina, even blood. Only love lasts."

She hid her face in her hands.

I turned and walked down past the calvaries towards Poppelsdorf. About halfway, I stopped and began to laugh to the inquisitive woods.

*　　*　　*

In danger is safety. Which is to say: In normal, daily life, in any given situation, it is possible to predict risk rather accurately in the light of experience. In a conflict on the field of normal, daily life, victory will go to the contestant with superior strength or resources. But as the peril increases, so the calculation becomes less simple, and the outcome becomes unpredictable. When, on Unter den Linden in East Berlin on May 2, 1983, I dived in front of the wheels of Brian Barchard's Daimler, it was an act that the GDR State Security had simply not provided for. It hadn't occurred to them that I would take such a risk or that, in the hail of grit on my face, the heat of the engine, the stench of petrol and lead and vulcanized rubber, I'd get away with nothing worse than a cheek gashed by a military numberplate and I'd be up and jumping into this mobile chunk of sovereign England before anybody could get a shot off.

So, on the evening of November 23, 1983, as I stood at the level crossing opposite the Käfer, with two behind me in a Mercedes, one beside me on foot, and one halted on a bicycle, I said to myself: They simply haven't considered it or rather, since these agents are better trained than your Stasi pavement-fodder, they just now are considering it, but it's too late. The Inter-City beats down on us, big as a mountain. I'm up on the gate. I plunge into the beam of light, steel, oil, stone and a bow-wave of white sparks. Something hits my wrist and spins me like a ballerina, into the far gate and over, head down among the gaping motorists. My hand! My hand! I left my hand behind! My left hand behind! I run on, jabbering, because if I stop I'll faint, into the Käfer, up the stairs, my legs beginning to jump and buckle, up to Inge Mohr's apartment, shouting:

"Inge! The packet!"

At the head of the stairs, I see a head of ginger hair and a pair of scraggy female buttocks vanishing behind a door jamb and, on Inge's face, above her nakedness, a look of unappeasable hatred. I can't deal with that now. I have my gun and the keys to the taxi. I have some Mozartkugeln sweets and a bottle of brandy, for which

I leave money, not as propitiation, but out of rapidly diminishing habit.

I sat in the taxi-cab on the Venusberg, sucking brandy and sobbing with pain, listening to the sound of shouting and music coming up from the Government District.

"I'll kiss it better," she said. She reached out, but was pulled short by her seatbelt.

"It's all right. I'll be fine in a moment. Then we'll go and see your dad."

"You shouldn't walk in front of a train. That was silly."

"It was silly."

At that moment, for the first and only time in this story, the contingent or fortuitous enters the narrative. The rear passenger doors opened and shut.

I shouted, "Rest period!"

In the mirror, I saw the florid, anxious face of the Speaker of the Lower House, and a young man, presumably his parliamentary private secretary.

I said: "No official vehicle, Dr Barzel?"

He switched on the back reading-light and opened his briefcase.

"No official driver, Dr Barzel?"

He slammed his forearm down on his papers. The young man put his face in the mirror. He said:

"Five hundred D-Mark. If you can get Dr Speaker in."

"We'll do it for love of country! OK, dear, now."

Rosa pushed the gearstick into drive.

The police still had the Ollenauerallee open; but under the trees of the Heussallee the lines were getting ragged. A crash barrier lay in the road. The shrieking faces seemed to narrow to a point ahead. I tucked in under the lee of a mobile water cannon, which was moving slowly forward in a drizzle of water and tear gas. Something heavy landed on the roof. A boy in a Palestinian scarf leaned on the barrier, kicking his legs for balance, and thumped the bonnet with his fist:

"NEVER AGAIN WAR! NEVER AGAIN FASCISM!"

"I want to go home," Rosa said.

I wriggled half out of my window, let the people see me: "Let the Deputies through! Let them through!"

There was a growl, neither yes nor no.

Barzel said, "The fall of the Weimar Republic began with the decay of parliamentary manners." He seemed to have lost his fear. It was as if the crowd, in prodding his upholstered body, had found the piece of metal in its centre.

"Is that Göbbels, Dr Speaker?"

"It is one my predecessors, the last Speaker of the Reichstag before Hitler, a gentleman by the name of Paul Löbe."

"I suppose you're right: the nationalist cat's out of the bag. We're in the equivalent of about 1928. *Um Gottes Willen!*"

A firecracker jumped on to Rosa's lap, hit me on the cheek, then vaulted into the back seat where the secretary screamed. I thought: Some kid's going to put a petrol bomb in here and we'll be barbecued. I pulled out from behind the cannon, pushed open the door, and standing on the seat, shouted: "I've got a No vote here, guys! Let us through!"

There was another roar, which beat against the sides of the taxi. A path opened. I jumped on to the accelerator. People and placards bounced to each side like spray from a speedboat. A woman sat on the bonnet and slipped, shrieking, off the side. I crunched over a crash barrier and burst through the police line. Inside the cordon, it was quiet. I swung up to the main door with a flourish. Men rushed down to hand out the Speaker.

The secretary was poking in his briefcase.

"No charge!" I said and drove round the corner, flicked off the lights and ignition and glided down into the Deputies' underground garage.

"Close your eyes. Tight. No looking."

She closed her eyes, tight.

I felt in the glove compartment for her Mozartkugeln and the pistol.

"Mr Fisher, what a surprise! And sweetheart!"

She sprung up from her keyboard and put her arms round Rosa, who stood stiffly in the embrace.

"Can I play with the computer?" I saw that Rosa was now worried about the adventure, the missed bedtime, her slippers and night-gown and chocolate face. She climbed on Adelheid Müller's chair, spun it and turned her back on us and retribution.

"Dear Mrs Müller!"

In those days, I believed that no time spent with the secretaries of great men was ever wasted.

She said: "Will you have some coffee? Deputy Dr Ritter is still correcting his speech. But what has happened to your hand?"

"Please don't bother, dear Mrs Müller. Unless you'll have some coffee with me?"

Round the door of the inner office, Ritter's head appeared. He looked irritated and then delighted.

"Richard! Welcome! Do you need a gallery pass?"

"Sebastian, I need to speak to you at once. Outside."

"Rosa! What are you doing here? Where's Nida?"

"Richard wouldn't let her come," she wailed. "He shut her in the . . ."

Sebastian looked at me, full of sorrow. At his shoulder, Adelheid Müller's face was white as new paper. The coffee cup she held tinkled, clattered, began to slop. I thought: Yes, I am Death, come to take your Perfect Knight.

"Mrs Müller! Please! Control yourself!" he said. "I would be grateful if you would keep Rosa here until I or somebody comes for her."

"Dad!"

She ran to him, her pink dressing gown billowing out behind

her. He knelt down and kissed her wet face. "It's all right," he said. "I'm not cross, I promise. I'm pleased. But I have to go now and work. I'll come back, I promise."

Down the corridor bustling with Deputies and reporters and tail-coated ushers, I sensed something I'd never noticed before: Ritter's physical strength. He could turn and throttle me, if he needed to. On the floodlit lawn of the Tulpenfeld, under the ragged chanting from beyond the police lines, he stopped and turned, holding his briefcase to his chest.

I said, "Sebastian, they're going to arrest you, in the Plenum, if necessary. Crimes against the Constitution. I've got a car and a weapon, but we must leave *now*. Peter knows we're coming and will get us to Damascus."

Ritter shook his head. "I have a speech to make. At 21.05, which is three minutes from now."

"Sod your speech, you imbecile Trot. They know everything, but everything: Beate, Klein, Moscow. They know because I told them. We have to leave now. You have responsibilities, if you hadn't noticed. To Rosa, if you remember."

He said: "I'd greatly appreciate it, Richard, if you would keep out of my family sphere. Let me just say this: We thought in 1968 that marginal groups alone, intellectuals, students, the privileged, could deputize for the working class and initiate a revolution of humanity without class distinction. Mere ideology, naturally. I have learned, over fifteen years, painfully, slowly and belatedly, that there is parliamentary democracy or no democracy at all. Will you excuse me? My whips will be getting anxious."

I said: "Sebastian, why did you tell me? About you and Beate and the little girl? Why did you give me those letters and papers? You must have known I'd unravel it all in the end."

"I don't fully know. I suspect that some secrets are too heavy to bear alone. I thought I should have a friend to share the burden. An error, as it turned out. Now I am leaving."

"We shan't meet again."

"Oh, on the contrary."

I finished the brandy on the stone benches in the middle of the Tulpenfeld. The speeches, broadcast into the reporters' offices, blew across the lawns at me. I heard Sebastian begin; a crash; then a howl of feedback; Petra Kelly shrieking; Barzel calling for calm; and ever fainter, Sebastian shouting:

"The insult to this High House . . ."

or something like that. I listened to other speeches: Kohl, Genscher, Vogel, Strauss, Kelly. I heard the division bell ringing through the Government District, Barzel announcing the result and the scream of pain and rage from the crowd beyond the cordon. I heard the cannons. Gradually, it became quiet. One by one, the lights went off in the offices. Footsteps passed me till, at the end, there was nothing left but, from the bureau of the *New York Times*, repeated over and over again: "This is the direct broadcast transmission from the German Bundestag. You are listening to the live transmission of the German Bundestag. This is the direct broadcast transmission from the German Bundestag."

Some time later, I thought I heard aircraft engines overhead and the end of my life and the beginning of real history.

I'm going to take a break now. You can finish this history as well as I can, probably better: Barchard in Moscow, matching Boris Nikolayevich glass for glass and sharing gypsy girls; Caroline mad as cuckoos in Dorubetskaya Street; Makhaev, nightly on NBC before the encircled Russian Federation Parliament, a Hero of August; Tully at Goldman Sachs; LaFrance blown to bits at Sarajevo Airport; John Chauncey Polk at the March of Dimes Ball at the Met; Barry Cohen in the rainforest; Julian Brown at the International Red Cross.

Peter Klein with his new Swiss face, at the top of his profession;

Beate Beck crying like a waif at her trial; Patty Livingston all alone, dozing in the sunshine before half a tortilla spread with honey.

Polina not in Woodstock, New York but Naples, Florida; Spratling in real estate. Polina in shopping-mall pastels, tracksuits, tennis jewellery. At some point — maybe she's sleeping around again, who knows? — Bill buys her a business: let us say, mail-order embroidery patterns, and she makes something of it, builds it up or chops it down, sells right at the top: one smart lady.* One hot morning, she puts on a T-shirt that reads *Paradise Beach Sports and Country Club* across the bust, walks into Bill's den and takes down, from the wall, one of his . . . Excuse me, I can't go on with this.

Sebastian on TV, in judge's chambers, in courtrooms that are now indistinguishable in my imagination: looking at me without recognition or turning to the President of the Court, his voice raised in forensic anger. I guess this is hell: to be condemned to betray him again and again and again through all the instances of German and European justice. Berlin, Bonn and Moscow spin in my head like the accursed playing cards in the Pushkin story. I suppose we'll one day get to Karlsruhe† and then to Strasbourg,‡ and he'll go free, but not for a while yet, not for a lifetime.

Ritter conducts his own defence, is reckoned brilliant; but some time, let us say in 1994 or 1995, he requests and is granted assistance of counsel. Of Rosa Luxemburg Ritter, what can I say? That with such a name, face, mother, father, how can she not waltz into history (beginning, naturally enough, with the cover of *Stern*)? Sometimes, when she's questioning somebody and I can see what she's trying to do a quarter of an hour before the witness, I think: And I kept you safe through the most dangerous years of your life; you are my present to Germany and history; and maybe Kohl's right and the Germans can't go on apologizing for eternity; and

* "One Smart Lady: Busy Fingers at Omaha Pattern", *Business Week*, August 25, 1987, pp. 16–17
† German Constitutional Court
‡ European Court of Justice

you, a mere girl, are the Parsifal who'll return the Grail of law, the spear of justice to this unhappy country.

I also do a non-Utopian, non-sentimental ending which, for some reason, takes place in a commandeered school. There's a terrific bombardment going on, but it must have been going on for a while, because nobody is much bothered by it. Ritter is coming down the corridor. His hair is all grey now. Military uniform suits him. I struggle up, stick out my hand, British-inhibited; but he slaps it down, goes on, hesitates, then strides on again. I don't know why Europe has gone back to fighting, if we're fighting on the same side, if I'm his prisoner or he mine. What I do know is that my power to make history – which only ever was love, not guts, or brains – has burned away, leaving just this residue: the hitch in Ritter's step, the wound in Polina Mertz's breast.

Then I have this ending, which doesn't really concern you. Actually, you lot can fuck off. I'm all right. I do small jobs that require the use of a handgun. But what I quite badly need is an answer to the question Goethe asked in the *Harz Journey in Winter* and Polina sang to the patient oaks and the jubilees of driving schools. Is there . . . father of love . . . a note that'll find its way . . . his busted heart . . . his thirsting soul . . . pull back those clouds . . . his blinded eyes . . . tum-tum . . . a million million winding streams . . . thirsting . . . thirsting . . . ?